KT-150-976

When disaster turns to passion

Welcome to an exciting new series of twelve books from Silhouette®, 36 HOURS, where danger is just a heartbeat away. Unprecedented rainstorms cause a 36 hour blackout in Grand Springs and it sets off a string of events that alters people's lives forever…

Martin Smith and **Juliet Crandall** were an unlikely pair, the dangerous mystery man and the quiet librarian. *Who was Martin Smith?* The sexy stranger had come to town in the midst of the storms, with no name and no clues to his past. Shy Juliet was fascinated—and willing to risk everything for him—but was he just 'too hot to handle'?

Marilyn Pappano

After following her career navy husband around the country for sixteen years, Marilyn Pappano now makes her home high on a hill overlooking her home town. With acreage, an orchard and the best view in the state, she's not planning on pulling out the moving boxes ever again. When not writing, she makes apple butter from their own apples (when the thieves don't get to them first), putts around the pond in the boat and tends a garden that she thinks would look better as a wildflower field, if the darn things would just grow there.

You can write to Marilyn via snail mail at P.O. Box 643, Sapulpa, OK 74067-0643, USA.

36 Hours

When disaster turns to passion

YOU MUST
REMEMBER THIS

Marilyn Pappano

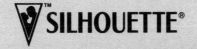

Silhouette and Colophon are registered trademarks of Harlequin Books S.A., used under licence.

First published in Great Britain 1999
Silhouette Books, Eton House, 18-24 Paradise Road,
Richmond, Surrey TW9 1SR

© Harlequin Books S.A. 1998

Special thanks and acknowledgement are given to Marilyn Pappano
for her contribution to the 36 HOURS series.

ISBN 0 373 65017 5

105-9909

Printed and bound in Spain
by Litografia Rosés S.A., Barcelona

36 Hours

When disaster turns to passion

For the residents of Grand Springs, the
storm-induced blackout was just the beginning…

Each book stands alone, but together they're terrific!

Prologue

Friday, June 6

The emergency room was bustling, with every cubicle occupied, every chair in the waiting room taken. Some patients waited quietly. Others were vocal about their discomfort—and their displeasure.

The man walked past all the waiting patients to the broad hallway, where a harried clerk stopped him. "Can I help you?"

He looked blankly at her. Did he need help? He wasn't in any pain except for the headache, and it would go away soon enough. The crack to his head had left him a little dazed, but that would go away, too.

"Sir? Are you hurt? Do you need to see a doctor?"

The bright lights in the hall made the ache in his head throb. When he closed his eyes to block the glare, he swayed unsteadily, and the woman took hold of his arm. "Sit down over here, and the doctor will see you as soon as possible. Did you hit your head?"

He sank into the chair against the wall and realized how good it felt to sit. It had been a long walk from the banged-up car on the highway to the well-lit hospital.

"Sir?"

Lifting one hand, he touched the knot raised when his head came in contact with some part of the car. "Yes, I…"

She crouched in front of him, pen poised over clipboard. "What's your name?"

He opened his mouth, but nothing came out. *Nothing.* In a flash, the muscles in his stomach knotted and panic surged through him. It was a simple question, the simplest question in the whole world. What was his name? It was…

Still nothing.

"Sir, I need your name for our records."

When he reached out, his hand trembled. When his fingers made contact with the clerk's hand, they wrapped tightly around it. She tried to pull free, but he didn't let go. Instead, he leaned closer, staring fearfully, desperately, into her face. "I don't know… I don't…"

Oh, God, he couldn't remember.

"Should I list him as John Doe?"

He lay on his back, staring at the ceiling, only half listening to the medical staff around him. He had been examined, poked and prodded, X-rayed and interrogated and, finally, medicated. His clothes had been searched for identification, but none was found. His wallet—if he'd had one—was gone. His driver's license was gone. His identity was gone.

On the up side, so was his headache.

"He doesn't look like a John to me. Can we pick another name?"

"How about Brad?"

"No…he's not the Brad Pitt type." The answer was dry and mocking and made him wonder for the first time what he looked like. Did he have blond hair and blue eyes, like the actor? If he saw a photograph of himself, would he recognize it? If he walked over to the mirror above the sink, would he find himself facing a stranger?

He didn't have the nerve yet to find out.

"Hey, I know what we can call him. Martin—"

The other female voice joined in. "Smith. Yes, of course. Perfect."

"Who is Martin Smith?" That was the doctor, sounding disinterested as he made notes in the chart.

"He's a character on the soap we watch. He's tall, blond, blue-eyed—"

One of the women gave him a furtive glance that he caught from the corner of his eye, then lowered her voice. "A hunk."

That was good, wasn't it? It meant he didn't look half as bad as he felt—and even without the headache, he felt pretty damn bad. He was scared.

Ever since he'd been brought back to the examination room, he'd been talked at, around and about. Finally, the doctor spoke to him. "You want to be Martin Smith?"

No. He wanted to be— He wanted to be whoever the hell he really was, not some soap opera pretty boy. He didn't say that, though. Instead he simply nodded. He could be someone he wasn't. He knew how to do that. Then, sooner or later, he would find out who he was.

Wouldn't he?

"All right, Mr. Smith. You can get up now. We're just about finished."

He sat up on the examination table so that he was facing the mirror. Once he found the courage to look, he saw blue eyes and blond hair. The man in the mirror needed a shave. He confirmed it by rubbing his hand along his own jaw. He combed his fingers through his hair, then touched his face again. The mirror image did the same.

He was looking at himself.

He was looking at a stranger.

"If you'll wait by the desk, Mr. Smith, I'll have the admissions clerk call the police. Maybe they can help you find out who you really are."

He nodded numbly, slid to the floor and followed the doctor to the desk. The chairs were still all full, so he wandered around the large room, pausing to look at bulletin boards and pictures, listening to the conversations around him to distract himself from his own problems.

"Yes, Doreen fell down the stairs when the lights went out. Doctor thinks she might have broken…"

"Melvin was in a wreck right downtown. The stoplights quit working, just like that, and some·idiot who had a red light before just kept on…"

"The lights went off, and—poof—Randi just disappeared. From her own wedding! I declare…"

"Isn't it awful about Olivia Stuart? To suffer a heart attack on the day of her son's wedding! The poor woman."

He stopped moving and pretended to study a poster advertising first aid classes at the local Methodist church. Olivia Stuart. Did the name mean anything to him? He couldn't say. It felt…not familiar, but different from Doreen, Melvin and Randi.

"I heard Josie Reynolds went to her house looking for her when she didn't show up at the wedding and found her unconscious on the kitchen floor. Bless her heart, maybe being the mayor has just been too much stress for her."

Olivia Stuart was mayor of this town. That must be why her name stood out. That must be why he felt some vague response to her heart attack. It probably wasn't anything—

"Mr. Smith?"

If the police officer hadn't spoken the name practically in his ear, he wouldn't have responded. How quickly he'd forgotten the soap opera hunk. Forgetting could be a fatal error, one he rarely made.

"Will you come with us?"

As he left the waiting room with the two officers, he smiled the faintest of smiles. This time he'd forgotten the biggest, most important, most vital thing of all.

He'd forgotten himself.

One

Juliet Crandall sat at her computer, her fingers resting on the keyboard, but her attention was distant from her work—about fifty feet distant, she estimated, at a table in the library's reference section.

The man seated there was one of Grand Springs's intriguing mysteries. He was called Martin Smith—an unimaginative name for such an intense and handsome man—but no one knew who he really was, he least of all. He was a regular at the library, poring over newspapers, magazines, old high school yearbooks—anything that might jog his memory. It looked as if it was yearbooks today.

She wondered why he wasted his time. Grand Springs wasn't so large that a student at one of the high schools could go totally unknown. If he had attended school here, someone would remember. A handsome face wasn't easily forgotten. Six foot three, lean and mean weren't very forgettable, either. No, if Martin Smith had lived here long enough to get his picture in a yearbook some twenty years ago, someone would know.

Though Juliet had been in town only a few weeks, she'd learned from library gossip that he'd been searching for ten months for some clue to his identity, and for ten months, he'd come up empty-handed. The police department—Juliet's other new employer—had taken his fingerprints and sent them off to the state crime bureau and the FBI, but they'd gotten back a not-on-file response. So he wasn't a cop or a criminal. He'd never been in the military, applied for a gun permit or held any sort of job that required a security clearance. Just like a few hundred million other people in the country.

Not. She'd seen her share of ordinary, everyday, average citizens, and Martin Smith, whoever he was, was definitely not like them. He was the stuff fantasies—hers, at least—were made of. Broad-shouldered, lean-hipped and long-legged. Carelessly tousled blond hair and stunning blue eyes that actors and models paid money to achieve with contacts. Skin of creamy gold as if he'd just finished up a month on a tropical beach instead of a winter of snow and ice in the Rocky Mountains. His clothes were casual—jeans, always jeans, faded ones that fit the way women wanted, and shirts, plaid flannel, chambray, plain white with the sleeves rolled up or snug-fitting T-shirts.

He was enough to distract even the most dedicated computer analyst-programmer-archivist from her work.

And she'd never even spoken to him.

He had sought help from the woman who'd held this job before her, but in her two weeks here, he'd never approached her. Maybe he'd developed a preference for working on his own. Maybe he'd simply run out of things to check. Maybe he just didn't think she had anything to offer him.

That wouldn't be a first.

With a sigh, Juliet forced her gaze from the window that was her small office's only interesting feature and tried to focus on the computer screen. Grand Springs was finally bringing its library into the age of technology, reorganizing and computerizing. It was her job—every Tuesday and Thursday, at least—to do just that. The rest of her work week was spent at the police department, upgrading their computer system to allow them to take full advantage of the FBI's new computer systems. When both jobs were completed, she'd be taking a full-time position in the police department as head of their records division. It wouldn't be exciting, but at least it was different from what she'd done previously.

She'd lived all her life in the same Dallas neighborhood—heavens, in the very same house. It had been cheaper to live at home while attending college, cheaper than getting a place of her own when she'd gone to work. After her father's death, she'd stayed to help her mother, and after her mother's death, she'd stayed because it was comfortably familiar. Just as she'd stayed at the same job all those years, sitting in the same cubicle at the same keyboard, seeing the same people. She had shopped at the same stores, followed the same routines and faced the same depressing future.

At least here things were different. Not perfect. No, she was still the same shy, quiet woman she'd always been. She still didn't have many friends. She still got all hot and tongue-tied at the idea of dealing with members of the opposite sex unless they were old enough to be her father or young enough to be her son. She still spent all her free time alone, and she still conducted her social life—what there was of it—in cyberspace.

She'd had hopes for more—that she would fit in here in a way she never had in Dallas. That she would make friends. That she might even meet the mysterious man she'd dreamed of since childhood who would sweep her off her feet with offers of marriage, babies and happily-ever-afters. After all, her last birthday had put her squarely in her mid-thirties. Time was slipping away fast. Just yesterday she'd been a dreamy teenager, lost in the books that were her refuge, convinced that some day her life would change. Tomorrow she would be a sad old maid, lamenting life's unfairness, regretting the emptiness and loneliness. Today was all she had.

"Excuse me."

For a moment, lost in the future she dreaded, Juliet didn't respond to the quiet interruption. When she finally looked up, she wished she hadn't. Her face grew warm, her mouth went dry, and her fingers went limp on the keyboard.

"You're the new computer whiz."

All she could do was stare and nod dumbly.

"I'm Martin Smith." His mouth twisted in what might have been meant as a smile but was actually a grimace. "At least, that's who I've been since last June." He came farther into the room and extended his hand.

Her palm was probably sweaty, but it would be too noticeable if she took time to wipe it on her dress. She shook his hand, then quickly drew back.

"You're...?"

The heat in her cheeks increased a few degrees. It was a simple process. He gave his name, and she offered hers. How could she forget? "Juliet. Crandall. I'm new. I replaced—" The other archivist's name flew right out of her memory. "Whoever used to do this. The computers and..." Sure that she had sufficiently embarrassed herself, she lapsed into silence with her hands tightly clasped in her lap. Too bad Martin Smith hadn't approached her via computer and modem. E-mail and real-time chats were so easy. JCrandall@gsc.edu could easily converse with anyone in the world. Juliet Crandall, face-to-face, couldn't talk to anyone.

Without waiting for an invitation—one she never would have thought of offering—he sat in the only other chair in the room. "I don't know if you've heard about me—"

"Oh, yes."

The abruptness of her answer made him blush. On her, a blush was just painful evidence of yet another embarrassment. On him, it was charming. It eased the hard lines of his face and gave him a boyish appeal. "Yeah, I'm the town freak."

"I didn't mean..."

He brushed away her words. "You didn't say it. I did. Actually, it comes in handy. I don't have to waste time explaining myself to anyone. Terry Sanchez—the woman who used to do this—said that you were really good with computers."

She shrugged. She'd been computer-friendly since the very first time she'd laid fingers on a keyboard. There were times, though, when she would have given up every skill she possessed to be a little more people-friendly instead. Now was definitely one of those times.

"Can you help me?"

Not ten minutes ago she'd wondered why he'd never sought her help. Now that he had, she wished he hadn't. Helping him meant spending time with him, and while that was certainly an appealing prospect on one level, on another, it was terrifying. She didn't do well one-on-one, especially with someone as handsome, intense and fantasy-quality male as Martin Smith.

But if she helped him, she *would* get to spend time with him. Maybe they could be friends. Maybe she could even learn something from him about relating to men.

"I don't know. If the police and Terry couldn't help…"

"I'm not a priority with the police. They ran my fingerprints and sent out a missing persons broadcast, and that was all. They didn't have the manpower, the budget or the interest in pursuing it any further. As for Terry…she says you're damn good with the computer."

She should be. The computers and the Internet were her life. She got her news and entertainment there, visited with friends, planned vacations she never took and had even sold her house in Dallas via an on-line real estate agent.

"I know there are ways you can do searches on the Internet," Martin continued.

"But you have to have something to work with. I understand you don't."

His gaze shifted away and thin lines appeared at the corners of his mouth. "Then it shouldn't take you long to hit a dead end. You won't be out much time, and I'll pay you for it." His jaw tightened, and his gaze returned. "Please…"

More than that last word, which sounded as if he were unaccustomed to saying it, it was the look in his eyes that got to her. Vulnerability in a man who, she was certain, had never been vulnerable. How awful his situation must be. She wasn't always happy with who she was, but at least she knew. It must be frightening to lose the very basis of who you are.

"All right," she agreed, and she saw relief sweep over him. "But I can't do it during office hours. Why—" Her voice choked, and she had to stop to take a breath. The last man she'd invited to her house had been an account executive with her previous company. He'd been charming, flattering and genuinely interested in her—or so she'd thought. After a half-dozen dates and one long memorable weekend, he had asked for what he'd really wanted: her help in hacking into another account exec's computer. There had been a big account up for grabs, and he'd needed inside information to be sure he got it.

He hadn't gotten the information, or the account.

But Martin Smith was being very up front about what he wanted from her. He wasn't lying, playing her for a fool and trying to seduce her into cooperating.

More's the pity.

"Why don't you come to my house this evening? We'll talk."

"Around seven? Is that okay?"

"That'll be fine." She scrawled her address on a piece of notepaper and laid it on the corner of the desk closest to him. He took it with a nod, then left the office, closing the door quietly behind him.

His fingers still wrapped tightly around the doorknob, Martin drew a deep breath. He hated this feeling, this tightness in his chest, as if he'd just faced some danger and survived. He hated asking for favors, hated pleading, hated like hell feeling helpless and incapable.

Especially in front of a woman like Juliet Crandall.

When Terry Sanchez had quit, she'd told him to ask the

new computer whiz for help, and he had fully intended to do so...until he'd seen her. It had been a Monday, her first day on the job, and he'd caught a glimpse of her over at the police department. She was pretty, quiet, apparently interested in little besides her machines, and she scared the hell out of him. It had taken him two weeks to find the courage to approach her.

It had been a long time since he'd been seriously attracted to a woman. At least ten months, he knew. Even longer, he suspected. He'd had a few dates since the accident, but nothing special. Just pleasant evenings with nice women. There had been no electricity, no heat, no potential.

Just seeing Juliet Crandall made him so hot he could melt ice.

She lived in a neat little house with a picket fence less than three blocks from his own place. The house was green, the fence white, the yard big enough for kids. She didn't have any, though. She didn't have a husband, either, or, as far as he could tell, anyone special in her life. The male population both in Dallas and Grand Springs must be stupid or blind or both.

Forcing his fingers to unclench, he walked away from her office and out into the warm April sunshine. He wondered if he preferred summer or winter. Would he rather be sweating somewhere under a blazing sun or racing down a mountainside on skis? He'd gone to Squaw Creek Lodge a couple of times over the winter with the intention of renting a pair of skis and taking the lift up the mountain, but fear had kept him from actually doing it. Fear that he would get to the top and be unable to ski down? Or fear that he would be able to? He hadn't known.

He wondered a lot about the fear. What had frightened him before the accident? Had he been a coward, or had he taken chances? Had fear been an occasional thing, or had he lived with it? He wanted to believe the former. He suspected the latter.

He *suspected* a lot of things. He suspected that the truth

was out there somewhere, if he could just find the smallest clue. He suspected that he might not like what he learned. He suspected that he might not like who he'd been.

But he had to know. No matter what it cost.

He walked down the hill, taking the turns that led to his place, a garage apartment that Stone Richardson, the detective who'd tried to identify him last June, had found for him. It wasn't anything fancy, but it was cheap, and, under the circumstances, cheap was important. He'd worked off and on during the last ten months, though mostly at odd jobs, so his income was pretty meager. Added to the money found in his pocket after the accident, it had stretched, but just barely.

Five hundred dollars and change. That was all he'd had on him when he wandered into the Vanderbilt Memorial emergency room. No wallet, no car keys, no jewelry beyond an inexpensive wristwatch. Just five hundred dollars and clothing that could have been bought in any of a hundred thousand places in the country.

His wallet and the car keys, the police theorized, had been left in the car following the accident. Unfortunately, when the mud slides had been cleared away and the roads had opened again, no car had been found. Maybe, with the keys in it, someone had taken it. Or maybe there had never been a car. Maybe something else entirely had happened, and his scrambled brain had substituted an accident for it.

He climbed the wooden steps to the second-floor landing and unlocked the door. Sometimes he hated coming home because it wasn't really home. Sometimes he hated leaving it, because at least it was safe. Inside these four walls he didn't have to be Martin Smith. He didn't have to be anybody at all, and he didn't have to pretend that he was coping with being nobody. He could be as angry, bitter and afraid as he wanted—as long as he got it under control before leaving again. Control was important. He remembered that, although he didn't remember why it was, or what would happen if he lost it.

The apartment was gloomy, and turning on the lights didn't help. It was one room with a kitchen in this corner, a bathroom in that corner, a closet over there and living quarters in the middle. The furniture had come with it—a bed and night stand, a sofa and chair, a table and four ladderback chairs. Everything was ragged and worn, but still functional.

Like him.

He wasn't a particularly neat housekeeper. The floor needed sweeping, and the rag rugs needed washing. There was dust on the tables and the lamp shades, and sections of newspapers were scattered everywhere. Ignoring the dirty dishes in the sink and the dirty laundry in the corner, he went to the bathroom and stripped out of his clothes.

Normally he tried to avoid the mirror hanging above the sink. He'd learned the art of focusing his attention so narrowly that he saw only parts—jaw, chin, cheeks—when he shaved, of combing his hair without seeing the face it framed. On occasion, though, he was drawn to the mirror. He could sit for hours staring at the total stranger whose face he wore, desperately seeking some connection, some tiny distant hint of recognition that never came. When he'd seen enough, it usually took far less time to get so drunk that he couldn't see, period.

This afternoon he stared, cataloging features that he knew by heart and yet didn't know at all. Blond hair in need of a trim, blue eyes, crooked nose. High cheekbones, thin lips, square jaw.

His gaze slid lower. There was a scar on his upper right chest—round, raised, the edges uneven. A gunshot wound, Dr. Howell had said. The long, straight, clean scar underneath it was from the incision made to remove the bullet. There were a matching set on his back and other smaller scars on his chest and back, plus one on his arm from something jagged—maybe a broken bottle or a dull knife that had torn instead of cut.

God help him, what kind of person had he been?

Violent.

Criminal.

Dangerous.

Had he been a dangerous man? He didn't want to believe it, but sometimes he did. Sometimes he dreamed that he had been exactly the sort of person who could threaten, intimidate and hurt—maybe kill—someone else. Sometimes the dreams were so vivid, so intense, that they terrified him, and he spent the rest of the night pacing the room to avoid falling asleep again.

That was the first thing he had to tell Juliet Crandall this evening. She hadn't wanted to help him in the first place. Warning her what kind of man he might be was only fair.

He'd never felt compelled to warn Terry Sanchez. But he had never seen Terry outside the library, and all he'd wanted was her assistance. He wanted a lot more from Juliet.

A hell of a lot more. But he couldn't have it. He might have a wife and kids somewhere. There might be warrants for his arrest. Whoever had tried to kill him before might try again. Before he could have any kind of future, he had to find out about his past. He had to find out whether he deserved a future or whether everyone would have been better off if one of those bullets had killed him.

Maybe, once he knew the truth, *then* he could want someone. Maybe then he could have someone.

Scowling, he turned the shower to hot and stepped into the tub. It wasn't yet four o'clock. He would be ready to go to Juliet's house three hours early. Or maybe he would *never* be ready to go to Juliet's house.

He bathed quickly, grateful when he got out that the mirror had fogged over. He dressed, combed his hair straight back, then stretched out on the couch to watch the clock. He didn't turn on the television in the corner or pick up the morning paper his landlady had brought over when she'd finished with it. He just lay there, wishing, wondering, regretting.

The minutes crawled, but finally the bedside clock read six-forty-five. He left the apartment, slipped through the gate in the back fence and made his way to the block where Juliet lived. Her car, a sensible gray sedan, was parked in the driveway, and the front door was open. He raised his hand to knock on the screen door, then stilled.

He could see a corner of the living room, an equal wedge of another room and down the wide hall to the kitchen. As he watched, Juliet turned the corner at the far end and started toward him. She was wearing a dress, a garden-party sort of dress of soft, flowing fabric, subdued flowers, ribbon trim and a row of little white buttons that ran from the modest V-neck all the way to the ankle. They were already fastened from the waist down, as if she had simply undone enough buttons to step inside the garment, and she was buttoning the rest now, her steps slow and leisurely, her head bent.

Maybe he stifled a groan or a board creaked or his skin was sizzling from the sudden influx of heat. Whatever the cause, abruptly she raised her head and stared at him through the screen. He felt dim-witted, thick-tongued and embarrassed, as if he'd been caught spying. He wanted to turn and walk away, to pretend that he'd seen nothing. Truth was, he *hadn't* seen anything. Just a narrow strip of pale skin that dipped between her breasts to her waist. Just her fingers working the small buttons. Just enough to know that he wanted more.

She turned her back. When she faced him again, the last button was securely fastened and her face was tinged pink. She held the screen door open a few inches. "Hello."

He took hold of the handle, but didn't pull, didn't step inside. Instead, in a masterpiece of clumsiness, he blurted out, "Before we start, I think you should know that someone tried to kill me."

"Today?"

"No. Several years ago." When she looked puzzled, he explained, "I don't know who I am—who I used to be—

but apparently it was someone with enemies. Someone who did something worth killing over.''

For a long time, she simply looked at him. Then abruptly she shrugged, making her hair sway. "Or maybe you were the victim of some crazy with a gun. Lord knows, there are enough of them around. Come on in."

He went inside, then flipped the hook on the jamb into the eye on the door. By the time he turned, she was already in the room on the right.

It had once been a formal dining room and still held dining room furniture. The pieces were old and oak—an oval table big enough to seat six, four chairs that matched, two office chairs on wheels and a china cabinet. The oak was heirloom quality, suited to a country house with a family to fill the chairs. Here it did duty as a desk, supporting the monitor, keyboard, tower and printer. The shelves of the china hutch held books, diskettes and program boxes. Packages of paper and printer cartridges were visible in the cabinet underneath before she shoved the door shut as she passed.

She sat in a bright blue chair in front of the computer but made no effort to turn it on. We'll talk, she had said, and that was apparently all she intended to do. Doing it here, he assumed, instead of the living room where they would have been more comfortable was her way of keeping it strictly business.

"I've been thinking about this all afternoon, and I'm not really sure I can help you."

He didn't want to hear that, pretended he didn't hear it as he circled the room. There were blinds on the windows, no curtains and nothing on the walls but a corkboard directly behind her. From across the room, he couldn't make out any of the notes thumbtacked to the board. When he pulled out the chair beside her, he still couldn't read them. Her writing was atrocious.

"Exactly what was Terry doing?"

"We went through old newspapers and school yearbooks, checked town records, looking for something I might remember.''

"You think you're from here."

"I know I've been here. From the start, I've had this feeling…" He wasn't one to talk much about feelings, or if he did, he disguised them with other words. Instincts. Intuition. Intuition told him he'd been in Grand Springs long enough to gain a familiarity with the place. Too often he knew what was around a corner he'd never turned. He'd known in September about the eighty-foot-tall pine that would be decorated for Christmas in December. There were places—the high school gymnasium, a restaurant downtown, a clothing store—where he *knew* he'd been at some time in the forgotten past.

"But if you had lived here or spent any length of time here, don't you think someone would recognize you?"

He scowled at the logic of her argument. "Maybe it was a long time ago. Maybe I've changed. Maybe I'm not that noticeable."

Juliet had to bite her tongue to stop from snorting scornfully at that last comment. Not noticeable? In what galaxy? She'd seen his effect on the females in the library, from giggly teenagers to white-haired grandmothers. There was no way he could have spent any time here and the women of Grand Springs not notice him. "When you appeared in Grand Springs, you didn't remember anything?"

"I remembered who was president of the United States. I knew that I've always liked Italian food. I knew I spoke fluent Spanish. I remembered plenty of things. Just nothing important, like who I am or where I'm from." He slumped in the chair, his feet stretched out so that they nearly touched hers. She swiveled her chair a few inches to the right.

"What happened the night of the accident?" She knew there'd been a wreck, that he'd suffered a head injury and now had amnesia, but the rumor mill was short on details, and details were desperately needed if she was going to help him.

"The first thing I remember is waking up with a hell of a headache. I guess I lost control of the car in the storm and hit the guardrail."

The storm. That was how the town referred to that weekend last June. Rains had saturated the area, and the downpour that Friday evening had been more than the ground could bear. There had been massive mud slides, closing the highways and causing a blackout that lasted into Sunday.

"Besides banging your head, were you hurt?"

He shook his head. "I left the car and started walking. The town was completely dark, so when I saw lights, I headed for them. It was the hospital. They examined me, gave me a name—"

"After the soap opera hunk," she said, and he scowled again. Which offended him more—the soap opera part or the hunk part?

"And called the police. They were busy with the blackout and the mayor's murder, but eventually they got around to me. They took my fingerprints and sent them to the FBI and the state. They didn't know who I was, either."

"So we know you're not a cop, you were never in the military, and you're not a crook."

"At least, not one who's been caught."

She ignored his mutterings and went on. "Before the accident, were you coming to Grand Springs or going away from it?"

"I don't remember."

"Which direction was your car facing when you regained consciousness?"

"I don't remember. I'd hit my head. I was disoriented."

"What happened to the car?"

He lifted his shoulders in a shrug. "Once things settled down and the roads were reopened, Stone Richardson took me out to find it. We couldn't."

"Why not?"

"I didn't remember where I left it, but wherever that was, it was no longer there. We drove all the way to the interstate and found nothing."

"So someone stole it."

"Or it got swept away by the mud slides."

"Is that possible?"

His look was dry, his voice even drier. "Have you ever seen a few tons of mud and rock come rushing down a mountainside?"

"I'm from Dallas. We don't have mountainsides. We don't even have many hillsides."

"A mud slide can uproot trees, tear down guardrails and destroy chunks of roadway. It can move a building off its foundation and carry it away, breaking it into splinters along the way. It can destroy a town, kill anyone in its way, and, yes, it can wash away a car."

"Didn't anyone search for the car?" It seemed a simple enough task to her: find the places where the mud had rushed over the highway, follow it down the mountainside and find the car. If it wasn't immediately visible, search any places where the mud was deep enough to cover it. Easy.

"When you moved here, you drove into town from the interstate, didn't you? You saw the drop-offs in some places along the highway, didn't you?"

She nodded. In a few places, the shoulder wasn't more than a few feet wide, and nothing more than a steel guardrail separated a car on the highway from a two-thousand-foot fall. Other drops were less dramatic, but there were plenty where a search would be difficult at best. "Do you think your car went over one of those drop-offs?"

"I don't know."

"So Stone took your fingerprints and checked missing persons reports and got nothing. Has he done that recently?"

"Why would he?"

"Maybe, when he checked, your family or friends or

employer hadn't yet realized that you *were* missing. Maybe you were on vacation and not expected back for several weeks. Maybe they filed a report a few days or weeks later." Picking up a pen, she made a note on the pad next to the computer. Tomorrow she would be at the police department. She would talk to Stone about trying again. "Do you have any scars, tattoos or distinguishing marks?"

He mumbled his answer as if he preferred not to acknowledge their existence. "Scars."

Her gaze followed his right hand to his left arm, where he rubbed the thickened skin. She made a note of its location and length even as she wondered what he had done to earn such an injury.

"It's a defensive wound."

Given a little time, she could have figured that out. The scar ran four inches along the inside of his arm, as if he had raised his arm to ward off an attacker. But who had attacked him and why? Had he been an innocent victim or an equally guilty transgressor?

She would like to believe "innocent victim," but it was hard to cast him as either innocent or a victim. On the other hand, it was easy to see him as aggressive, strong, take-charge, bold. It was easy to imagine him meeting an attacker head-on, giving as good as he got.

Unless his attacker was someone he couldn't defend himself against—a woman, perhaps, a friend or an authority figure. Or unless he believed he deserved the attack. Which brought her back to her original question: what had he done?

Knowing that he could offer no more information than her wild imagination, she pressed on. "You said scars. What about the others?"

"What does it matter?"

"The more identifying information we can provide, the better the chances of getting a match."

"Assuming that there was someone who cared enough to file a missing persons report."

"You don't think there was?"

His fingers knotted, and his eyes turned the bleak blue of a sunless wintry day. "I don't know."

Under the best of circumstances, it was a vaguely dissatisfying answer. When it applied to every area of your own life, when it answered even the simplest, most basic questions—What is your name? How old are you? Where do you live?—it must be frustrating as hell.

"You weren't wearing a wedding ring?"

"No. No tan line, either."

"Which proves nothing. There has to be someone—a wife, a girlfriend, friends, neighbors, co-workers. You can't have lived so isolated that *no one's* noticed you're gone."

"I *don't* know." Rising from his chair, he paced to the other side of the table. He was restless, edgy, and he made her feel edgy. She fiddled with her pen as she watched him.

"What about the other scars?"

For a long moment, he looked at her, then answered in a rush. "I've been shot twice—once in the back, left side, down low, and once in the chest, upper right side. There are two entry wounds, plus two surgical scars where the bullets were removed. Based on the way scars mature, the doctor says one is a couple of years old, the other probably a couple of years older than that."

"And the scar on your arm?"

"It's older. I've had it since I was a kid."

"The doctor told you that?"

"No. I just know...." Frustrated, he gestured toward the computers. "What can you do with those?"

She could do anything, go anywhere, be anyone. His interest, of course, was much narrower. What could she do for *him?* It was her turn to parrot his answer. "I don't know. I need a name, a town, something to go on."

"If I had a town, I'd be there, and if I had a name, I wouldn't need—"

You. She smiled faintly. She knew that, of course. If she didn't have something tangible to offer, he would have no interest in her. Too bad that she had nothing to offer—just lots of questions and no answers. "You said you've had this feeling of familiarity about the town. What about the people?"

He shook his head.

"No one seems familiar? No one brings a particular response?"

He stood at the window, back straight, very still, and stared out. The sun's last rays shining through the partially opened blinds cast a pattern across his face, with a shadow across his mouth and another over his eyes. At last, he answered, his voice so grim that she didn't want to see his eyes. "Olivia Stuart."

Juliet drew her feet onto her chair seat and wrapped her arms around her knees to contain a shiver. For such a short time in town, she'd learned a lot. Olivia Stuart had been widely admired in Grand Springs, hailed as the town's best mayor ever. Her death last June, presumably from a heart attack, had stunned everyone. The news that the heart attack had been drug-induced had sent shock waves through the town. Last October the police had arrested one of her murderers—a professional killer by the name of Joanna Jackson—and were still looking for another of those involved, Dean Springer. Springer had hired Joanna, but to this day, no one knew whom he was working for. No one knew why his mysterious boss had wanted Olivia Stuart dead.

Maybe Martin Smith knew.

As if he knew the direction her thoughts were traveling, he smiled mockingly. "I was questioned and cleared. At the time the mayor was given the fatal injection, I was somewhere out on the highway. A couple of Grand Springs's respectable citizens can vouch for that."

But that only meant that he hadn't been the one to actually give the injection. Could he be the one who had ordered it? Could he have held a grudge against the mayor with lethal consequences? Juliet didn't ask the questions aloud, but Martin had already asked them and failed to come up with answers.

"Could you have known Olivia?"

"Maybe."

"Could you be a relative?"

"No."

"How can you be so sure?"

"She had a son and a daughter. I've met both of them, and they don't have a clue who I might be."

It shouldn't take you long to hit a dead end, he'd said this afternoon, and he had been right. She was running out of questions, and they had learned nothing. "What kind of response does she bring?"

He shrugged but continued to stare out. "That night in the ER, I heard that she'd had a heart attack, and...I was sorry. I didn't have any idea who she was, but...it mattered. It was as if her death—or her life—was important to me in some way."

"Maybe you'd done business with her. Maybe you were on your way here to meet with her."

"Stone checked her appointment book. Everyone listed in it is present and accounted for."

"Maybe your business with her was personal."

He shook his head. "She was very organized. She kept track of her personal business as well as her professional matters."

"It's human nature to feel some measure of sadness when you hear someone has died. Maybe that's all it was. You were just being human."

With another shake of his head, he closed the blinds, then faced her. "I don't think I'm a very empathetic person."

"What do you think you are?"

He rested his hands on the back of the chair across from her, and his fingers automatically tightened. "I don't know, but I think..." He took a deep breath as if it were the only way to force the words out. "I think I'm afraid to find out."

Two

"Do you want something to drink?"

Martin nodded as Juliet got to her feet. They'd been at it more than an hour—lots of questions, lots of the same depressing answers. *I don't know. I don't remember.* Why did she bother asking? Why did he bother repeating? Why didn't they just accept that, for all practical purposes, his life before last June no longer existed? At least not in a place where *he* could get to it.

After a moment alone in the quiet office, he left his chair and stepped into the hallway. The living room was dark, but he could make out overstuffed furniture in dark stripes, the kind made for stretching out on, and a television, silent in the corner. There were two doors between him and the kitchen, one probably a closet, the other open to reveal a bathroom. A third opening on the opposite side was another hallway, one that presumably led to the bedrooms. That was where he'd first seen her this evening, buttoning her dress, unknowingly teasing him, tantalizing him, turning him on.

He remembered sex—not with any particular person, not at any particular time, but he remembered the need, the raw, aching hunger, the torment in a slow, leisurely seduction and the pleasure in a quick, hard completion. He remembered the sense of power at what he could make a woman feel and the very real vulnerability at what she could do to him.

Sweet hell, what Juliet could do to him, if only he could remember. If only he knew his past.

He walked the length of the hallway, not allowing himself even the quickest of glances down the shorter hall to the bedrooms. She stood at the counter, her back to him, filling glasses with pop and arranging cookies on a plate, and he took advantage of her lack of awareness to study her. Her feet were bare—had he always found that erotic or was this a postconcussion fetish?—and her skirt swirled around her ankles as she moved. The dress was loose and full from the waist down. It clung like a second skin from there up, snug enough that he could tell by the uninterrupted smoothness that she wasn't wearing a bra. He *knew* she wasn't wearing one, because he'd seen that pale delicate skin, so soft and inviting that his fingers ached to touch it.

She was humming softly to herself, with her head bent so her hair fell forward, revealing her neck. It was long, pale, probably soft, definitely erotic. All he would have to do was walk across the room, brush a few strands of hair aside, touch his mouth to her skin, and he would be so damned hot that he just might burst into flames.

He was moving toward her, closing the distance between them, only a few feet away, when she turned from the counter and saw him. Startled, she dropped the glasses she held. Pop, ice and bits of glass went everywhere, splashing her skirt and his jeans, as color flooded her face. "Oh, my God, I didn't know— Don't you make noise when you walk?"

Though he hadn't meant to frighten her, he felt guilty, anyway. He should have spoken from the doorway, should have let her know that she was no longer alone, but he'd seen her, and everything else—except wanting her—had fled his mind. "Sorry," he said stiffly. "I'll clean that—"

"I will." She snatched up a towel from the counter and crouched, careful to tuck her skirt tightly around her legs. He found a broom and dustpan in the corner and, while she mopped up soda, swept the broken glass into a pile. When he knelt to scoop it into the pan, he found himself closer to her than he'd ever been, closer than he should ever be.

Close enough to see that her eyes were just a shade more blue than hazel. Close enough to touch her. Close enough to hurt her.

Startled by the thought, he moved back, swept the glass into the pan and got to his feet, quickly putting the length of the room between them. Why the hell would he hurt her? Was that what he did? Hurt vulnerable, helpless women? Maybe even kill them?

Like Olivia Stuart?

The thought had occurred to Juliet earlier that maybe he had given the order for Olivia's murder. She hadn't asked, but he knew she had wondered. He wondered, too. Had he been coming to Grand Springs to harm the mayor? To help her? Or was his response to the news of her death nothing more than human nature, as Juliet had suggested? Damn it, he didn't know.

But, as he'd told her, he didn't think he was a very empathetic person. He thought he might be a coldhearted bastard. Maybe a cold-blooded killer.

She stood up, wet a handful of paper towels, then crouched to give the floor a thorough swipe. "Sorry about the mess. I'm used to being alone, and you do move quietly. I was just surprised."

"It was my fault." He didn't look at her, but he could see her peripherally—a swirl of soft colors, blond hair, bare feet. What was wrong with all the people she'd known that she was used to being alone? Why weren't there men lined up at her door? Why wasn't she spending her evenings with a husband and family instead of a computer? Instead of with *him?*

"Just give me a second and I'll have everything—"

"Don't bother. I should go." He looked at her finally and saw disappointment flare in her eyes before her face flushed and she turned away to needlessly rearrange the few items on the counter. Disappointment. She didn't want him to leave. Was she crazy or just lonely?

He knew loneliness intimately—the empty, aching need

to share at least some small part of your life with someone special. He'd made friends here, but even with them, he still felt the need. He still wondered if there was someone out there somewhere who was lonely for him. Was there someone special, someone he'd loved, someone whose life was incomplete without him?

He didn't think so. Maybe it was sentimental bull, but he believed that if there had been someone special, some part of him would know. Maybe not his mind, but his heart. His soul. But his heart was too empty. He was too alone. Too attracted to Juliet.

Juliet, who was avoiding facing him, who was embarrassed, who was lonely.

He swallowed hard. Knowing he shouldn't, he said, "If it wouldn't be any trouble…"

She flashed a relieved smile. "No, not at all."

He stayed on his side of the room while she took two more glasses from the cabinet, stretching high to reach, pulling taut fabric even tighter. Stifling a groan, he turned his attention to the back door. It stood open, the screen door unlatched, giving him a glimpse of a night-dark yard with shadows and gloom for cover.

"You need a light in the backyard," he commented. "Either a floodlight or a motion sensor. And you should keep the screen door latched. Better yet, you should replace both your screen doors with storm doors, the kind with a keyed lock. You need a dead bolt on the door, too—at least a one-inch—and…"

The wary look she gave him made him stop. "This isn't Dallas."

"No, it's Grand Springs. In the ten months I've been here, the mayor has been murdered, her daughter and granddaughter were kidnapped, the bank was robbed, and someone tried to kill a couple of cops and the town treasurer. Don't confuse small with safe. Keep your doors locked." Though his advice might be coming a little late.

She had already let *him* in, and that just might be the worst mistake she could make.

She offered him a glass. He had to cross the room to take it from her. "Maybe you worked in the home security business."

"Maybe I worked in the home invasion business."

"If you were a criminal, you must have been very, very good to reach your age without getting caught. By the way, what age have they settled on for you?"

"Late thirties, maybe forty." Forty hard years, judging by the lines on his face and the damage done to his body, and he could account for only ten months. The knowledge made him feel less than whole.

After latching the screen and locking the door, he followed her down the hall. He expected her to turn into the semibusinesslike dining room. Instead, she went into the living room, switching on lights before settling on a crimson-and-green love seat. She put the plate of cookies on the table between the love seat and sofa, then gestured for him to sit. He wanted to choose the armchair across the room, beneath a hanging lamp, but he obeyed her and sat on the couch instead.

Munching on a cookie, he gave the rest of the room a look. It was homier than the dining room, with pictures on the walls, and books, plants and collectibles scattered around. It was a comfortable room, the sort of place— maybe minus the family photos—he imagined he might have had in another place in another life.

"These are good. Did you bake them?"

"I bought them at the bakery near the college. They were out of their wonderful little fried pies—"

"With cherries, apples and apricots."

"You've been there?"

He shook his head. He just knew. Sick of things he should remember but couldn't and things he knew that he shouldn't, he changed the subject. "Why did you come here?"

The question made her uncomfortable. She was fine asking hard questions of him, but the simplest question about her turned her face pink and made her gaze shift to the family portrait on the opposite wall. "I wanted a change."

"Are your parents still in Dallas?"

"No. My father died five years ago. My mother died two years later."

"No brothers or sisters?"

"No. A lot of aunts, uncles and cousins, but none I was particularly close to."

"Why Grand Springs?"

"The job came open, and I liked the idea of living in the mountains."

"Wait until you've spent your first winter here, then see if you like it. Do you ski?"

"No."

"Hike?"

"No."

"Camp? Fish? Take long bike rides?"

"No."

"Then what do you do?"

"I work, and I spend time on-line."

He glanced across the hall at the computer. There were few, if any, people in her life, but she had her computer. Cold company, but better than what *he* had. Nothing kept him company but loneliness, frustration and fear. Fear of who he had been, of who he was, of who he might never be. Fear of knowing and of never knowing.

Grimly he forced his attention back to her. "What do you do on-line?"

"Talk to friends. Read the paper. Check movie reviews and weather forecasts. Order books." She shrugged. "Everything."

"Have you ever met these friends before? In person? Face-to-face?"

Discomfort edged into her expression. "I don't do well face-to-face."

Maybe she was more comfortable hiding behind a computer screen. The men among those on-line friends didn't know what they were missing. Even if she had described herself as five-five, blond and blue, it would say nothing about the stubborn line of her jaw or the way she turned that delicate pink when embarrassed. It didn't give a hint of the shape of her mouth or the silkiness of her hair or the fragile air that surrounded her. "Five-five, blond and blue" could be a man's worst nightmare...or his sweetest dream.

"So you get on the computer and talk to people you've never met. How do you know they are what they say they are? How do you know they're not scam artists, stalkers, rapists or killers?"

"How do we know that about anyone?"

How did she know it about *him?* Point taken.

"These people don't know me, either. They only know what I choose to tell them."

"Wouldn't you rather talk to a flesh-and-blood person? Someone you could see, hear, touch?"

Again she looked uncomfortable. "I'm talking to you."

He was definitely flesh and blood—very hard flesh, if she came near him, and very hot blood. His smile was thin and unamused. Here he was, warning her about the men on-line, but *he* was a bigger threat than any of them. He knew how she looked, moved, sounded. He knew where she lived. He knew he wanted her.

His muscles tensing, he forced his thoughts to a safer path. "Your boyfriend must have been sorry to see you leave." Yeah, that was good. Juliet with another man, a man who was special to her, getting intimate, making love—that was a definite turnoff.

Or not, he admitted as an image popped into his head: Juliet naked, her skin slick with sweat, her soft little moans erotic and torturous to hear. It didn't matter that the hands rubbing her body and the mouth suckling her breasts belonged to someone else, didn't matter that another man would fill her, pleasure her and finish with her. It was arousing as hell. Scary as hell.

"I haven't been in a relationship in a long time."

He hadn't, either, not once in his entire life of ten months and a few days. His body was more than ready. Unfortunately, his spirit wasn't. He needed answers. Reassurances. Some reason to think that he might be worthy of a relationship with someone special.

"Have you ever been married?"

With a faint smile, she shook her head.

"Ever come close?"

Another shake.

Fools. The entire state of Texas was nothing but fools.

"Have you considered leaving Grand Springs?" she asked, turning the conversation away from herself and back to him. He let her.

"Where would I go? What would I do?"

"To look for someplace familiar. What do you do here?"

"Work occasionally. Try to remember always."

She showed interest in his first answer. "Work. What do you know how to do? What skills do you have?"

He knew where she was leading. Every time he'd seen someone doing a particular job, he had wondered, Did I do that? "Odd jobs, mostly. At Christmas I worked in a couple of shops downtown. I wasn't much of a salesman. I filled in on a framing crew when they were shorthanded, and they agreed that I was no carpenter. I've bussed tables and washed dishes at the Country House Restaurant." He shrugged.

"Nothing seemed familiar?"

"No."

"Correct me if I'm wrong, but you've only forgotten things of a personal nature. You remember who's president, how to drive, how to tie your shoes."

He nodded.

"Maybe you don't *want* to remember the personal stuff.

Maybe there's a reason deep in your subconscious that you've blocked it, like a marriage falling apart or the death of someone you loved or—''

"I *do* want to know—more than you can imagine." But maybe she was right. Maybe his fear was stronger than his desire to know. After all, right now the front-runner for his previous occupation was "criminal"—or worse. He had good cause to wonder. He noticed things, like how easy it would be to gain entry through her unlocked doors. He was familiar with police procedure, more so, he suspected, than the average law-abiding citizen. Someone had tried to kill him.

And there were the dreams. The nightmares.

He tried to pretend they didn't exist, tried to go through the day without acknowledging them, to face the night without fearing them. He'd never told anyone about them—not Stone, not Doc Howell, not the shrink named Jeffers they had sent him to. They were too frightening, too threatening, with someone dying in every dream. The details were different—the identity of the victim, the place, the means of death—but one thing always remained the same. *He* was always there. Innocent witness? Or brutal killer?

"Have you seen a psychiatrist?"

"For a while. He couldn't make me remember."

"Make?"

Her voice was soft, her tone far from accusatory, but it made him defensive, anyway. "He couldn't *help* me remember." All Jeffers had done was interview him at length, give him a diagnosis of generalized amnesia and a prognosis that, at some time, it would probably resolve itself and he'd be back to normal. No help at all.

"I thought most computer whizzes were odd little guys who turned to computers because they couldn't relate to people, or spoiled, overindulged teenagers whose parents wanted them out of their hair. How did you get interested?"

"I was an odd little overindulged teenager who related

better to machines than people. Have you considered hypnosis?''

"We're talking at cross-purposes here. I'm tired of talking about myself, and you don't like to talk about yourself. Why is that?''

A blush and a shrug. "I know all about me.''

"I don't.''

The blush deepened. "We're here to try to learn about you.''

He wasn't. Oh, he wanted her help, of course, if she had any to give, but he was here because two weeks and one day ago, he had taken one long, hard look at her and fallen. He was here because he wanted to know more about her, because he wanted to watch the unconsciously sensual way she moved, because he wanted to torment himself with what he shouldn't want, should never have.

He was here for pleasure. She was here for business. It had never occurred to her that they could be one and the same. It never might.

Okay, hypnosis. "The shrink tried hypnosis, but not everyone's a good candidate. The results were less than satisfactory.'' In fact, it had been an exercise in futility.

She stifled a yawn, and he checked the time. It was only nine—not too late for him, but he didn't have to go to work tomorrow. He could stay up until dawn and sleep till noon, and no one would care.

Setting his empty glass aside, he got to his feet. "I'd better go.'' Even to himself, he sounded tentative, as if one word from her could change his mind. Stay. Don't go. Spend the night.

He doubted he had ever been particularly fanciful, but his imagination had run wild in the last two weeks, all without the slightest encouragement. To Juliet Crandall, he was a mystery, no more. A puzzle with its pieces jumbled. She probably hadn't thought of him even once as a getting-involved, kissing-and-seducing, making-love-and-babies-

and-a-future-with kind of man.

She probably never would.

Juliet stood in the doorway, watching as Martin walked into the night. He moved quickly, silently—stealthily, she thought—into the shadows, disappearing from sight.

Was he a criminal? Was that why he moved like that, why he'd been able to sneak up on her in the kitchen tonight? Did that explain how he'd been able to take a few seconds' look at her door and yard and find the weaknesses from a security standpoint?

She closed and locked the door, then went into the dining room. By the time she settled in her chair, the computer was up and running. There was a batch of E-mails awaiting her. She scanned the list, but didn't open any messages.

What did she really know about these people? What did it say about her that her only friends were virtual strangers, hiding behind screen names and identities that were as likely fabricated as truthful? They'd told her their names, marital status, occupations, but on-line, it was easy to be something you weren't. Heavens, they thought *she* was interesting, and on-line, she *was.* Her fingers never tripped over words the way her tongue did in a real-life conversation. If she embarrassed herself—as she'd done in the kitchen—no one was there to see it. As far as they were concerned, she was friendly, outgoing, competent and fun.

Geez, maybe they *were* scam artists, stalkers, rapists and killers.

But more likely they were just average people, a little lonely and a little lost. Like her. Like Martin.

Exiting the mailbox, she called up her favorite search engine and typed in one word. The lights in the lower corner of the screen blinked as the modems communicated and transferred data.

Her search was far too general, giving her every site listed that contained the word *amnesia.* There were nearly seven thousand hits. Rather than try to narrow it, she began sorting through them one by one, occasionally stopping to link to another site. By midnight her eyes were gritty, her back was aching, and she'd increased her knowledge of amnesia a hundredfold. But she hadn't learned anything that could help Martin.

Did it matter? Now that he knew how little she could do, he would probably keep his distance. She sincerely wished she could help—she wouldn't mind his gratitude at all—but she wasn't a miracle worker. She had to have *something* to work with.

Still, she couldn't help feeling as if she'd somehow let him down.

She would do what she could—send out a missing persons bulletin again—and that would be the end of it. It was just as well. She didn't want any man simply because he was grateful for what she'd done for him. If he couldn't appreciate her for herself, it was his loss. Wasn't that what her parents had always told her?

But they'd been wrong. It was her loss, too. Living alone, being alone, seeing other women her age with husbands and children and having no opportunity for her own family in sight—those were her losses, and she lived with them every day.

Clicking the mouse, she backed out of the sites she had accessed, thought for a moment about reading her mail, then shut down. She turned off the lights as she made her way to the bedroom.

It was a nice size, with room for the furniture that had been her grandparents' and a thickly padded chaise that was her favorite place to curl up on a sleepless night. It was a pretty room, too, painted pale peach on two walls and deep coral on the others. The linens were a coral-and-teal floral, the curtains at the window frilly coral, the slipcover on the chaise frilly teal. There were ruffled pillows on the bed and the chaise, and lacy crocheted doilies—gifts from Grandma—everywhere.

It was a woman's room, she acknowledged as she undid the buttons on her dress. Everywhere she looked, she saw ruffles and frills. Only a man secure in his masculinity could lie in that bed or stretch out on the chaise without being totally overwhelmed.

Martin came to mind.

Her fingers stopped on the buttons as she turned to face the mirror, to see what he had seen when he'd first arrived. The fabric gapped to her waist—not a lot, not immodestly, but enough. The material was soft and pretty, like an impressionist watercolor, and the skin that showed was pale. Tentatively she touched herself, just one fingertip at the point of the vee, drawing it slowly along exposed skin to her waist. Closing her eyes, she did it again, only this time, in her mind, the hand was dark, the fingertip callused, the touch incredibly sexual. It was enough to make her shiver, then flush.

She wasn't so terribly needy that she had to fantasize over a man who clearly held little interest in her as a woman. It hadn't been so long since she'd had sex. It had lasted the weekend—the *entire* weekend—and had been the best sex she'd ever experienced, and it had been only...

Only twenty months ago. She scowled. She *was* needy enough to fantasize about Martin Smith. But it was only fair. He was so well suited for feminine fantasies.

Giving herself a shake, she finished undressing and got ready for bed. She was lucky enough to be a sound sleeper, and she slept through the night, awakening in plenty of time for breakfast before work. The job at the library was okay, but she liked her three days at the police department better. The clerk who worked in the office, Mariellen, required constant supervision, but Juliet liked everyone else and she liked the work.

She was only a few blocks from the house when she spied a familiar figure ahead. Martin didn't have a driver's license, according to Tracey at the library. He didn't have any official documents at all. There must be some provision for obtaining them when you truly had no idea who you were, but maybe he wasn't interested. Maybe he couldn't face becoming Martin Smith officially. Maybe he feared that would somehow rob him of the man he really was.

As she drove the half block that separated them, she debated, then pulled to the curb. "Can I give you a ride?"

When he turned her way, he looked exhausted. His eyes were bloodshot, his features fixed in a scowl. "I'm not going anywhere."

A curious answer. "Then how about a ride home?"

After a moment's hesitation, he climbed in beside her. He was so tall and broad-shouldered that immediately the car seemed to shrink by half.

"Tough night?"

He tilted his head back and closed his eyes. "Yeah. I couldn't sleep."

She wondered how hard he had tried. His jaw was unshaven, his hair disheveled as if he—or someone—had combed it with his—or her?—fingers, and he still wore the same snug jeans and emerald shirt he'd worn to her house last night. She could see the pop stains on the lower leg.

She had assumed, when he'd said good-night, that he was going home. Now she wondered. Not that it was any of her business.

Realizing that they weren't moving, he looked at her. "What are you waiting for?"

"I don't know where you live."

He gave her the address, only five blocks in the opposite direction. She made a U-turn and tried very hard to think of something to say, anything at all to break the silence that pricked at her and didn't seem to bother him in the least. Before she came up with a single, simple, asinine comment—*nice day,* for God's sake—she was pulling into his driveway.

The house was old and lovely, three stories, big enough for a family or two or three. She looked at it, then him. "You live here?" *Brilliant, Juliet. He told you he did, didn't he?*

"Back there." He gestured toward the back, and she saw

the detached garage with an apartment overhead. "Thanks for the ride."

That was it—no goodbye, no mention of last night, no small talk, nothing personal at all. *Thanks for the ride.*

"You're pathetic, Juliet," she berated herself as she backed into the street again. "Any other female in town could have done better than that. Five blocks, and you don't say a word—not a word! And you wonder why men don't go nuts over you."

No, that wasn't true. She never expected men to even notice her. Last night Martin had suggested that he might have been unnoticeable in his previous life, which was laughable. She knew unnoticeable, because *she* was. All her life people had been looking through her. Maybe she could have gotten by okay being plain and too smart, but shyness on top of plainness and braininess was the kiss of death.

And she wasn't kidding herself: she *was* plain. Only her parents had ever thought differently, and they were supposed to think she was beautiful because they loved her. She had always thought that someday some man would also think she was beautiful, because that would surely mean he loved her, but it had never happened, and it probably never would.

Even if it did, it wouldn't necessarily mean he loved her. It might just mean his vision wasn't so great.

Her office in the Grand Springs Police Department was nothing fancy. Since she would soon be doing the job, she was already situated in the records supervisor's office, a square room with a big window, like her other office, that gave her a view of the daily workings of the department. She rarely had time to look…but she'd always managed to find a few minutes whenever Martin had come in to visit one detective or another.

She locked her purse in the bottom desk drawer, picked up her coffee cup and headed for the machine in the outer room. Once the cup was filled, she stopped at Stone Richardson's desk. The detective was typing a report using the old reliable hunt-and-peck method on a less-than-reliable typewriter and grumbling under his breath. "Once we get the system up and running, that'll be a lot easier," she commented as she sat in the chair next to his desk.

"Typing's typing."

"Yes, but you won't be dealing with paper, so correcting mistakes is easier. I'm designing a computer report template with the same field identifier blocks, so all you'll have to do is pick the appropriate report from the menu, then fill in the blanks."

He didn't look impressed. "And it will be available when?"

"Soon. The desktop terminals should be in next week."

"Unfortunately, this report can't wait." He sat back in his chair. "What can I do for you?"

"I talked to Martin Smith last night. He said you guys did a missing persons broadcast right after his accident."

"Yeah. We got a couple of possible hits, but they didn't pan out. You have an idea?"

"I'd like to do it again. Maybe, at that time, no one was aware that he *was* missing, but surely after ten months, someone has realized that something's wrong."

"Good idea. The file is in your office. Go to it."

With a smile of thanks, she took the coffee back to her office, pulled the folder and settled at the National Crime Information Center terminal there.

She was working on the required state certification as an NCIC terminal operator, along with her other duties, but she'd been granted access in the meantime. It was slow going, though. Ditzy Mariellen, whose desk sat right outside the door, could have the information typed in and the broadcast sent in the time it would take Juliet to thumb through the manual that would help her locate and fill out the proper form.

But she didn't hand the file to Mariellen. She opened it and studied Stone's notes. A John Doe white male, approximately forty years of age, six-three, blond and blue.

Not much of a description for the best-looking man she'd come across in recent memory. There were notes on the scars—six in all, the last attributed to a burn—but no other identifying marks, no tattoos, no birthmarks. Of course, six scars were enough.

He feared he'd lived a violent life, and the evidence seemed to be on his side. Innocent people did become victims, but three times, possibly four?

She just couldn't imagine him as a criminal. And why not? Because he was handsome? A quick look through the mug books would confirm that handsome men did, in fact, commit crimes. Because he seemed so lost? She couldn't call any figures to mind at the moment, but she suspected that lost, lonely people were more likely to commit crimes than happy, well-adjusted people with everything going their way. Because she was attracted to him? Heavens, she'd been attracted to losers before. The last man in her life had been unethical and immoral. Criminal was just one short step down.

Still, she didn't believe Martin Smith had been a criminal before his accident. Even if he had been, he was a different man now. People could change. Wasn't waking up a new person one of her favorite fantasies? With his accident last summer, Martin had been given the perfect opportunity to start over new, with no name, no memories and no past to haunt him. He could be anyone he wanted to be, could correct old mistakes and make right bad choices. It could be a dream come true.

The questions were the only downside. To fully accept and enjoy his new life, he had to know about his old life. Were there parents who missed him, a wife who mourned him, children who were slowly forgetting him? Or had he been alone, with no one to care?

They would find out soon enough. A loving family surely would have turned to the police for help when he failed to return from his trip. Surely they would be searching for him, distributing flyers, showing photographs, asking questions. Surely there would be a response to this broadcast she was about to send to every law enforcement agency in the country.

And if there wasn't?

Then he was more than likely a free man, free to make a new life for himself. The odds of him including her in it, even temporarily, weren't great, but she could always dream, couldn't she?

Three

The Courthouse Deli was located across the street and down a block from the police department. It was busy from noon to one, but after that a diner looking for privacy couldn't find a better place. Bringing along official-looking reading and choosing a table in the distant corner helped keep most people away…but Martin wasn't most people.

He walked past two dozen empty tables to the back, stopping beside the empty chair. "Mind if I join you?"

Juliet looked surprised but didn't say a word as he slid into the chair and folded his hands together on the table. "They told me over at the department that you usually eat lunch here." A simple statement that wasn't entirely true. One of the dispatchers *had* told him that—a week ago—and she'd said "always." *She always eats at the deli and sits in the back facing the wall to discourage anyone from noticing her.* The only problem with that was that he wasn't so easily discouraged and she was far from unnoticeable.

"That doesn't look like light reading."

She glanced down at the newsletter. "It's about the NCIC 2000."

"Which is?"

"NCIC is National Crime—"

"Information Center. I know. What's the 2000?"

"Their new computer system. Once it's up and running, it'll offer image processing, automated single fingerprint matching, new databases, linkage fields and automated statistical collection. With the equipment that will be available in the patrol cars, an officer in the field will be able to take photographs and scan a single fingerprint, then send them to the bureau and have a response back in no time. It will be—'' She broke off abruptly and shrugged. ''A big improvement.''

For a moment there she had been supremely confident, as she should be. The instant the thought had occurred to her, though, that she might be talking too much, the confidence had faded away with the words. Too bad.

''So part of your job is getting the Grand Springs PD up to speed for this new system.''

She nodded.

''It can't be easy. Some of those guys are still using manual typewriters.''

''Once they realize how much easier the system makes their job, they'll love it.'' She fell silent while the waitress came to take his order, then said, ''I sent out another missing persons broadcast this morning. Maybe we'll get somewhere this time.''

''How long will that take?''

''I don't know. I'm still pretty new at this.''

Stone had told him the last time that a positive response was difficult to predict. It could take a few hours or, if a department was really swamped, a few months. If there was no missing persons report out there that matched his description, there would be no response at all. That had been hard enough to face ten months ago. It would be even harder now, finding out that he'd been the kind of person who could simply disappear from the face of the earth and no one cared.

The suspicion that he'd been exactly that kind of person made him uneasy. Deliberately he changed the subject. ''Did you work in law enforcement in Dallas?''

''No. I worked for a large corporation that had its fingers in a little bit of everything. I set up their systems, wrote programs specific to their needs and kept everything running. When this position came up, I applied and was hired.

The library job seemed okay, but the police department job sounded ex—interesting.''

Exciting. To a computer genius who spent more time with machines than people, even the fringes of police work probably did sound exciting. "Is it interesting?"

"It beats cataloguing library books." She said it with a smile, too light and sweet for the likes of him. He stared at her until it faded, until her blue gaze dropped away from his and familiar discomfort came into her manner.

The waitress served their meal. After scraping the lettuce from her sandwich, Juliet asked, "Did you get some sleep this morning?"

Such an innocent question to spark such intimate images linked one to another: sleep, bed, Juliet, naked, hot, needy, desperate. Fumbling for his glass, he took a drink, swallowed hard and blinked to clear his vision. "Yes." He had spent half the night pacing his apartment and the other half roaming the streets. He'd had a glass of milk at the all-night diner—the cook's remedy for insomnia—and walked until he was exhausted. He'd needed the ride she'd given him—had been half asleep before it was over—and had slept the sleep of the dead the rest of the morning.

All because last night he had dreamed the dreams of the dead.

"Have you had insomnia since the accident?"

His throat was still tight, his voice still husky. "I don't have insomnia."

"But this morning you said you couldn't sleep."

And she had assumed, as everyone else did, that by couldn't, he meant physically unable to. That was what he wanted them to think, wasn't it? "I wouldn't let myself fall asleep last night." His tone was halting, his gaze fixed on his hands. They were familiar, yet strange. Long fingers, callused skin, strong grip, capable of all the things hands were designed for and maybe more. Capable, maybe, of inflicting great pain, of stealing someone else's very life. "Sometimes I have dreams...."

She leaned forward, and her voice brightened, as if the subject had suddenly become ex—interesting. "About your past?"

"I think so. I don't know. Maybe not." *Please, God, no.*

"What kind of dreams?"

"Just dreams."

"You don't remember them?"

His silence let her believe one answer, but the truth was completely different. He remembered too much. Not enough.

"Are you in these dreams?"

"Look, I'd rather not—"

"But they may be important. Maybe the key to your memory is in these dreams, Martin."

It was the first time she'd said his name. Such a plain, simple name, serviceable but nothing special. But it sounded special in her voice. "Look, they're just dreams, nothing more. They don't mean anything. They're not important."

"But they disturb you."

He scowled, wishing he'd let her believe, like everyone else, that he was an insomniac. Since it was too late for that, he chose instead to turn the conversation in a direction that was sure to make her forget his sleep problems. "Not as much as you do."

She stared at him, her face turning as red as the cloth on the table. "I didn't…" She fidgeted, then straightened and sat primly. "I don't know what you mean."

"No, Juliet, I'm sure you don't," he agreed quietly, then lightened up. "When you were in school, did the kids tease you about your name?"

Her look was wary, her tone cautious. "Of course. How could they resist?"

"'What light through yonder window breaks? It is the east, and Juliet is the sun!'"

"My mother was a fan of Shakespeare. What can I say?"

"There are worse things in the world to be named after."

"Like a soap opera hunk?"

He nodded.

"I did some reading about amnesia last night."

"You keep medical books around the house?"

"On the Internet."

He'd left last night so she could go to bed. If he'd known she was going to stay up late, he would have hung around until she'd shoved him out the door. He would have delayed going home and to bed himself, would have delayed the nightmares. "Learn anything interesting?"

"Lots, but nothing that might help."

"I don't think I was computer-friendly. All this on-line stuff seems like a whole new world to me."

"It is a whole new world. It can offer some pretty vast possibilities."

"It can also isolate you. It offers so many possibilities that you lose the need for real people in your life."

"But if you don't have real people in your life, it's a decent substitute."

He wondered about that. Maybe standing on the sidelines watching life go by via a computer monitor was okay for her, but he suspected it would make him just that much hungrier for human contact.

He was already pretty damn hungry for contact with *her.*

Finishing with her meal, she tucked the computer newsletter in her bag, picked up her tab and got to her feet. "I've got to get back to work."

"I'm heading that way. Mind if I walk with you?"

Her only response was a shake of her head.

The weather was springtime warm, which didn't mean they were safe from a cold snap or even snow. After all, it was only late April. They could easily wake up any time in the next month and find themselves snowed in.

He knew where he hoped he would be in the event of such luck.

The block-long walk passed quickly. Too soon they were inside the police department, and Juliet was looking eager to gain the privacy of her office. He tried to think of something to say—some excuse to see her again, some courage to ask for another evening of her time—but the words didn't come. With a faint smile and a murmured "See you around," she went down the hall to her office. A moment later he saw her through the window, taking a seat at her desk, turning her attention immediately to the computer there.

"Look, Jack, a Peeping Tom right here in the department."

He glanced over his shoulder to find Stone Richardson and Jack Stryker, another detective who was working the Olivia Stuart homicide, standing behind him.

"What's so interesting?" Stryker looked, then shrugged. "Oh. The computer person." He said it as if Juliet were of no more interest than the grandmotherly secretary sitting outside the chief's office, as if she weren't the prettiest woman to set foot in Grand Springs in a long time.

Come to think of it, Stone didn't seem particularly impressed, either. Granted, both men had gotten married in the last year—Jack to Josie Reynolds, the town treasurer, and Stone to Jessica Hanson, the bookkeeper at the ski lodge—but did that mean they'd lost their ability to recognize beauty when they saw it?

To each his own, so the saying went, and apparently it was true. After all, while Martin liked what he knew of Josie and Jessica, he personally didn't find either particularly attractive. It was clear, though, that their husbands thought differently.

"You looking for us?"

The two detectives were so far from the reason for Martin's presence in the department that, for a moment, Stone's question didn't register. Finally, though, he offered a noncommittal shrug. "Any news?"

"On Olivia's case?" The cop shook his head. "Still no sign of Springer."

Dean Springer had lived in Grand Springs without attracting anyone's attention for years. He'd been a nobody, a loner who kept a low profile and minded his own business. Somehow his business had come to include the mayor's death. The woman who had actually carried out the murder had identified Springer as the man who'd hired her, but there was no question that he'd merely been the go-between. He was neither smart enough nor prosperous enough to arrange a murder-for-hire, and there was the little matter of lack of motive. No, he'd been working for someone else. If the police ever located him, maybe they would find out who.

What if it was Martin?

"Juliet sent out another broadcast on you today."

Still troubled by his doubts, he gave Stone little attention. "Yeah, she told me. I'd better get going." He had a job this afternoon, and for the next few days, over at Grace Tabernacle on Aspen Street. Reverend Murphy had hired him to help with a renovation project too small to hire out to professionals. Considering his luck with construction in the past, he hoped the preacher was more experienced with such work.

He wasn't, he announced when Martin met him on the front steps of the church. "But I'm a great believer in miracles."

"As long as you're praying for one, ask for one for me," Martin said dryly. He didn't think he'd been a church-going man before the accident, and he hadn't converted to one after, but he was sure he believed in God, both before and after. Sometimes in his dreams, he prayed—frantic, panicked pleas—and sometimes he could manage no more than the deity's name—*Oh God, oh God, oh God.*

"I've been praying for you from the beginning," the reverend said as he opened the door and led the way inside.

The glass doors led into a short, broad hallway. Straight ahead, up three steps and through another set of doors, was the sanctuary with pews on either side and a burgundy carpeted aisle down the center. The door on the left led to a kitchen, and a hallway at the back of the sanctuary led to Sunday school rooms and bathrooms. Martin *knew* all that even though he'd taken no more than five steps through the front door.

Reverend Murphy stopped at the second double doors and looked back. "Although the Lord would like to see you in one of his houses on Sundays, he's not going to smite you for coming Wednesday afternoon instead."

"I've been here before."

"When? I don't recall—" The reverend turned back from the doors and approached him. "You mean before the accident. What do you remember?"

The harder he tried, the less there was to remember. The déjà vu faded, taking with it the faint images of the rooms behind the closed doors. "Nothing," he said flatly, disappointment almost too strong to bear. "I don't remember anything."

When she left the police department after putting in an extra hour, Juliet had nothing more on her mind than going home, putting on her nightgown and vegging out in front of the computer. When she saw Martin leaning against the fender of her little silver car, everything fled her mind, including all words more intelligent or complicated than "Hi."

"Hey." He straightened and shoved his hands in his hip pockets. "Working late?"

She nodded. "Too much to do, too little time. Are you waiting on someone?"

"You."

Her gaze automatically shifted away, her smile trembled and disappeared, and a rush of nerves gave her a shiver. She waited until she was sure—or, at least, hopeful—her voice wouldn't quiver, then asked, "Why?"

"I thought maybe we could get some dinner."

She wanted to ask why again, but she already knew his answer. He hadn't yet accepted that there was no help she could give him. He wanted to talk, wanted her to find some answers for him. It wasn't the same as being wanted for herself, but, hey, it wasn't as if she had any better offers to consider. "All right. Where would you like to go?"

"The Saloon is just down the street. The music's kind of loud, but they have good greasy burgers."

Greasy burgers did sound good. So did loud music to fill in the silence when conversation failed her, as it always did. "We can take my car—"

"I'd rather walk, if you don't mind. It's a nice night."

She agreed. They walked a block or more in silence, giving her an opportunity to window-shop. Grand Springs had a lovely downtown with a hundred percent occupancy. Everything was closed now, but as summer drew nearer and tourists began using the town as a base for their mountain excursions, the shops would keep later hours.

"Busy day?"

She caught a glimpse of Martin's reflection in the plate glass, staring straight ahead, presenting a handsome if less than perfect profile. His nose was crooked, and so was his jaw. In fact, there was a little asymmetry to his whole face, one side not quite matching the other, but it didn't detract from his appearance. She'd been lusting after him for more than two weeks now, and she'd never noticed the flaws until the evening sun had highlighted them.

"Busy enough. The department's computer system was outdated when they bought it—precisely why they got such a good deal on it—so I'm trying to get it upgraded, and I've got to get certified to use NCIC, so I'm working on that, and my clerk is years behind in entering data on the computer, so I'm helping her with that. I could use another clerk—"

"Or maybe just one who actually does her job."

She smiled. "You know Mariellen."

"She dots the *i* in her name with a little heart."

"It's a star now. How do you know her?"

"She asked me out."

Juliet gave him a surprised look that made him laugh.

"I know. I don't need to know how old I am to know that she's way too young for me."

"Some women prefer older men." And *all* women liked some combination of sexy, handsome, tough, endearing, vulnerable, mysterious and lost. Martin scored on all counts.

"Mariellen got that job when she was dating a cop," he said. "She thought working at the same place meant spending a lot of time together. Then they broke up and he moved off to take a job in Denver, and she kept the job. She's not particularly good at it, but—"

"She's young, pretty and sweet. You can't help but like her and overlook her shortcomings." Juliet had once been that young, and underneath all her shyness, she'd been sweet, too, but no one had ever been willing to overlook her failings—maybe because she hadn't been pretty, too? Instead, she had worked extra hard at having no failings. She'd knocked herself out to be the best employee her boss could ever ask for. In the department, everyone was satisfied—herself included—if Mariellen showed up for work less than thirty minutes late.

"So you didn't go out with Mariellen. Do you see anyone in particular?"

The look he gave her was long and chiding. "Would I be here with you if I did?"

She was saved from answering because they'd arrived at the Saloon. She puzzled over his response, though, as they made their way to the booth farthest from the door. What did a girlfriend have to do with his presence with her this evening? If this were a date, sure, she could see the conflict, but it wasn't. They were here to discuss the problem of his missing identity and the possibility, however remote, that her computer skills could be of use to him.

Weren't they?

She slid onto one bench, laid her purse aside and folded her hands together. She felt prim and stuffy, out of place in the dim lights, loud music and smoky atmosphere of the bar. Of course, her navy suit and plain white blouse didn't help any. At least with his jeans, boots and T-shirt, Martin fit right in. All he needed was a cowboy hat over that nice blond hair.

"Do you like country music?"

"I can take it or leave it." Truthfully, she never listened to it—not always an easy feat to accomplish living in Dallas.

"What do you like?"

"A little rock, a little classical. The blues."

"B. B. King, John Lee Hooker, Buddy Guy? 'Stormy Monday'?"

"I love that song." He grinned, and she found herself smiling back. "Maybe you're from the South."

"Because I like the blues?"

"Because when I came out of the office, you said 'hey' instead of 'hi.' Isn't that a Southern thing?"

He shrugged. "I don't have a Southern accent."

"As far as I can tell, you don't have any accent at all. Maybe you just lived there."

Another shrug. "You have an accent. You sound Texan—lazy and sultry and—"

The waitress, dressed in a short little flirty denim skirt, a snug red cowboy shirt and red cowboy boots, interrupted with "What'll you have?"

More of what he was saying, Juliet thought, both dreamy over his comment and disappointed that it'd been cut short. *Sultry.* No one had ever called her anything even remotely close.

She ordered pop, and so did Martin, and she followed his lead in ordering dinner: burger with cheese and spicy fries. When the waitress brought their drinks a moment later, Juliet scanned the room. Martin seemed to be the only man in the place without a long-necked beer clutched in one hand. Not that he needed beer to prove his masculinity. He could walk to the bar and order a glass of warm milk, and no one would have the nerve to say a word about it. "Do you drink?"

"Occasionally, but I have to be careful not to overdo. It's too big a risk for me."

"Do you think that, or do you know it?"

"I know it." He didn't offer an explanation of how he knew, just a grim, almost bleak look and the slow, unconscious stroking of his fingers over the scar on his left arm. Souvenir of a drunken barroom brawl? Maybe he'd been an alcoholic in his previous life, or someone else important in that life had had a drinking problem.

"What did you do this afternoon?" she asked, seeking any mundane topic of conversation that could chase away the sorrow in his eyes.

"I'm doing a little work at one of the churches—some stripping, painting, minor remodeling."

"I thought you weren't a carpenter."

"I'm not, but I'm cheap, and the church doesn't have much money. I just follow the pastor's directions, and he prays for the best."

"Sometimes that's all it takes."

The music went quiet as, across the room, a young man bent over a guitar and tuned the instrument. There were others on the bandstand with him, kids who looked too young to drink where they played. After a few minutes fiddling with the instruments, the band was ready. Without ado, the young man stepped up to the microphone and eased into the first song.

"The bands around here are usually kids from the college," Martin said. "Some of them are pretty good."

Grand Springs College was a small school that co-owned the library with the city. They provided Juliet with Internet access both on and off the job and had tempted her with the possibility of earning a graduate degree someday. At least it would be something to fill her evenings.

Even if she preferred filling them this way.

"Do you like to dance?"

There were only a few couples on the dance floor, couples much better acquainted with each other than she and Martin. They must be, to get so close, to move so intimately. Her cheeks turning pink, she looked back at him. "Actually, I don't know how."

"What do you mean you don't know how? Didn't you go to your high school dances?"

"I was on the decorating committee for both the homecoming dance and the prom, but no, I didn't go."

"Why not?"

The pink in her face turned red. "No one asked me, and frankly, if anyone had, I would have turned him down."

"Were you too shy to date?"

She nodded, though "too shy to get anyone's attention" was more like it.

"I think I probably liked shy girls."

Although she was convinced he was wrong—he'd probably been the captain of the football team, and he'd probably dated the pretty, perky, every-boy's-dream head cheerleader—she humored him. "Why do you think that?"

"Because there's something damned appealing about the women they become."

Her flush turned to heat—lazy, indolent, seeping into every pore, warming her blood, threatening to steam. If she could swallow, she would. If she could pick up her pop for a cooling drink without making the glass sizzle, she would. If she could come up with something smart or provocative or witty to offer in response... *Smart* she knew—*provocative* and *witty* she didn't—and *smart* said don't make assumptions. Don't fall for a line. Keep it business.

She was seeking something perfectly businesslike to say when he spoke again. "I can teach you to dance."

Her gaze shot to the couples on the floor, each holding the other so close that there wasn't room for a breath between them. She'd never been that close to a man in her life unless they were both naked and doing something wild. To get that close—even fully dressed and in public—to

Martin required more courage and grace than she'd ever possessed. "I couldn't."

"Of course you could." He rose from the table, took her hand and pulled her to the edge of the dance floor. "Put your arms around my neck and come closer…closer…. Relax…just let me move and you follow. It's as easy as sex—"

God was in heaven, and he took pity on her. The song ended, and the band moved without pause into the next, a rousing tune that required more dexterity than her feet were capable of. Gratefully, she pulled free of Martin and returned to the booth. His expression as he sat down opposite was part regret, part teasing. "You do indulge in sex from time to time, don't you?"

Wide-eyed, she stared at him. Not in a long time, too long, and never with a man like him.

"Oh, well, next time," he said as the waitress set plates in front of them.

Next time. She'd waited all her life for *this* time. With her luck, next time would never come.

The food was good, the music by turns loud or low and mournful. She ate, watched everyone but Martin and tried to think of something to say. When the silence was finally broken, though, it was by Martin. "What would you rather be doing?"

"What do you mean?"

"You look like you're a million miles away. Doing what? And with whom?"

He sounded defensive, which made her answer with more honesty than she normally would have offered. "Looking for something to talk about. With you. I never really developed a talent for small talk. I learned to speak when I had something to say and not to chatter the rest of the time."

"So let's talk computers. You can tell me all about them."

"Except that you don't want to learn all about them. Your interests are more physical. Active. Outdoors."

He grinned. "I don't know about the outdoors part, but I do like physical and active." His sexy grin spelled out for her exactly what he was referring to, then he controlled it. "That's the thing about amnesia. You never know what your interests are or how they stack up against what they used to be. I like spicy food. Did I always, or is this something new? I have a weakness for blue-eyed blondes. Has that always been true, or before the accident did I prefer green-eyed redheads? Did I like country music and wear suits and work nine to five, or would I have chosen smashing a steel guitar over listening to one?"

"You may never know."

He shook his head adamantly. "No. I can't live with that."

"You may have no choice, Martin."

"No. I at least have to know if I'm—" Breaking off, he shook his head again.

If he was married? If he was a criminal? If he was someone he could bear to be? She regretted that she had no answers for him.

"Are you ready?"

"Let me stop by the ladies' room." She had to cross the dance floor and circle the opposite end of the bar to reach the narrow hall that led to the bathrooms. On her return trip, she didn't make it to the end of the hall before a cowboy with the requisite beer blocked her path.

"Whoa there, darlin'. The evenin' is young. No one's in a hurry."

"Excuse me." She stepped to one side, but he blocked her again.

"I haven't seen you in here before. Jimmy Ray knows everybody in the Saloon. I ought to, considering I spend my every evening here."

"You're right, Jimmy Ray, you haven't seen me here

before. Now, if you'll excuse me—'' When she tried to slip past, he caught her wrist in his free hand.

''What's your rush, little girl? You come and have a drink with Jimmy Ray and maybe a two-step or two. I can show you a real good time.''

She bet he could, if she weren't too smart and he weren't too drunk. He was young and cute, and, like most women, she had a fondness for cute cowboys. Drunk, pushy and manhandling ones, though, weren't her style.

She tried to twist free, but he held her tighter, his fingers biting into her skin. ''I'm not interested in a good time. I'm going home now, so let go or—''

''Or what, sugar? What're you gonna do?'' He pulled until she was against his chest and barely able to breathe. ''I'll tell you what you're gonna do, darlin', you're gonna have a dance and a beer or two with me, and then you're gonna—''

''Let her go.''

Relief swept through Juliet at the sight of Martin standing behind the cowboy. In the cramped hallway, he looked taller, broader-shouldered and tougher than he ever had before, and his voice was cold enough to freeze fire.

''Go away, man. Find your own woman. This one's already taken.''

She wriggled, but the cowboy's arm was around her waist now, and all she accomplished was rubbing suggestively against him. ''Let me go, Jimmy Ray,'' she pleaded. ''Don't cause any trouble.''

Martin clamped his fingers around the cowboy's arm and bent it up behind his back, freeing Juliet in the process. As she scrambled away, he shoved Jimmy Ray face first into the wall, then leaned close. ''You're right. She *is* taken. She's mine. Now, apologize to the lady.''

''Listen, man, I'm sorry, I didn't know she was with you—''

''To her, not me.''

''It's okay, Martin. Let's just go—''

"Tell her you're sorry and it'll never happen again."

He squirmed, but when Martin twisted his arm higher, a spasm of pain crossed his face and he became still. "I'm sorry. I didn't mean no harm."

"And it'll never happen again."

"It won't, I swear it."

"It's all right. Please, Martin, let him go."

After a moment, Martin shoved him away. Jimmy Ray stumbled, hit the opposite wall, then staggered off into the men's room, complaining as he went about the pain in his shoulder. After another moment, Martin faced her. His eyes were grim enough, his expression savage enough, to frighten her far more than the drunken cowboy ever could. She swallowed hard, then touched his hand. "Thank you."

Slowly, the worst of the threat seeped away, and he gestured toward the door. "Let's get out of here."

Darkness had fallen, but the street was brightly lit. Martin wished for shadows as they made their silent way back to the police department and Juliet's car. This wasn't the first time since the accident that he'd gotten into a situation that could have easily turned violent, but this was the first time that he'd *wanted* it to. He'd wanted to smash his fist into the cowboy's face, to break a few bones and loosen a few teeth so that the next time the bastard wanted to harass some woman, he'd think twice.

But Martin could well imagine Juliet's reaction if he'd taken it any further than he had. Hell, he didn't have to imagine. He'd seen the fear in her eyes for a split second before she'd swallowed over that lump in her throat and thanked him. Fear. Of *him*.

They were only a few yards from her car when he finally spoke. "I would never hurt you." But the promise didn't come out as absolute and unwavering as he'd intended, because the awful truth was, he didn't know whether he would. He knew he could have killed that cowboy. He knew, suspected—feared—that he'd killed in the past. When he remembered that past, when he again became the man he'd once been, who knew what he would be capable of?

Not hurting Juliet. God help him, he *couldn't* be capable of that.

She fished her keys from her bag before looking at him. "If I thought you would, I wouldn't be here with you." She stated it simply, flatly, not open to argument. "Can I give you a ride?"

"I would appreciate it." He settled in the passenger seat, the shoulder and lap belt fastened. He'd been wearing the seat belt that night, in the storm. Unfastening his seat belt was his first memory after the fact that his head hurt like a son of a bitch and the realization that he'd smashed up the car.

"Do you need to stop anywhere?"

"I would like to make a detour, if you don't mind. It won't take a minute." At her nod, he directed her to Aspen Street and Grace Tabernacle. She pulled to a stop in front of the building, and he leaned forward to see past her. The building was still and dark, except for one yellow light burning inside.

"Is this the church where you're working?"

"Yeah. I've been here before. I knew how the rooms looked, how the floor plan was laid out, before I saw it. I remembered…"

"Maybe when you were here before, you attended services here."

"Maybe. I don't feel like the church type."

He felt the wryness of her look. "What type do you feel like? The sinner?"

He'd certainly indulged in sinful thoughts, especially since she'd come to town.

"Maybe you lived here for a time when you were a boy, and your family attended this church, but you moved away while you were still young. That would explain how you know things about the town and why no one knows you."

He thought his connection to Grand Springs might be

more than that—worse than that—but he accepted her suggestion with a shrug.

"We could talk to the minister or some of the church members. Maybe they could narrow what you remember to a specific time period."

"And then what?"

"I don't know. See if the church still has records on members back then. Locate some old city directories and find out who left town during that period. See if the schools still have records on students from that time."

"Talk about your needle in a haystack. That sort of search would take forever."

"Time is the one thing you have plenty of."

That was true. And even if the search was fruitless, at least he would have a few names to add to his list of people he wasn't.

"Maybe I've never been here," he remarked as she pulled away. "Maybe I'm remembering things that someone else told me."

"I suppose it's possible."

And it meant that he would never find out who he was unless that someone happened to return home and recognized him.

When she would have turned toward his apartment instead of her house, he stopped her. "I'll walk home from your place."

"I don't mind. It's just a few blocks—"

"Not too far to walk." He would rather see her safely home, would rather increase the odds of being asked in for a while.

With a nod, she turned and, a moment later, parked in her driveway. The house was dark, not even a porch light shining, and looked less welcoming, less homey, than last night.

She didn't ask until she was on the porch and he stood at the bottom of the steps. "Want to come in?"

"Sure." More than she could imagine. More than he could admit.

She opened the door and switched on the porch, hall and living room lights. While she did so, he stopped just inside, listening, smelling potpourri and the scent of her cologne, faint, tantalizing, like bits of a forgotten dream. He knew her clothes smelled of the same fragrance—he'd smelled it in those few seconds he'd held her stiffly in his arms on the dance floor—and wondered if her skin did, too. It would be so easy to find out, to strip off the plain suit that didn't flatter her and the businesslike blouse that did, to lower his head until his mouth brushed against her, to stroke the places that might reveal the scent—the tender skin on the inside of her wrists, the long line of her throat, the soft, pale skin between her breasts.

Ah, hell, why didn't he just go find one of those two-thousand-foot drops they'd talked about last night and throw himself over? It couldn't be any worse torment for him, and it would certainly be less dangerous for her.

She sat down on the sofa. He went only as far as the armchair. She again wore the look that meant she was trying to find something to talk about—small talk. He wasn't interested in small talk. He wanted to know everything there was to know about her. He wanted to confide the last little detail of his dreams to her. He wanted to vent his frustration over yet another day of not knowing who or what he was. He wanted—

"I appreciate your intervention with Jimmy Ray at the Saloon."

She had called the cowboy by name earlier, but it hadn't registered. From the instant he'd looked up and seen the man grab her, he'd been too furious to notice anything else. They could have been the only three people in the world for all he'd known. Now he wondered. "You know him?"

She shook her head.

"But you know his name."

"He introduced himself, along with an invitation for a

beer and a two-step.'' She smiled faintly. ''He was just drunk and probably harmless—''

''Men are rarely harmless, and a drunk man will do things he would never even imagine when he's sober.''

Another faint smile. ''I'm grateful for your help.'' She removed her shoes, sensible flats, and tucked her feet beneath her. ''You said last night that you feel a connection to Olivia Stuart, that her death or possibly her life was important to you in some way.''

Her reminder put him on guard, tightening the muscles in his neck and jaw. He didn't want her to remember that she had wondered if he had played some role in the mayor's murder, didn't want her to think of him as a man who might have ordered the killing of an innocent woman. He didn't change the subject, though. He just waited.

''Does anyone have any idea why she was killed?'' Juliet asked.

''Just theories. The most popular one involved coal mining. Her last word before she died was 'coal' or something similar. There's been a lot of strip mining in the region. One of the companies wanted to come into the county right outside town, and Olivia was against it.''

''Why? Every town needs economic development.''

''Many people feel strip mining is best for the company's economic development, not the town's. After a while, the mine shuts down and moves on, their employees are out of work, and the county is left with a scarred mountainside that doesn't do much in the way of attracting tourists. A lot of people around here are against it. Olivia happened to be one of the most vocal.''

''Is the mining profitable enough to make killing one opponent a reasonable solution?''

''If you're the sort of person who finds killing for any reason reasonable,'' Martin replied.

''What other theories?''

''Apparently there were some problems in town before she was elected mayor. She's credited with cleaning them up. Maybe someone held a grudge. Or maybe it was personal and had nothing to do with her position as mayor."

"But from what I've heard, it doesn't seem she had an enemy in the world," Juliet remarked.

He gave her a dry look. "With the police looking for someone to blame for her murder, would you admit it if you'd wanted her dead?"

When she broke her long silence, it was with a quiet question. "You wonder if *you* wanted her dead, don't you?"

He didn't succumb to the denial that came so easily. "Yes. I wasn't here when she was drugged, but maybe that's why I was coming here—to see for myself that she was dead and to pay the people hired to kill her."

"You didn't have much money on you when you showed up at the emergency room."

"No, but it could have been in the car."

"What would it take to find the car?"

"An act of God. Either it was stolen or it's buried out there under tons of mud in one of those deep ravines. I don't think I'm ever going to see it again."

She fell silent again for a time, then gave a great sigh. "I don't know how to prove who you are, but maybe we could prove who you aren't."

"Who aren't I?"

"Olivia Stuart's murderer."

"How would we do that?"

"By finding the person who is."

"The police have been trying for ten months. How are we going to succeed where they've failed?"

"I don't know, but at least we've got something to work with. It won't answer all your questions, but it will ease your mind on that one."

"And what if we prove that it *is* me?"

"We won't."

"You can't go into this with preconceived ideas or prejudices. What if we prove that I did order Olivia's murder?"

"Then we'll deal with it."

He liked the way she said *we,* as if they were a team. It made him feel not quite so alone. But the reality was, if Juliet proved him a killer, *he* was the one who would deal with it. He was the one who would go to prison for it. "So where do we start?"

She looked at a loss. She was a computer whiz, he reminded himself, not a cop. Still, she was probably logical and methodical—two important qualities in a cop. "I guess we start with Olivia. You said she had two children."

"Hal, a city councilman, and Eve Redtree."

"Redtree. Rio Redtree's wife?"

He nodded. After a long estrangement, Eve Stuart had married the local reporter last fall, giving their little girl Molly a real family for the first time in her young life.

"What about a husband? Did Olivia have one?"

"I've never heard any mention of one. I assumed she'd been divorced a long time."

"Did she have any other family here? Had she always lived here?"

Leaving his chair, he picked up the pad and pen next to the phone and handed them to her. "Make a list. I'll get some answers tomorrow."

Four

"Are you busy?"

Her head was bent, her eyes on the computer screen, her fingers typing away on the keyboard. What about that picture *didn't* look busy? Juliet groused silently as Mariellen plopped down in the chair across the desk. She finished the list she was typing, then looked at her young clerk. She'd often wondered just how much work Mariellen got done on Juliet's library days, with no one to supervise her. She suspected not much. "Why aren't you at work?"

"I was. I took an early lunch."

"It's not even ten-thirty yet."

The clerk shrugged. "I heard you ran into a little trouble at the Saloon last night."

Grand Springs was, for all its size, still a small town at heart. It didn't take long for gossip to circulate, even about something as insignificant as her run-in with the drunken cowboy. "It was no big deal."

"Jimmy Ray's not usually such a pain. In fact, he's a pretty nice guy. He does like to party, though. He must have tied on a few too many, to be hitting on you." The young woman's voice caught, and embarrassment crept in. "Not that there's anything wrong with hitting on you—I mean, unless you don't want him to. I imagine there must be plenty of men somewhere who would make a pass at you if you wanted them to, but..." She blew out her breath. "You're just not Jimmy Ray's type."

Resisting the urge to point out to her clerk that she'd

been at the Saloon with a man who had turned *her* down, Juliet looked at her. "Now, that's a relief."

"Oh, hey, he's a lot of fun, really. He just likes young and less...settled women."

Juliet's fingers returned to the keyboard, typing in commands. She'd been wrong last night when she'd thought that she had once been as young as Mariellen. She'd *never* been that young. If that was "less settled," then hooray for settling in.

"He said some mean son of a bitch practically dislocated his shoulder. From his description, I knew it could only be Martin Smith. He likes older women, of course."

Annoyance crept into Juliet's voice. "Is there anything you need, Mariellen? Because if there isn't, I know for a fact that you've got enough work piled on your desk back at the department to keep you busy until this time next year."

"I just wanted to tell you that Jimmy Ray's not a bad guy. I've known him all my life. I lived just down the street from his grandparents, and we played together practically since we were in diapers."

Finally she was interested enough to turn away from the computer. "You were born and raised here, weren't you?"

Mariellen nodded. "You want to know anything about Grand Springs, if I don't know it, I can tell you who does."

"Tell me about the mayor. The last mayor. Olivia Stuart."

"Oh. Well, her son Hal is *real* cute, but he's kind of old—like, nearly forty or something. I grew up with Eve. She's just a year or two older than me."

Inwardly Juliet scowled at the description of Hal Stuart. He was cute, but as for old, her best guess was that he was a few years younger than her, and she was still closer to thirty—just barely—than forty. "What about Olivia's husband?"

"She wasn't married when she died."

"What about the kids' father?"

"Oh, him. He's dead. He died years ago, when Eve was just a baby. I probably wasn't even born yet. I don't know how, but it wasn't a natural death, like, he didn't drop dead of a heart attack or anything. After Olivia died, I heard my parents talking about how hard it must be for Eve and Hal to lose both parents the way they did."

"Did Olivia have any enemies?"

"Oh, no way. Everyone liked her. She was cool."

At least one person hadn't liked her enough to send Dean Springer to hire a killer, and Springer hadn't cared enough to try to foil the plot. It hadn't been Martin. She was convinced of that...almost. Of course, she didn't want to believe that she was attracted to, spending time with and having lustful thoughts about a murderer, but some cautious part of her knew his self-incriminating theory was entirely possible. He'd been on his way to town at the time of her killing. After the accident, when nothing else had held any significance for him, not even the sight of his own face, her death had mattered. He knew things that it seemed only a cop or a criminal should know, and he was no cop—the lack of fingerprints on record with the FBI proved that. Then, there were the scars.

And last night. Simmering under his anger last night had been barely leashed brutality. He could have torn Jimmy Ray apart limb by limb without breaking a sweat. He was no stranger to violence.

But that didn't make him a killer.

Whatever he had been before the accident didn't have to affect what he was now. He'd been given an opportunity to become a different man, and regaining his memory didn't have to change that.

"Hello? You in there, Juliet?"

Fingers waved languidly in front of her face. Startled, she refocused her gaze on Mariellen.

"Sometimes I think communicating with you would be easier if you had a keyboard attached. What were you thinking about?"

"Nothing. What were you saying?"

"Nothing much. If you're really interested in Olivia, you should talk to Donna Sanderson, the chief's wife. They were good friends and ran the charity fund-raiser together every year. I'd better get back to work. See you tomorrow." Mariellen stood and smoothed her skirt over her hips before sashaying away. Her blouse fitted snugly, and the skirt stopped just a fraction above what was decent, leaving mile-long legs exposed. In her own simple cotton dress that reached almost to her ankles, Juliet felt overdressed, overly modest and dowdy.

The dress was a twin to the one she'd worn two nights ago—that one in a soft pastel print, this one a bold cranberry solid—and Martin hadn't looked as if he'd found the style the least bit dowdy. In fact, he'd looked…

She thought back to the moment when she'd realized she was no longer alone, when she'd looked up and seen him standing so still. There had been guilt and embarrassment, but before that, just for an instant, there had been arousal. Just the tiniest flare of arousal.

Ignoring the longing deep inside, she scoffed at her own thoughts. Martin Smith could have any single woman in town and more than a few of the married ones. All he had to do was give his chosen one a wink and a wicked grin and she would come running. He wasn't likely to settle for *her,* especially when she was already helping him, no strings attached.

But maybe he *was* willing to settle. Hadn't he described her voice as sultry? And claimed something appealing— *damned appealing*—about the women shy girls became? Hadn't he wanted to dance with her, pulling her onto the floor, urging her in his own sultry voice, *Closer…closer…just let me move and you follow…as easy as sex…* Hadn't he told the cowboy, *She is taken. She's mine*?

With a frustrated sigh, Juliet lowered her head until it bumped against the desktop. None of it meant anything. He was a charmer. Flattering and pleasing women—all women—was just part of who he was. It didn't mean a thing.

"I admit, there are times when the computers make me bang my head against the nearest hard surface, but I thought you were above that."

She turned her head to one side and through a curtain of hair saw Tracey Mendez, one of the reference librarians, in her office door. With another sigh, she sat up. "Computers don't frustrate me. Everything else in the world does."

"So you're a mere mortal, after all." She offered the folder she held. "I copied the Stuart clip file as you asked. I would've thought the police would already have copies of all these articles."

Juliet's smile was faint as she accepted the folder. She hadn't actually said that the copies were for Stone or Jack, but she also hadn't admitted they were for her and Martin. The fewer people who knew they were snooping around, the better, so when Tracey had made the assumption, she had let her. "Thanks a lot."

Tracey lingered at the door. "I heard about last night."

Heat seeped into Juliet's face. Was she also convinced that Jimmy Ray had been drunk because he'd chosen to make a pass at *her*? Was that what everyone in town thought? "It was just a misunderstanding."

"Yeah, Jimmy Ray Bullock thought tight Wranglers, scuffed boots and a charmingly youthful grin were enough to get him any woman in the house." Then she grinned delightedly. "There are times it's enough to tempt *me*. Of course, I don't have Martin Smith hovering around ready to defend my honor. *He* could tempt me anytime."

She waved on her way out, and Juliet responded with a nod while staring at the manila folder. It was such a temptation to open it and dive in, but this wasn't business. It could wait until later.

It did wait. Her workday officially ended at five, but it took her fifteen minutes to convince herself to try to find

Martin and another fifteen minutes to find out that he'd left the church and was most likely at his apartment.

She climbed the steep stairs, caught her breath at the top, considered leaving again, then forced herself to knock. It had been about ten years since she'd shown up uninvited at a man's apartment. She'd met Jerry in a computer class at the university, and he'd evolved from fellow nerd to study partner to her only truly serious relationship. Then, out of the blue, he announced that he had fallen in love with an empty-headed ditz who couldn't find the on button to a computer if it was painted Day-Glo green and whistling Dixie. Her parents had thought her heart was broken. It wasn't.

Martin opened the door, bringing her back to the present. *He* was a heartbreaker. Not Jerry.

His hair was wet and stuck up at angles, and a towel hung around his neck, obscuring all but a tanned strip of chest. His button-front jeans rode low on his hips with the top two buttons undone, and his feet were bare. The sight was enough to take a woman's breath away.

She shouldn't have come, she thought, her gaze riveted on those unfastened buttons. Even if he'd been fully dressed, this was his home, and she hadn't been invited, and his bed was just a dozen feet behind him, and there was no way she could go inside or even stand here outside and make intelligent conversation. She should give him the file to go over alone or invite him to her house or, better, to some restaurant where noise, lights and other diners would distract her and give her half a chance at not making a fool of herself.

"Hey. Come on in."

"I—" Her feet ignored her brain's command and carried her over the threshold. The place was dark—not enough windows—but basically neat. The bed dominated the room—big, empty, unmade. In the months he'd lived here, how many women had slipped between the plain white sheets and helped rumple the covers? In the years before he came here, how many women had shared his bed?

He closed the door, then started for the bathroom. "Have a seat. I'll be done in a minute."

She watched him, catching a glimpse in the dim light of one of the scars from when he'd been shot in the back. Had he been running away, trying to save himself, or had his attacker been too cowardly to face him and instead ambushed him from behind? And why had this unknown person wanted him dead? What had Martin done to deserve such an attempt?

She straightened the pillows on the couch and sat down. It faced the bed and made thinking impossible. Quickly she moved to the chair, but she could still see the bed from the corner of her eye. Calling herself pathetic, she moved to the small square dining table, pulled out the chair that would put her back to the rest of the room and sat down.

In the bathroom Martin listened to the soft tread of her footsteps as he finished drying off, then pulled on the shirt hanging on the door hook. She was slow to settle. It probably wasn't easy when everything centered on the bed, when she surely must suspect by now that bed was exactly where he wanted her. He was surprised that she'd even had the nerve to come here. He would have bet that she was too shy, too needy of her own turf, to set foot in his apartment.

If she'd delayed five or ten minutes, he would have been out of here, on his way to her house to compare notes on the Stuarts. He was glad she hadn't, though. As uncomfortable as it surely made her, he liked the idea of her and a bed in the same room. He wanted to look at her and see the bed, wanted to imagine her naked in it, wanted to taunt himself with thoughts of what they could do in it. He wanted the sweet, hot suffering, wanted to believe that someday it could come to fulfillment.

If he found out who he was, what he was. If he could live with what he found out.

He combed his hair, tucked his shirt in and buttoned his jeans, then opened the door, his gaze going straight to the couch, the chair, the bed, all empty. She was sitting primly at the dining table, nothing in front of her but a wall that needed painting. At least she was still here. She'd found the only seat in the house that avoided the bed, but she was here.

"Want a soda?"

She didn't look at him but shook her head.

"It's safe to look. I'm all buttoned up and decent and everything," he teased softly as he slid into the chair across from her.

She lifted her gaze, but her face warmed at the hint that he knew she had noticed his unbuttoned jeans. Her voice quavered as she laid the folder she'd been clutching on the table between them. "I have copies of every article the *Grand Springs Herald* has ever published about any of the Stuarts."

"Going back how far?"

"Ten years. Anything older than that is on microfiche and will take longer to find. But I can't imagine anyone holding a grudge that long, then suddenly deciding to kill the person."

"Maybe the grudge wasn't worth killing over to start with. Maybe over a period of years it festered and grew until the person felt he had no choice but to kill her."

She shrugged but didn't look convinced.

"You've never hated anyone, have you?"

"Not enough to wish them dead. Certainly not enough to kill them." Then, hesitantly, she asked, "Have you?"

He regretted his answer, regretted even more that it was Juliet hearing it, but he couldn't lie to himself and certainly not to her. "Yes. I think."

She didn't ask exactly what he thought—that he had wished someone dead or that he'd actually taken steps to kill someone. She was probably afraid to know. So was he.

For a long time she stared at him, her face pale, then blindly she opened the folder. "We should get started."

He laid his hand over hers on the top photocopy. She tensed but didn't pull away. "I asked a few questions around town today. Olivia and her husband came here from Denver right after they were married. There's no other family in the area. They had three kids—"

"Three?"

"The oldest was a son named Roy Jr. He's been gone so long that most people have forgotten he existed."

"Gone, as in dead?"

"He ran away from home more than twenty years ago. He apparently didn't get along with his father. Olivia believed he was dead. She was convinced that he would have contacted her sometime over the years if he were alive to do so."

"What about her husband? Mariellen said he died when Eve was a baby."

"Roy Stuart was a drunk who knocked his wife around until he got tired of it, then started on the kids—the boys, at least, especially the older one. He doted on Eve and never laid a hand on her. Sue Marie Harper, who was friends with Olivia from the beginning, thought that was why the older kid ran away. He got tired of playing punching bag. Anyway, one night about twenty years ago, Roy got drunk as usual, got into an argument at home and grabbed Olivia. She pulled away, which threw him off balance, and he went tumbling down the stairs. The fall killed him."

"Lucky Olivia."

"I doubt she felt lucky. She had two kids to take care of on her own."

"She obviously did a good job. Hal and Eve would make any parent proud. It's a shame about the older boy, though. It must have been hard for her, believing that he was dead but never knowing for sure."

"Maybe if she'd done something to protect him while

he was here, he wouldn't have disappeared and she wouldn't have had to wonder.''

''That's a hard-hearted attitude,'' she said, quietly censuring him. ''She was abused, too.''

''She was his mother. She should have protected him. If she couldn't get help for herself, then she should have done it for her children.''

''She did the best she could. The services, assistance and acceptance that a battered woman can find today weren't always available twenty years ago. She had three children to consider, one of them a baby. She made the best choices she could—''

''She wasn't a helpless woman. After her husband's death, she took care of those other kids, worked and went to college, then law school, all to give them a better life. Yet before that she stood by and let her bastard of a husband beat the hell out of her oldest child and did nothing to stop it.''

Juliet was giving him a sympathetic look that made him wish he could call back all his words and bitterness. She was wondering if his old man had knocked him around, something he'd wondered himself when the anger had started building as Sue Marie Harper had talked this morning. It didn't take a shrink to know that he'd either been some adult's adolescent victim or had been close to someone who was. He didn't like the image of himself as victim. He felt more comfortable with the idea of avenger.

''You're right. She owed her son better than that. She should have killed her husband the first time he laid a hand on the boy instead of waiting for him to fall down the stairs in a drunken rage.'' She slid her hand free, then tapped the newspaper articles. ''Do you want to look at these now or get some dinner?''

He wanted dinner, preferably without any mention of the Stuarts, last June's accident or his memory loss. He didn't want a single reminder that he had no right to the kind of intimacy he wanted with her. ''Dinner.'' Then maybe a movie. Or a walk around town. One slow, sensual dance. A night in her bed. Then tomorrow they could talk about business. Or next week. Maybe next month.

She closed the file and slid it into her bag. "I have a roast in the slow-cooker at home, or we could go out."

"At home sounds fine." Better than fine. Private. Promising.

Torture.

He got his shoes on, locked up, then followed her to the car. Five minutes later they were inside her house with its familiar shadows and scents, along with the new aromas this evening of roasted beef and vegetables and, courtesy of the timer on the bread machine, a loaf of fresh bread.

They ate at the kitchen table and shared clean-up when they were done. Stretching above her, he placed the serving platter on the top cabinet shelf, then, as he lowered his arm, brushed his hand across her hair. Her hands became still in the sink of sudsy water, and for a moment, she stopped breathing. So did he.

Her hair was cool, silky, and slid between his fingers. He could wrap both hands in it and pull her head back for a kiss, but he would never stop with one kiss. He wouldn't stop until it was too late and they would both be sorry. One thing he wanted was to never make Juliet sorry.

She bent her head, pulling her hair through his fingers, and he let go. He put distance between them, moving as far away as the job allowed to dry the remaining dishes.

After rinsing the sink and drying her hands, she looked at him but didn't quite meet his eyes. "Do you want to go in the living room and read the articles?"

"How about showing me your computer?"

The request surprised her, but with a nod, she led the way into the office, booted up the computer, then glanced at him. "What are you interested in?"

Things that couldn't be found on any computer screen, at least not with the right faces on the bodies. But he was good and didn't suggest anything that might make her blush. "I don't know. Travel."

"To where?" To his shrug, she responded, "Since you say 'hey' instead of 'hi' and 'soda' instead of 'pop,' how about the South? Atlanta?"

She did a little pointing and clicking and a little typing, and in a moment a full-color picture of Atlanta's skyline filled the screen. He didn't think he was familiar with it, didn't think he would have recognized it without the text to identify it.

"Are you interested in shopping? Restaurants? Tourist attractions?" A few more photos appeared, nothing that struck a chord. At his silent response, she returned to the search feature. "How about Raleigh?"

They took five-minute tours of several more cities before she got to Miami. When she would have clicked past a particular photograph, he laid his hand over hers. Now *that* was a shot he remembered—the downtown building all lit up at night. He'd seen it before.

The look she gave him was apologetic. "That building's pretty recognizable. It's been in the opening credits of a TV show, on postcards, in magazines and a music video or two."

Sure, he'd seen it. Probably everyone in the country had. "What else can you do on here?"

"Do you like to read? Want to see what Stephen King's up to on his web site? Maybe order a book or two from an on-line bookstore? We can check the local weather or see what's on television tonight. We can read the *Washington Post* or— What's today? Thursday? We can check the new bestseller list in *USA Today*. We could browse through a few thousand sites on amnesia, or we could run Roy Stuart Jr., for a phone number."

"Do that." He sat back and watched. In only a matter of minutes, she came up with no matches on three different searches. "So what does that mean?"

"Maybe he doesn't have a phone, or it's unlisted."

"Or maybe he's dead."

She shrugged. "Maybe he changed his name. Maybe he has a roommate and the phone is in his or her name."

"Do yourself."

She did, and the screen displayed a Dallas address and phone number. "It'll be updated to show this address within a few weeks."

He had probably never imagined that he would be envious of a phone listing, but he was. Juliet Crandall knew exactly who she was, where she was and where she had been, while he lived with a name borrowed from a fictional character and chosen for a reason as frivolous as hair color.

"Want to read the newspaper articles?" Her voice was soft, tentative, as if she sensed the downturn in his mood.

"Yeah, sure."

She disconnected the modem, then exited the program, leaving the menu on the screen when they left the room.

A thick stack of papers later, his eyes were bleary, the muscles in his neck were tight, and he'd learned nothing. By all accounts, Olivia Stuart had been a pillar of the community, a progressive mayor and a model citizen. She had worked tirelessly for her favorite charities—one of which funded searches for runaway children—and had been active in her church. She had been fair in her running of the city, had compromised when it was in the people's best interests and stood her ground when it wasn't. She'd given no one a reason to kill her.

But someone *had* killed her.

"It must have had something to do with the mayor's office."

Juliet, comfortable on the couch, blinked before focusing on him. He knew how she felt. "Why do you think that? There was never anything really controversial going on, other than the strip-mining business, and the town never would have approved that, regardless of Olivia's opinion. Everyone in authority was against it."

"Whoever wanted her dead hired a professional killer to

do it. That pretty much rules out a crime of passion or a personal grudge.'' He didn't like the argument he was about to offer, but he offered it, anyway. ''If I hated you so much that I wanted you dead, I would want to kill you myself, not pay someone to do it for me.''

''Unless an alibi is important.''

''But an alibi is important only if I believe I'll be a suspect, if my grudge against you is well known. Everyone swears Olivia didn't have an enemy in the world.''

Juliet resettled on the couch, stuffing another pillow behind her back, stretching out her legs on the sofa cushions, fixing her gaze on the lamp hanging above his head. ''But these articles cover all the mayor's business the entire time Olivia was in office. There was nothing worth more than a few harsh words.''

''Maybe it was something that hadn't come out in the papers yet.''

She nodded. ''If we could see her records and papers…''

''Everything that pertained to city business would have been turned over to the acting mayor—her son Hal—until the new mayor was elected. My guess is the personal stuff went to Hal, too, and his sister.''

''Do you think they would let us look at it when we don't even have a legitimate interest? I mean, we aren't cops or anything.'' She didn't sound hopeful, and Martin shared her feelings. She'd never met either Stuart, and what little they knew about *him* wasn't likely to persuade them to turn their dead mother's personal papers over to them.

Still, he tried to ignore his own pessimism. ''The cops have been trying to solve their mother's murder for ten months and haven't done it yet.'' He shrugged. ''Maybe they're ready to give someone else a crack at it.''

They weren't—or, at least, Hal Stuart wasn't.

Friday afternoon found them in the Redtree living room—Juliet and Martin, Eve and Hal. Even though Hal was the city council liaison to the police department, it was the first time Juliet had met him or his sister. She took an immediate liking to Eve. The young woman was only a year or two older than Mariellen in age but years ahead of her in experience and maturity. Of course, Mariellen had never had a reason to grow up, but Eve had, in the form of her brown-eyed little girl, born when Eve was still a child herself.

Juliet didn't take such a liking to Hal Stuart. He was, in Mariellen's words, real cute, but in too polished a manner for her taste. She preferred a little rough and rugged, someone who might pick up a hammer or hike up a mountain, someone who didn't consider himself too good for honest manual labor, who wasn't afraid to defend a woman from a drunken cowboy. Hal looked the type to worry more about his suit wrinkling or his salon-perfect hair getting mussed than his dinner companion's safety.

From his seat at the end of the coffee table, Martin had finished their request and was waiting for an answer. Eve looked intrigued. Hal didn't.

"You want us to hand our mother's personal papers over to you." Hal shook his head. "No."

Juliet spoke for the first time. "Mr. Stuart, we just want to help find the person responsible for your mother's death."

"Evidently, you're a little confused in your job description, Ms. Crandall. You're a computer operator and records clerk. You're not a police officer, and you're certainly not a detective. Why don't you toddle on back to your computer and do the job you're being paid to do instead of interfering with *real* police work?"

She stiffened, her fingers knotting tightly together. As the records supervisor and a soon-to-be-certified NCIC full-terminal operator, she was authorized access to any and all records within the police department. Granted, she *wasn't* a cop—her job was administrative—but she wasn't just a dumb little clerk, either, and she resented like hell his saying so. "Mr. Stuart—"

He rose to pace behind the sofa where his sister sat. "You people are something. A clerk and a—a handyman, both of you strangers, both of you obviously with too much time on your hands and with delusions of grandeur, waltz in here and expect us to just happily give you everything left behind when our mother was brutally and senselessly murdered, so that *you* can try to do what the best and most experienced detectives in town can't. Give me a break."

A clerk and a—a handyman. For a moment, Juliet had been afraid he was going to say something worse. Town freak, Martin had called himself when he'd come to her office at the library, and she had half expected similar words to come from Hal Stuart. Instead, he'd settled for simplistic descriptions and chilling disdain.

"Forget it," Hal said, his tone final. "And if you bring this up again…" He gave her a cold, hostile look. "I'll speak to the chief." With a great sense of drama, he left the room and the house, slamming the door behind him. A moment later she heard his car drive away.

In the heavy silence, Eve sighed. "I apologize for my brother. Our mother's death has been difficult for him."

"We didn't mean to make things worse," Martin said quietly. "It's just that… From my first night in town, I've felt some…connection to your mother. I wanted to find out whatever I could. Juliet and I have time to spend on this that the detectives don't. And sometimes, a fresh perspective can reveal clues that others have missed."

"A fresh perspective always makes everything clearer." Eve sat silent for a moment, clearly debating with herself, then reached a decision. "All right."

"All right?" Martin echoed.

"You can have the papers."

"But your brother said—" At Martin's warning glance, Juliet cut the words off.

"My brother thinks he's head of the family now that everyone else is gone and that his word is law." She smiled wanly. "But Mom's records are in *my* attic, and I said you can take them."

"If he finds out—"

"He won't, unless you tell him." She rose from the sofa and gestured to them to follow. They climbed the stairs to the attic, finding a half-dozen neatly labeled boxes. "Mom never threw anything away. She's even got drawings I did in first grade in here."

With Eve's help, they moved the boxes to Juliet's car in two trips. After Eve returned to the house, Juliet slammed the trunk shut on the last three, then murmured, "Hal's going to be furious if he finds out."

"Like she said, he won't find out if we don't tell him."

She hoped Martin was right. She liked her job and wanted to keep it, and getting on Councilman Hal Stuart's bad side didn't seem the best way to do it.

She glanced at the clock after backing into the street. She'd skipped lunch today to make this meeting instead. No way was she going to give anyone a chance to accuse her of slacking off on the job, especially an obnoxious, smug person like Hal Stuart. She would be back at her desk precisely when she was due, but she still had time to take the boxes home.

"You didn't like him, did you?"

She glanced at Martin. "I don't like anyone who takes that patronizing, superior-male attitude and tells me to 'toddle' off."

He laughed. "I didn't think that would sit too well with you. You have to wonder, with that attitude, how he got along with his mother. She was a very strong woman, and, as mayor, she pretty much ran the city council."

It would be easy to let her dislike for the man color her conclusions, but she reined her feelings in. "Apparently they got along very well. He loved and respected her. She was his mother, a lawyer and the mayor. I'm just a little clerk."

"With an IQ double his and the know-how to make him disappear into cyberspace."

It was a lovely thought that she had indulged in on more than one occasion. She'd never done anything of that nature herself, but she knew people with the ability, who could teach her step by step how to disrupt someone's life.

She wished they could teach her how to reclaim someone's life. But once Martin knew who he was, he'd be out of here, wouldn't he? He would have a life, family and friends to return to, and no reason at all to stay in Grand Springs. In that secret little place inside that liked the idea of stealing Hal Stuart's identity, she liked the idea of Martin never recovering his own if it kept him here.

Her selfishness shamed her and made her face hot. Of course she wanted Martin to find himself again. She wouldn't wish the uncertainty and fear he was living with on her worst enemy. But she also wanted him to stay, for a while at least. Until he got tired of her. Until he turned his attention to someone else. It was bound to happen. Every man she had ever been involved with had eventually turned to another woman, and none of them could compete with Martin in sheer masculine appeal.

At her house, he unloaded the boxes, stacking them in the dining room corner, while she put together two sandwiches. They ate on the way back to their respective jobs, Martin finishing his lunch as she pulled to a stop in front of the church. "You'll be over this evening?"

"Sure."

"I can pick you up if you don't mind waiting."

He shook his head. "I'll have to go home and clean up. I'll meet you." He got out, then bent to see her through the open window. "Hey, Juliet? Thanks."

She watched until he disappeared inside, then gave a soft sigh. A few days ago, she had thought gratitude from a man like Martin Smith was perfectly fine. Today she wanted more—a whole lot more. She was used to wanting and not having. It was a way of life. But this time not having just might be unbearable.

And having just might break her heart.

Five

"Maybe I was an accountant." Martin's words broke the silence that had settled over the dining room nearly an hour ago and brought Juliet's attention from the stacks of papers in front of her to him—exactly where he wanted it to be.

"And why do you say that?"

"Because there's something familiar about this." He took in the entire room with his gesture—the empty boxes, the countless stacks and piles of papers, the last two boxes waiting for sorting. "I feel like I've done it before. We know I wasn't a cop. Unless I was a very methodical criminal, maybe I was an accountant. Maybe I was an auditor with the IRS, and that's why no one would admit to expecting my visit."

She didn't smile at his joke, but returned to the statements she was sorting as she absently asked, "Are you good with numbers?"

"I don't know. Try me."

"What's two hundred thousand divided by three?"

"That's an easy one: 66,666.66 for one, .67 for the other two."

Holding up an official-looking document, she shook her head. "It's the amount of life insurance each of Olivia's children received following her death."

"She divided her life insurance three ways?"

"One-third to each of her children: Hal, Eve and Roy Jr. I thought she was convinced he was dead."

"That's what Sue Marie Harper said."

"I wish we'd asked Eve yesterday."

It would have been kind of hard to work into the conversation, he thought as he sorted a half-dozen credit card statements from a pile of utility bills. *We'd like to go through all of your mother's personal records to see if we can prove that I didn't have anything to do with her murder, and, oh, by the way, did she believe that your brother, who ran away when you were a baby, was still alive, or had she finally given up hope?*

"What's the date on the policy?"

She turned to the last page. "It was signed thirteen months ago. Maybe she'd heard from Roy Jr."

"Without telling anyone? Not even her other children?" It didn't seem likely. Hal and Eve had just been kids when their brother disappeared, but surely their mother would have told them if he'd contacted her. "Maybe she just never gave up hope." Hope died hard—his was still hanging on, and he imagined it was nothing compared to a mother's hope for her eldest child.

Juliet laid the life insurance policy aside and reached into the box at her feet for yet another handful of papers. Olivia never threw anything away, Eve had said, and the boxes proved her right. Unfortunately, she hadn't been particularly organized, at least in this area. Kids' drawings from twenty years ago shared space with utility bills from last year. Credit card and bank statements were spread through every box, along with yellowed Christmas cards, long-done to-do lists and personal correspondence.

Most likely Olivia had meant to organize the boxes at some future date. She had never intended to die and leave her personal things in such a mess.

Suddenly antsy, Martin pushed himself to his feet and stretched. "Let's go somewhere."

"Where?"

"I don't know. The hardware store. I'll change your locks this afternoon."

She looked wary. "Do you know how to do that?"

"Of course. You drill a few holes and install the lock set. No problem." He waited until the caution faded, then added, "Besides, the directions are on the back of the package."

When she smiled but didn't immediately get up, he wheeled her chair back from the table and pulled her to her feet. "Come on. It's too pretty a day to stay inside with a bunch of old papers."

She let him pull her as far as the doorway, where she tugged free. "Let me get my shoes."

He glanced at her feet. He liked her habit of going barefoot at home. It gave a certain intimacy to a situation that she made a real effort to keep on a business level. He wondered why. Was he so far from her type that the idea of anything personal between them had never occurred to her? Was she cautious enough that she would never allow herself to get involved with a man without a name or a past? Or was she insecure enough to think that business—her help—was all he wanted from her?

Someday he would find out.

While she went to the bedroom, he walked around the table. They'd worked last evening and all morning, together yet separately. He'd sat on the floor, the wall at his back, sorting stacks around him. She had worked at the table, and her stacks were neater. The credit card statements that he'd put in one pile she had sorted by company and year. She'd even sorted the kids' artwork by signature. The biggest stack was Eve's work, the smaller pile Hal's. There were only three items in Roy Jr.'s pile—a Mother's Day greeting, a construction-paper Christmas card and a drawing.

He held up the drawing by wrinkled corners. The crayon lines were childish and crooked, but the forms were easily identifiable: a yellow house with a woman standing on one side, a baby in her arms and a child at her side. On the other side stood a tall, menacing figure. Instead of stick-fingered circles for hands, the figure's hands were clenched, colored in black, and his scowl was fierce. The sky on the mother's side of the house was sunny and blue. Above the father it was gray and threatening.

Roy Stuart Jr. couldn't have been older than seven or eight when he'd drawn the picture, just a little boy who should have been innocent, carefree and ignorant of the evil in the world. But he hadn't been. His father had seen to that.

So had his mother.

"It's not a pretty picture, is it?" Juliet stood behind him, her hand on his arm. For an instant, the drawing was forgotten. All he could think of was how warm her touch was, how slender and perfectly formed her fingers were. All he could want was more—both hands touching him, hell, her entire body touching his. Too soon, though, she drew away, squeezed his arm, then walked to the door. "I'm ready."

So was he. How unfair that he was ready for something so much more intimate than she was offering.

He returned Roy Jr.'s drawing to the table, moving it to the bottom of the pile, before following Juliet out.

At the hardware store, she paid for the two dead bolt locks he chose, then they returned to the car. "Back home?" she asked over the roof.

"Want to drive up the mountain? We can see…" The image of a place popped into his mind, a clearing ringed with large boulders, with a pine-needle carpet and a view to forever. The picture was so clear and exact that he knew he'd been there before—in that nebulous *before* that haunted and eluded him—and he knew exactly how to get there.

He would give a year off his life to know *how* he knew.

Juliet slid behind the wheel, started the engine and waited for him to climb in. He gave her directions out of town, turning off the main highway, switching from one road to another as they climbed higher through the forest. After six, maybe seven, miles, the last road they'd taken came to an end, and he sat still, staring.

Yes, he'd been here. A number of times. Important times.

Leaving Juliet and the car, he walked between two granite boulders taller than he was and through the clearing. It climbed up at a gentle slope, then abruptly dropped straight down two hundred feet or more. Years ago, a split-rail fence had been built a few feet back from the cliff for safety's sake, but time and the elements had tumbled most of it. Vandals had played a role, too, burning the fallen wood in a makeshift fire ring in the middle of the clearing.

"Oh, Martin, it's beautiful." Juliet had stopped a few feet away, and her gaze was directed to the northeast, where the mountains spread out as far as the eye could see. It *was* beautiful. Breathtaking. Awe inspiring.

"On a clear day, you can see…" *All the way to heaven.* Where had he heard that? Who had told him?

"Forever." She tore her gaze from the vista to look at him and sobered. "This is one of those places you remember."

He nodded.

"Did you come here often?"

Instead of giving the answer he'd come to detest, he turned his back on the mountains. Except for the view, there was nothing special about the clearing. The same boulders, trees, mosses and wildflowers that made up this area could be found in a million other places in any direction he turned. Awe-inspiring views could be found all over, too. So what made this place special?

Damned if he had a clue.

"Can we sit down?"

"Sure." He started toward the rocks nearest the fire ring. They were just the right size for huddling around a fire but only a fraction of the size that apparently interested Juliet, who was looking for footholds to reach the top of a ten-foot-tall boulder. "Go to the other side," he advised, and she disappeared from sight. A moment later she reappeared on top.

"Come on up."

How had he known that the jagged surface on the opposite side of the rock served as well as any staircase could? Had he come here with family, friends, girls, all of the above or none of them? Had he shared picnic lunches, camped around the fire or created his own private lovers' lane?

As he reached the top, his gaze fell on Juliet, sitting cross-legged and straight-backed. Recreating that last pos-sibility—if he'd ever created it in the first place—certainly held merit. Right here on this boulder would be a hell of a place to make love. Maybe the act itself wouldn't be the best—he felt damn near like a virgin again—but the loca-tion would make it memorable.

Juliet would make it memorable.

He sat down, close enough to touch her if he let himself, not so close that he would be tempted to let himself. For a long time she simply looked out. For a longer time he sim-ply looked at her.

Gradually his watchfulness made her uneasy. She glanced at him, gave half a smile, looked away, then glanced back. It wasn't an uncomfortable or negative un-easiness but more of a self-consciousness. An awareness. A beautiful-woman-to-lonely-man sort of thing.

He forced himself to look away, to shift away, putting solid rock between them. Supporting himself on one elbow, he stretched out and offered conversation that was as harm-less as he could imagine—and a world away from what he wanted to say, something along the lines of, Do you want to make love on top of the world? Do you want me? Would you have me? "Did you ever imagine growing up in Dallas that someday you'd be living in a place like this?"

"Growing up in Dallas, I never imagined that a place like this existed." She moved away, too, finding a place where stone jutted up to provide a backrest. "My family has lived and died in Texas for more than a hundred years. I didn't expect to be any different."

"I'm glad you are."

Juliet clenched her teeth as she felt her face warm. He

said that as if he meant it. Of course, he did—on a business level. It was a fair guess that no one else in the city of Grand Springs could match her ability with computers, though there were probably some kids who came close, and she was possessor of a logical mind and strong deductive reasoning. For all the good it'd done him. So far her computer had told him that Roy Stuart Jr. didn't have a listed phone number. Wow. Big deal.

"It's not as if I've been much help."

He grinned. "It's not as if I'm talking about your help. Overall, I'd have to say that losing my memory has *not* been a particularly pleasant experience, but if there is an upside to it, it's meeting you."

To hide her nerves, she clasped her hands together in her lap, stretched out her legs and crossed one ankle over the other. He recognized her discomfort, anyway, and gave a dismayed shake of his head. "The men in Dallas are idiots. They deserved to lose you."

She laughed in spite of herself. "Trust me. I didn't leave any broken hearts behind."

"You could break my heart."

"You could have left behind a few broken hearts yourself."

"Does the idea bother you?"

That there might have been some significant woman in his life? A girlfriend, a lover, maybe a wife? It made her jealous. It saddened her because she could imagine too easily how deeply it would hurt if the man she loved just suddenly and without warning disappeared from her life. But did it bother her? Would it make her refuse anything he might offer because some woman, whoever she may be, back home, wherever that might be, had a prior claim to him?

She slowly, hesitantly shook her head. That was in another life, when he was another man. She had no place in that life, and that life had no place in *her* life.

Her answer seemed to give him something to think

about. With a nod, he rolled onto his back, folded his arms under his head and gazed up at the sky. He looked thoughtful. Troubled. And just a little bit satisfied.

Heavens, her answer gave *her* something to think about. He could be a married man. He could have children who mourned their daddy and begged for him to come home. She could be falling for another woman's husband. She could fall in love with him, and his memory could return, and he could realize that she offered nothing compared to the life he'd lost. He could break her heart.

Or not. His memory might never return. Or maybe it would, and there would be nothing to return to. Maybe there was no lover, no wife, no children. Maybe he had nobody, like her. It was hard to imagine, but it was possible. Anything was possible.

Even a woman like her attracting the interest of a man like him.

Wanting to save such a fantasy for later, when she was alone, she turned to face him. "Where did Olivia live at the time of her death?"

He didn't open his eyes or turn his head. "In a house on Poplar."

"What did the kids do with it?"

"I guess it belongs to them. No one's living there. That's where she was found, you know."

She knew. She'd filled in the gaps in the gossip with the newspaper clippings she'd brought home Thursday. It had happened on a Friday evening last June. Olivia had left the office early and gone home to get ready for Hal's wedding to Randi Howell at the ski lodge. When she didn't show up, Josie Reynolds—now Stryker—had gone looking for her and found her unconscious on the floor in her kitchen, suffering from an apparent heart attack. It was nearly a week later that the real mechanism of death had become discovered: the injection of pure potassium into her system that caused her heart to stop.

"I wonder if there's anything at the house that might help us."

Finally he did look at her. "It's a fair bet that Hal isn't going to let us in to find out. I don't know about Eve."

"Well, if they say no, couldn't we just go, anyway? Just for a look around?" As his expression turned disbelieving, she realized what she had suggested and flushed. "Just go, anyway" was a sorry euphemism for breaking in, and even if they did just look around and didn't take anything, it was still wrong.

It would be easy, though. They would go at night, of course, to diminish the risk of being seen. Martin could probably pick the back door lock, or maybe there was a window that could be easily opened. People in small towns were notorious for trusting their neighbors, leaving locks undone or settling for substandard security. They could take flashlights, close the drapes, make a leisurely search of the premises and be gone with no one the wiser.

And what if it wasn't so easy? If one of Olivia's neighbors suffered with insomnia? If someone called the police? Even if she and Martin could convince them that they had simply been looking for clues, Hal Stuart would have her fired for sure. If they couldn't convince the police, she would have a tough time finding another job with a criminal record.

"Forget I said that," she mumbled. She had too much to lose on what would probably be a fruitless quest, anyway. If the police hadn't found anything of value in the house, it wasn't likely she and Martin would, either.

"Don't get caught up in this. Playing cop can be fun, but don't ever forget that that's *all* you're doing—playing." He rolled to his feet and offered her a hand up. When she was standing, he didn't immediately release her but turned her to face the mountains, then moved close behind her, his arms around her shoulders, his body warm and solid against hers. "You should see this place in winter, when there's snow everywhere. The trees get so heavy with snow and ice that the branches break. You can walk through the woods and hear the cracking. Everything's cold and clean, and the sky turns the clearest, sharpest blue.''

''I'd like to see that,'' she said softly. Maybe next winter, if he was still here, he would show her. Maybe next winter he would have no interest in her. Maybe she would have to be satisfied with this: snow on the distant peaks, slopes covered with a thousand shades of green and dotted with massive outcroppings of stone and, nearer, the delicate colors of wildflowers.

For a time he held her, and she let him. She didn't lean into him, didn't snuggle closer, but stood motionless, arms at her side, and savored the feel of him.

''Juliet?''

''Hmm.''

''Want some lunch?''

He could have asked a dozen questions that wouldn't have disturbed her warm, enveloping sense of well-being— Are you comfortable? Do you like this? Can I touch you? Can I kiss you? Something so mundane as lunch, though, disrupted the coziness of their position. So did the sudden growl of her stomach.

His chuckle stirred her hair. That was all it was—not a brush of his cheek against it. Not the touch of his mouth to it. Just the rush of breath when he laughed. ''I'd call that a big yes.'' He released her and started to the ground.

Before following, she turned for one last look. She would come back here in the summer and the fall. She would bring a blanket, a picnic and a wish for an artist's talent to capture the scene.

Martin jumped the last few feet to the ground, then offered her a lift down. For a moment his hands lingered at her waist. For a moment his gaze met hers and she thought he was going to kiss her. She was wrong. He released her and turned toward the car. Stifling a disappointed sigh, she went after him.

They ate lunch in town, then swung by the church so he

could borrow the tools necessary to install the locks. She had wondered, when he'd brought it up that morning, if she wouldn't be better off calling a locksmith, but, in spite of his teasing, Martin knew what he was doing. She helped, if standing there handing him an occasional tool could be considered much help. When he was finished, he gave her the new keys, then went out into the backyard to take a look around. "You need a dog."

"A dog." She said it as blankly as if he'd just advised buying a machine gun. Never in her life had she considered owning a dog—or any other kind of creature, for that matter. The lack of pets was a long-standing Crandall family tradition. "Why in the world would I want a dog?"

"For protection."

"I don't want a mean dog."

"He doesn't have to be mean, just noisy. No burglar wants to deal with a barking dog."

Was that just common sense or did he know from experience? She pushed the thought from her mind. "*I* don't want to deal with a barking dog."

"Well, of course he's not going to be barking all the time. You've got a great yard for him, and he could keep you company in the evenings, and he'd keep an eye on both you and your house."

She would prefer that Martin keep her company in the evenings and look out for her safety, but, of course, he wasn't always going to be there. But a dog just wasn't her idea of a companion.

She looked over the yard. It *was* great—fenced all around, not too wide but deep, with lush grass that would require mowing soon. It was one of the reasons she'd bought the house, and she had big plans for it—shrubs along the back fence, bulbs and perennials on one side, more bulbs and annuals on the other, a brick patio with room for a grill, a table and chairs and maybe even a fountain close to her bedroom so she could open the windows at night and sleep to the sound of bubbling water.

She *didn't* have room in those plans for a dog who would poop on the lovely grass, dig up the flower beds and probably pee in the fountain, all while annoying both her and the neighbors with its incessant burglar-warning bark.

Considering the matter closed, she opened the screen door and waited. "Are you ready to get back to work?"

They went inside, finished the job of sorting, then merged their two sets of papers. "Now what?"

He sprawled in the chair beside her. "When you checked the other night to see if Roy Jr. had a listed phone number—can you do it the other way?"

"You mean a reverse search? Put in a number and ask for a name? Sure."

"Why don't you take the most recent phone bills and check her long distance calls? I'll start with the bank records."

She turned on the computer, accessed the Net and went directly to the uniform resource locator, or URL, she needed. Checking Olivia's long distance calls for the last year of her life wasn't much of a task. Business calls had been made at the office on the city's bill, and personal calls were few and far between.

At least until the March preceding her death. Once a week for three months there was a call, usually between 7:00 and 8:00 p.m., lasting an hour or more, to a number in Miami Beach, Florida. Curious, she typed in the number, hit the enter key and waited. "You ever hear of a Jason Scott?"

Martin shook his head.

"Olivia called him regularly for three months. The last call was the week before she died."

"Call him."

She disconnected from the modem, then picked up the cordless phone from the china hutch and dialed the number. "And say what? 'Hi, you don't know me, but I was just wondering what your connection to Olivia Stuart was?' As if any sane person would actually tell me."

He grinned. "If he's a red-blooded man, he will, if for no other reason than to hear you talk some more."

On the second ring, a recording came on. *The number you have dialed has been disconnected....* She reconnected to the Internet server and tried a search for Jason Scott in the Miami area. There were a number of hits, but the addresses were different. "So what do we do? Call every one and ask if he's the Jason who used to live at that address?"

When he shrugged, she printed the listings, then began dialing. It didn't take long to hit a dead end. After the last wrong number, Martin took the phone and placed one call. Eve Redtree had never heard of Jason Scott and knew of no reason her mother would place so many calls to Miami.

"Maybe Scott is a private investigator and she had hired him to find Roy Jr.," Juliet mused. "Maybe he *is* Roy Jr. Maybe when he ran away from here, he knew his mother would try to find him, so he changed his name."

"She left him more than fifty thousand dollars. Don't you think, if she knew he'd changed his name or had known where to find him, she would have mentioned it to her attorney, her children or the insurance company?"

"Probably. Anything interesting in her bank statements?"

"Maybe. She wrote a couple of large checks to Hal, one a year before she died and one five months later. Repaying a loan?"

"Or maybe making one."

He shook his head. "Hal's a lawyer. He makes decent money. He's not married, has no kids and no obligations besides himself. Why would he need to borrow twelve thousand dollars from his widowed mother, who certainly wasn't rich herself?"

"You don't drive a car like his or wear clothes like his on a *decent* salary. Hal's got very expensive tastes. Maybe that's how he pays for them—Olivia gave him his inheritance while she was still living."

"Then, in all fairness—and Olivia was a fair woman—there should be similar checks to Eve, but there aren't.''

Perhaps she'd given Eve her share in cash—and Martin hadn't come across the withdrawal yet—or in property. The money could have been Olivia's contribution to Hal's ill-fated wedding, or he could have gone in debt buying those expensive things and his mother had bailed him out. There were plenty of possibilities.

"Wouldn't you like to see a credit history on Hal?''

Of course she would. She was as nosy as anyone else. "You think you can talk one out of Stone?''

"I doubt it. I'm not a suspect, but as long as we don't know who or what I am, I'm not a trusted confidant, either. Besides, he'd probably just tell us to mind our own business and leave the police work to the police.'' He grinned. "You think you can sweet-talk one out of that computer?''

She had the contacts to accomplish it, but it would be illegal and probably wouldn't have any relevance whatsoever to Olivia's murder. If they both didn't dislike Hal, the subject never would have come up. "Only as a last resort. This isn't real, remember? We're playing.''

He grinned again, a slower, lazier, make-a-woman-weak grin. "I can think of a lot better games to play, darlin', especially with you as my playmate.''

If she were a braver woman, she would duplicate that wicked grin and the husky bedroom voice and issue an invitation no red-blooded man could refuse. But she wasn't brave or wicked. She was blushing and fluttery, flattered and skittish. She was no temptress.

But, oh, how she wished she was.

Dragging a thirty-gallon trash can, Martin made his way to the Dumpster out behind the church Monday afternoon. He hefted the can, filled with debris from the remodeling job, to the lip of the Dumpster and was about to up-end it when movement inside caught his attention. Slowly he let the can slip back to the ground, then moved a chunk of

Sheetrock to better see the puppy who'd been scrounging inside.

He wasn't the sort of cute, lovable and oh-how-adorable puppy who would easily find a home. He was skin and bones, more than half starved. His coat was filthy, coarse and marked with scars from his nose all the way back to his rump, and he looked likelier to bite a hand than lick it.

"Hey, buddy." Martin removed his gloves, then rested his arms on the edge of the Dumpster. He didn't reach out. "If you're looking for food, pal, you picked the wrong place. This is a church. The only time you'll find food in this trash is when they have their annual bean supper, and that's not for another six months."

The dog backed into the corner, settled his rump on a two-by-four and gave him a wary look. Black and tan, he appeared to be a mix of Lab and hound and about six or eight months old.

"I have a sandwich inside. If you'll wait here, I'll get it." He'd stopped at the deli on his way to work and picked up a club sub for lunch, but then he'd run into Stone and Jack, who had invited him to the diner with them. He'd decided to save the sandwich for dinner, but the dog needed it more than he did.

When he returned, the puppy was standing near the Dumpster, watching him with dark brown eyes. As soon as he crossed the invisible line of the dog's comfort zone, the pup darted away, then turned to watch again.

Martin sat down on the ground, his back against the trash bin and unwrapped the sandwich. At the first whiff of food, the dog became still, his gaze riveted on it. Martin fed him slowly, tearing the sandwich into pieces, tossing them a few feet away. When it was all gone, he and the puppy watched each other for a time.

"Life hasn't been too kind, has it?" He wasn't an empathetic person, he'd told Juliet, but he could certainly relate to this scruffy, scarred creature. All the puppy wanted was food in his belly and a safe place to sleep. All he'd gotten was hunger, fear and abuse. All Martin wanted was a name of his own and Juliet. All he had was nothing.

He hadn't seen Juliet since Saturday evening. They had finished working late, and she had stood at the door and watched until he was out of sight. He had stood in the shadows and watched until she locked up, until the lights went off in the dining and living rooms, until only one dim light had burned in the front hall. He had remained there in the dark, imagining her getting ready for bed—brushing her blond hair, washing her face, unbuttoning every tiny button on her long, flowery dress, then sliding it off her shoulders and letting it drop to the floor, leaving her wearing damn near nothing, all pale delicate skin, small breasts, narrow waist—

Squeezing his eyes shut, he forced air into his constricted lungs. And so he had stayed away Sunday. He had given her a day's peace to do all the things she'd normally done before he'd intruded in her life. He had stayed locked up in his apartment, but his thoughts had been two and a half blocks away. His desire had damn well been with her. He'd considered himself lucky to survive the day.

"Hey, Martin, what's taking so— Oh. You found a mutt." The preacher walked straight toward the dog, extending his hand.

"Don't—"

The dog went still, the hair on his back rising, and a low, threatening growl rumbled through him. Before Martin could finish his warning, the puppy snapped at the preacher, closing his jaws only a breath away from the man's hand.

"Hey, he tried to bite me!"

"If he'd meant to bite you, he would have. That was a warning. Don't ever approach a strange dog with your hand out like that. He could take your fingers off."

"Well, don't encourage him to stay around here. The kids play outside after the service, and he might seriously injure them."

"I won't. If he'll come, I'll take him home with me."

As if he needed a dog in his apartment…but he knew some-one who *did* need one in her backyard, even though she didn't realize it yet.

After emptying the can, he left the dog with a backward glance. Back inside he picked up more rubbish while Rev-erend Murphy double-checked measurements for the new wall they were building. "This carpet used to be bur-gundy," Martin remarked as he scooped up Sheetrock and insulation.

The preacher looked down at the plastic-covered carpet. "It's been green since I came here, and that was fifteen years ago."

"Then maybe before that."

"If it's important, I can ask some of our long-time mem-bers. A number of them got married here. It might show in their photographs."

"Do you have a list of members from twenty years ago or so?"

The preacher shook his head. "We're a small church, and we're a little informal. Other than marriages, births and deaths—and our financial records, of course—I doubt we have anything going back more than ten years. I'd be happy to put you in touch with some of our older members, though."

"Thanks." Though, frankly, Martin wasn't sure it would help. Finding out when the carpet was changed from bur-gundy to green would narrow the time span when he had visited or lived in Grand Springs the first time, but probably not significantly, not in a church that kept the same carpet fifteen years or longer. He already knew he must have been young, for no one to recognize him now, but old enough to remember.

When they finished work for the day, Martin emptied one last load of trash, then looked around for the dog. He was still there, curled in a tight ball with the Dumpster at his back. Martin crouched a half-dozen feet from him, folded his fingers tightly and offered the back of his hand. The puppy didn't wag his tail or come close to sniff.

"Okay, pal. I'm going home now. If you want to come with me, feel free. If you choose to stay here, I'll bring you some lunch tomorrow. It's your choice."

He'd gone more than a block before he heard the scratch of claws on the sidewalk. A glance back showed the dog twenty-five feet behind him. He stopped when Martin stopped and walked when Martin walked.

At home Martin gave the mutt water and a bowl of the only food he could find: canned green beans with a slice of bread torn over the top. The dog wolfed it down, turned in a circle three times underneath the steps, then wedged himself into the corner where the stairs met the outside wall.

They were two of a kind, Martin thought as he went upstairs to clean up for his evening with Juliet. Scarred, nameless strays, allowed to stay only through the kindness of strangers. The dog was luckier, though. Juliet would take one look at those big brown eyes of his and change her mind about having a pet. She wasn't as easily taken by Martin's blue eyes.

Oh, she was *interested,* but everyone who knew he had amnesia was interested. From her he wanted infatuated, in lust, maybe more. Maybe the rest would grow out of the interest. After all, when he'd put his arms around her up on the mountain Saturday, she hadn't pulled away. Granted, she also hadn't moved any closer or laid her hands over his or leaned against him. She had stood stiff and unyielding, but she hadn't pushed him away, not even when he'd kissed her hair.

And what if she did come around? What if she decided that she wanted the same things he did—a real relationship, intimacy, sex, possibilities? He still didn't know who he was, whether he was free to feel anything for her, whether he was deserving of anything with her. Was he willing to overlook the fact that he might be married, a criminal or crazy?

He shouldn't...but he'd been alone a long time, more

alone than any man should ever be. He would like to be strong and noble and keep a safe distance from the world until he discovered the truth about himself, but that might never happen, and while he waited, he still had to live. He couldn't do it alone.

But he could with Juliet.

When he was fairly sure she would be home from work, he left the apartment. The dog immediately jumped to his feet and waited. "You know, you need a name. The ER nurses named me after a character on television. I guess we could name you after a TV dog, but you don't look like a Lassie or a Rin Tin-Tin, and you're the wrong color for Old Yeller. And those are the only Hollywood dogs I know. Hell, if you're going to live with Juliet, maybe she should name you."

He circled the garage, and the dog trotted along behind, keeping a safe distance for two and a half blocks. Juliet—wearing one of those pretty, flowing dresses and no shoes—was just going into her house with the mail when she saw him. She held the screen door open for him, and the dog shot around Martin, raced inside and disappeared down the hall.

"Hey! He can't just come in here!"

"Looks like he already did, darlin'."

"Find him and make him leave."

Stepping inside, Martin whistled, but there was no response. He figured the little mutt had headed for the kitchen—something certainly smelled good there—but the room was empty. Along the back hall only one door was open, and it led to Juliet's bedroom. "Smart dog," he murmured as he walked through the door. Over his shoulder he said, "Romeo's found himself the most comfortable bed in the house." Exactly the same bed Martin had *his* eye on.

"Romeo? *Romeo?* Oh, no. Uh-uh. I'm *not* having a dog, and I'm *certainly* not having a dog named Romeo. For heaven's sake, I get enough jokes as it is. Do you think I want my neighbors to see me outside with that mutt and say, 'Oh, there's Romeo and Juliet'?" She came through the door, stopped abruptly and scowled at the dog stretched out on her bed with his head on a pillow. "Oh, please... He's on my bed, and he *smells*."

"Of course he smells. He's been on the road a long time. I'll give him a bath." Eventually. When the dog trusted him enough to actually let him touch him. Maybe in a month or so.

"He's probably not housebroken."

"I'll do that, too."

"I bet he has fleas."

"I'll take him to the vet and get those flea pills."

"I work all day."

"He'll sleep all day once he has a safe place and doesn't have to be constantly scrounging for food. He's half-starved, Juliet. You can't put him out."

"If I did, you would take care of him." She heaved a sigh, and a little of her dismay slipped away. "He can't sleep in my bed."

He certainly couldn't, because if luck ever turned his way, Martin intended to claim half of that bed for himself. "Just give him a bed of his own and tell him no when he gets on yours. He'll learn."

"And what would I feed this creature?"

"Dog food—though he's partial to green beans and club subs."

"He'll probably dig up my flowers."

"You haven't planted any yet. He'll learn to leave them alone. Come on." Claiming her hand, he pulled her to the side of the bed. "Hold your hand like this—" moving behind her, he folded her fingers "—and hold out your hand. Romeo, meet your new—"

"*Not* Romeo."

"Okay." He moved a step closer, inched her hand a bit farther. "Not-Romeo, meet your new mother—"

"Owner."

"Juliet. She may be a little prickly at first, but you'll warm up to her. Trust me." *He* certainly had. In fact, right now, with her body pressing against his, he was damn near steaming.

The dog lifted his head from the pillow, sniffed, then licked her hand.

"Hey, he likes you."

The look on her face was closer to disgust than delight. "And that's how he shows it? With his *tongue?*"

"Darlin', people have been expressing affection with their tongues since the beginning of time."

"*I* haven't."

"Oh, right. Any kiss that's worthy of the name…" He turned her so she was facing him, so that she was close enough for some serious dancing. For some serious loving. "Like this…" He raised her hand to his mouth, touched his tongue to her palm and felt her shiver. "And this…" Brushing her hair back, he traced the shape of her ear. "And this…"

Her mouth opened to his as if they had kissed a thousand times before. After a moment, she slid her arms around his neck and swayed naturally, subconsciously, against him as he stroked her tongue with his. He remembered this kind of kissing, as if it were an ingrained part of him, but not this kind of pleasure. Sure as hell not this kind of need. One kiss, one sweet little unending kiss, and he was hard and hot and all too aware of the bed only a few feet away. All he had to do was move her a step or two, lower her to the mattress, get that dress off of her and—

The mattress dipped under their weight, and the dog growled a long, low threat. Startled, Juliet pulled away. Her cheeks were flushed, her mouth soft and well kissed, and she looked as guilty as any schoolgirl caught in the middle of something naughty. She was so damned innocent… and he found that so damned erotic.

She got to her feet and would have fled to the door if he hadn't grabbed her hand. She kept her back to him, her head bowed. "I—I'm sorry. I—I don't normally do this...."

"You don't normally kiss men in your bedroom? I'm glad."

"I didn't mean to— You don't have to— I'll still help you—"

"Juliet." He gently turned her to face him again and ducked his head to peer up into her downturned face. "*I* kissed *you,* darlin', and I did it because I've been wanting to ever since the first time I saw you. I did it because you're a beautiful woman and you're sweet and you have a voice to make a man ache and I like your bare feet and your dresses and your blushes. It's got nothing to do with your help. I did it because I wanted to. Hell, I did it because I wanted you. You knew that, didn't you?"

Silently she shook her head.

He gave his most endearing grin. "Consider yourself warned."

Six

Juliet now knew more about Martin Smith than she had an hour ago—that he had a soft spot for helpless creatures. That he was far and away the best kisser she'd ever had the luck to know. That he made her want more than ever to be a brave, wicked temptress. And that he was certifiably insane.

He was the best-looking man in town, probably in the entire state. He could have anyone, but he wanted *her*. Even if he hadn't told her so straight out—it still made her shiver that he had—she would have known. Heavens, she'd been pressed against his body from chest to thigh. She had felt every bit how much he'd wanted.

Maybe it was a gratitude thing. Maybe he'd been celibate since his accident and was looking for someone whose expectations wouldn't be so high, who wouldn't know if he was less than fantastic. Maybe—

"I think he needs to go out."

Shaken out of her thoughts, Juliet turned to see the dog pacing the kitchen.

"Let's go out with him—give him plenty of time to take care of business so you don't have any messes to clean in the morning."

She dried her hands, left the sink full of dishes from their dinner and followed them outside. The dog immediately raced away while Martin walked to the edge of the light that spilled through the doorway. "He needs a name."

"I know. I was trying to think of something dignified," she lied. Better than admitting that she'd been trying to figure out exactly what it was Martin wanted from her and why.

"Oh, yeah, he's a dignified sort of guy. He's peeing on everything in sight, but he's dignified."

She pretended to ignore his teasing, but it made her feel warm inside. In her experience, men didn't usually tease *with* her. They teased *about* her. There was a lovely difference. "What is he besides mutt?"

"He's not mutt at all. I think he's half hound, half Lab."

"Lab. That's a retriever, isn't it?"

He grinned. "You really don't know much about dogs, do you?"

"I told you, I've never had one. But I'll find out. There must be a site on the Net for Labs."

He shook his head. "You know, the Internet isn't the answer to all of life's questions."

"No, but it's close. It entertains me, educates me, informs me, amuses me—"

"It can't arouse you."

She gave him a smug look. "Obviously, you haven't been to the places *I* have."

He moved into the shadows, shifting into a faceless form and a throaty, aroused and arousing voice, drifting out of the darkness to wrap around her. "It can't hold you or kiss you. It can't make you weak. It can't turn your blood to fire. It can't make you want and need so desperately that you beg for release, and it can't give you that release. It can't satisfy you, Juliet." *But I can.*

Those last words were soft, a whisper, maybe a wish of her own creating. He was all too right. The Net could do wonderful things, but it couldn't replace a man in her life. It couldn't satisfy her. But he could. If he wanted. If she trusted him enough to believe.

The dog came toward them, nose to the ground, stopping periodically to bend one front leg. "He's tracking," Martin commented.

So are you, she wanted to reply. The only difference

between her and the rabbit or squirrel whose trail had caught the dog's attention was that she *wanted* to get caught.

She just didn't want to lose.

"How about Hunter?"

She glanced at him. "Hunter who?"

"The dog. Labs and hounds are both hunting dogs. Why not name him Hunter?"

"I can live with that. I'm just not sure I can live with him."

"If you can't, I'll take him. I'll find him a home."

She'd been teasing, she realized. The dog was the first gift, such as it was, she'd ever received from a man not related to her, and she would learn to appreciate him. Besides, he was kind of cute—or would be once his skin no longer drooped from his bones and that awful smell no longer emanated from his coat. He had soulful eyes, a tail that curled like a big question mark and the biggest feet she'd ever seen on an animal. He might prove good company on lonely nights.

"We'll see," she said quietly. But there really wasn't anything to see. Hunter the Lab hound had found himself a home.

Once they were settled in the dining room, with the dishes done and stinky Hunter curled in a corner, Martin brought up business for the first time. "The preacher is going to put us in touch with some of the older church members. It's a long shot, but maybe we can find out something about my past visit to Grand Springs."

She nodded. The better she got to know him—the more she came to care for him—the less thrilled she was with solving the mystery of his identity. The mystery of who killed Olivia Stuart, though, still held her interest. "I ran the rest of the phone numbers on Olivia's bills. They mostly belong to relatives. Some Stuarts, some Davises—her maiden name—and Eve. I've gone through the last three years of her credit card statements, and there's nothing unusual there. She paid off the high-interest ones every month, ran a balance on the low-interest ones and never used her gas cards anywhere but Grand Springs and on occasional trips to Denver.''

"When did you do all this?''

"Yesterday.'' Saturday evening, soon after he'd given her that lazy, wicked grin and that lazy, wicked assurance—*I can think of a lot better games to play, darlin', especially with you as my playmate*—he had gone home, and he hadn't come back Sunday. She had waited all morning, then spent the afternoon encouraging herself to go somewhere—to lunch, shopping, for a drive up the mountain. But she hadn't gone, and he hadn't come, and by bedtime she'd told herself that she was glad he hadn't. She'd gotten a good bit of work done. She'd answered the E-mails that had gone ignored all week and spent more time on the Net in one day than she had in the preceding five. It was the way she'd spent every Sunday in the three years since her mother's death. It was normal, routine, comfortable. She'd told herself that she was grateful for the respite, that she appreciated the hours alone with the computer.

She had lied to herself.

"You know, it's perfectly permissible to take a day off and do nothing.''

Was nothing what he'd done? Had he slept in late, kicked back and watched baseball and movies all day, or had he gone out with friends—a female friend, in particular? She was jealous enough to care, but she would never ask. She would never admit that, while he was enjoying his day away from her, she had sat here missing him.

"I also sorted the correspondence.'' She picked up a box from the floor that held rubber-banded stacks of letters and handed the batch on top to him. "Look what I found.''

The envelopes were mostly the larger envelopes of greeting cards, and each one was addressed in Olivia's graceful penmanship to her older son. The oldest was yellowed and wrinkled, the newest clean and white.

"There are thirty-one of them. My guess is birthday cards, mostly, and some letters. The flaps aren't sealed, just tucked in. You can open them if you want."

He flipped through the stack, then, with a shake of his head, handed them back. She hadn't read them, either. A mother's letters to the son she had failed, then lost, were much too personal for a stranger to read. Olivia had poured her heart and soul into every word contained in those envelopes, and if Roy Jr. ever came home, if he was alive to come home, he deserved to know that he was the first— and, if he wanted, the only—person to read them.

"You've been a busy little thing, haven't you? If I'd known you were going to work all day, I would have been over here as soon as the sun was up to drag you out of the house and away from the computer."

Nice idea, but the fact was, he *hadn't* come over or called. He hadn't shown any interest in spending the day with her.

But he'd made it clear this evening that he was interested in spending the night with her. All she needed was the nerve to say yes.

One more kiss like that one in the bedroom, and she wouldn't have to say a word. When she stripped off both his clothes and her own, he would get the idea.

"So what do you want to do now?"

His question was innocent. The response that popped into her head wasn't, and it made her blush. She had to clear her throat to speak. "Someone needs to read her letters."

"Not me. I've got bank statements to finish."

"I feel like such a snoop."

"That's what police work is about. Cops are nosy. They want to know everything about everyone."

"Stone says he's blessed with inordinate curiosity."

"Or cursed, depending on your point of view."

Average citizens like her were blessed that people like Stone were out there. She could see, though, how people on the wrong side of the law might consider it a curse. There was no doubt which side Martin was on now, and she didn't care which he had been before—citizen or criminal—but she wondered. So did he. The difference was her wondering was idle curiosity. His was fearful expectation.

Olivia had apparently been a great believer in written correspondence. There were piles of letters spanning twenty years. How many personal letters could Juliet find in her own collection? Two? Maybe three. That was what came from living in the same city with your entire family and never making a friend close enough to write when she moved on.

She divided the letters by author, then started with the most recent and read back, finding little to catch her attention. What finally did was a brief note at the end of one letter: *So sorry to hear about Hal. Hope all is resolved. I know how you worry since Roy Jr....* She read it aloud to Martin. "It's from a woman named Dara. As far as I can tell, they were friends before Olivia moved here."

"Is there any mention of Hal in the letter before that one?"

She skimmed it quickly, then shook her head.

"What's the date on it?"

"November, year before last."

He checked the notes he'd made. "That's when she wrote the second check to Hal. So he was in trouble and needing money. For what?"

She shrugged. "Debts. Taxes. Gambling losses. Woman trouble. There are a million reasons people need money."

For a long time, he sat silent, his gaze distant. When he finally looked at her, there was a troubled look in his eyes. "We talked about getting a credit report on Hal."

"You can't possibly think he was involved. Olivia was his *mother*. He *loved* her."

"You know that for a fact?"

Now it was her turn for silence. All she knew was what she'd been told. Everyone in town believed that Hal had loved Olivia. Maybe he had, maybe he hadn't. Maybe he truly was grieving, as his sister had explained, or maybe it was a camouflage for his resentment. Maybe he had been desperate. He'd accepted twelve thousand dollars from her. Maybe he'd been in deeper trouble and had thought her life insurance was the only way out. Sixty-six thousand dollars wasn't a lot to kill someone for, but maybe he'd expected half instead of only a third. It still wasn't a lot, but to a desperate man…

At worst, Hal Stuart's credit history would be interesting reading. At best, it could clear him or implicate him. But how to get it? Martin could go by the credit bureau and charm it out of a susceptible clerk—meaning anyone female and breathing. It could cost the clerk her job—and her freedom—if anyone found out, but women had done foolish things for handsome men since the beginning of time.

Juliet could explain to Stone or Jack Stryker what they were doing and ask one of them to get it for her. Likely, all she would get was a reminder that she was a clerk, not a cop, and a warning to stay out of police business.

She could try to get it herself. Usually, when one of the detectives wanted a credit report, they went to the bureau in person to request it, but the working relationship was positive enough that, on occasion, someone would call over with a request and get the report faxed back. If she called and convinced the clerk that she was asking on Stone's behalf, then managed to be standing next to the fax machine when the report came in…

She wasn't a liar. She could never pull it off. Her voice would quaver, her hands would shake, her face would flush, and she would burn in hell. She would lose her job, and they would know nothing new.

"I don't know of any means of obtaining the report that doesn't include the risk of arrest for either one or both of us."

"Forget it, then."

"The credit reporting agencies have pretty sophisticated security. There were problems with hackers a few years back, and they all upgraded significantly. That doesn't mean it can't be done—not by me, but there are a few people out there who are brilliant enough, determined enough." And she happened to have gone through college with one. There wasn't a system in the country she couldn't penetrate, Susan had bragged. She'd been so good at it then that she now earned a comfortable living helping design those security programs.

"Forget it," he repeated. "You wouldn't like jail."

"You know that for a fact?"

For a moment his eyes turned bleak. "I think so."

"How? You don't have an arrest record. You're not a cop. You weren't a jailer or prison guard, because all jailers and prison guards have prints on file."

"Is it possible I do have a record, and by mistake they didn't get a hit on the prints?"

"They ran them through the FBI computer."

"The FBI's not infallible."

"But their computers are." When he didn't offer an argument, she returned to the letters in front of her. She ran Dara's through the multifunction printer to make a copy, then moved on to the next.

There were no other references to Hal and trouble, no mention of problems either professional or personal. Maybe, as a rule, Olivia kept her problems to herself, or perhaps her life was as carefree as it seemed. And yet someone had killed her. Not a very carefree thing to do.

"It doesn't make sense."

Martin looked at her. Her feet were drawn up in the chair, her face was wrinkled in a frown, and one fingertip tapped her mouth. Her eyes were so clear, the blue a perfect complement for the pure blond shadings of her hair. Even scowling, she was... Not pretty, not like Eve Redtree or Stone's wife. No, Juliet was as beautiful as her namesake.

"What doesn't make sense?"

"How could someone hate Olivia enough to want her dead with no one else around knowing it? That kind of passion can't be easily hidden."

"Oh, I don't know. *You* keep your passions fairly well hidden." He had first judged her—as a lot of people had, considering the gossip around the police department her first week—as cool and serene and more than a little aloof. After the way he had kissed her this evening, after the way she had kissed him back, he would never think of her as cool again. Her kiss had been wicked enough to tempt a saint, innocent enough to torment a sinner. If Hunter hadn't objected to their invading his space, they would still be in her bedroom, and they wouldn't be sleeping.

"Computers are my passion," she said primly. "Everyone knows that."

"Yeah, right," he snorted. "So, back there in your bedroom earlier, why were you thinking about interfacing with *me?*"

Her face turned scarlet, and she squirmed in her chair. Interesting. The heat and restlessness of embarrassment weren't really so different from the heat and restlessness of arousal. Which would win out if he stopped talking and started doing? If he kissed her, touched her, stroked her? If he coaxed her out of that chair and onto the floor, if he stretched out beside her, beneath her, on top of her?

It was no contest. He would win. But would she?

He wished he knew. She would enjoy the moment, but he couldn't offer any guarantees for the future, and he wanted that. He wanted to be able to assure her that there *was* a future, that he would never hurt her, that she would never have any regrets.

But life didn't offer guarantees. You buy your ticket, and you take your chances. But he was better equipped for taking chances than Juliet was. All her life she'd been protected—by her parents, by her shyness, by her career that surrounded her with a buffer of machines to keep other humans at bay. He'd been on his own literally longer than he could remember, had looked out for and protected himself. He knew all about taking chances, while he was the first and biggest chance Juliet had ever taken.

He got to his feet and stretched. "I'd better go home."

"I can give you a ride."

"Nope. You can walk me to the door, though." When she did, he grinned. "Now you can lean over here and give me a kiss good-night."

"I don't think so." Her voice was even, but her breathing wasn't. It quavered just enough to catch his attention.

"Then I'll kiss you." Holding her hands, he drew her closer and was about to lower his head when a convincingly chilling snarl sounded.

"I don't think so," Juliet repeated.

Hunter stood a few feet away, his unwavering gaze fixed on Martin, his lip curled back to bare his teeth. Martin gave him a wounded look. "Is that any way to treat the man who helped you find a new home?"

The mutt gave him a look that was utterly unrepentant.

"He's not going to be mean, is he?"

"Nah. He's just looking out for you. We'll do some training over the weekend."

"What kind of training?"

"Teach him to protect you."

"You know how to do that?"

Yeah, he did, he realized. He didn't know how, but...

For a long moment, she regarded him solemnly, then smiled faintly. "You're full of surprises, aren't you?" Stepping forward, she brushed a kiss to his cheek, then opened the door. "I'll see you."

He remained on the porch until he heard the lock click and her soft, sexy voice trailing away. "Come on, Hunter, let's find a place for you...."

Too bad she wouldn't take in one stray as easily as the other.

Martin went home and to bed, stretching out across the

mattress to watch a late-night movie. The reception wasn't the greatest, though, the picture fading in and out, the voices giving ground to static that built, then receded once more into words. For a time he hovered between sleep and wakefulness, then sleep won out.

Then the dream came.

Like the movie on television, the images appeared, faded, reappeared. The words were indistinguishable, the voices harsh and angry. He was watching, listening—the recipient of the anger or the cause of it?

Wake up. You don't want to see this. That voice was his own, also angry, pleading, damn near desperate. *Damn you, wake up! I don't want to see this!*

But he couldn't wake up. The pure, overwhelming, sweat-breaking terror wouldn't let him. It held him paralyzed, unable to speak or think or move, unable to do anything but feel, and he felt too much. Pain, fury, hatred, horror, grief, shock, sorrow. The smells were nauseating—burning flesh, blood, sickness, despair, death.

Then a whisper, frantic, panicked. *He's dead! Oh, my God, you've killed him! You've killed him!*

For one brief instant, he felt satisfaction, peace. Then the images began shifting in rapid succession. Different voices, same sickness, another death, another and another until he couldn't bear anymore, until he knew that, if he didn't wake up, he would start screaming and never stop. With a strangled cry, he jerked awake, clamping his hands over his face to muffle any sound, to rub away the images that burned. His breathing was loud and ragged, his skin damp, his throat tight.

He had no doubt that the voice in the dream had been talking to him. He didn't know who was dead, didn't know what had happened, but *he* was responsible. He had taken another human being's life. He had no proof, but he *knew* it.

He rolled from the bed and pulled on the jeans he'd discarded a few hours earlier. Restlessly he prowled the perimeter of the room, shutting off the buzzing television before stopping at the window that faced Juliet's house. He couldn't see it from here, of course. Trees and other houses blocked his line of sight. But he knew it was there, knew *she* was there. He could see the pretty little green house with its porch and darkened windows, the yard where she wanted flowers but now had a dog. He could see through the closed door, down the hall and around the corner into her bedroom, could see her in bed, wearing nothing at all, snuggled under the covers with her hair falling across the pillow.

And Hunter standing guard at the door, of course.

What would Juliet think if he showed up in the middle of the night, seeking comfort and distraction? She would probably offer something soothing to drink, an ear for his problems and maybe a bed in the guest room, but she wouldn't offer herself, not in the way he wanted her.

She would never offer if he told her about the dream, if she knew that he had killed someone and, for an instant, had been glad. She would be appalled, frightened. Hell, *he* was, and he lived with the dreams.

But she had a right to know. Before things got any more serious, before he kissed her again, certainly before he made love to her, he would have to tell her. She had to know who she was inviting into her life…and her bed.

He just wasn't sure he could bear it. He'd made friends in his months here, but none like Juliet. If he lost her…

He would have nothing.

With a sigh, he glanced at the bed, wondering if he could sleep again, if the dreams would return. He decided not to tempt fate. It took him only a moment to finish dressing, grab a jacket and leave. He thought about going to Juliet's—not to disturb her, only to stand outside—but decided against it. If the neighbors saw him and called the police, it was a toss-up who would be more embarrassed: him over getting caught or Juliet over his interest in her being made public in such a way.

Not that it was likely anyone would see him. He knew how to blend into the night, how to avoid detection. He could go anywhere unnoticed, could do almost anything unseen. The fact that he didn't know whether that was good or bad was depressing.

The neighborhood was quiet—no barking dogs, no prowling cats. He headed downtown, away from Juliet's house and his own. He walked straight to the diner, took a seat away from the counter and accepted a glass of warm milk and a sympathetic smile from Pete, the night cook. "Trouble sleeping again?"

Martin shrugged.

"Have a turkey sandwich. It's good for what ails you."

"I'm not hungry."

"It's not food. It's medicine. Haven't you ever fallen asleep after Thanksgiving dinner? It's the turkey. Scientists have proved it."

He didn't know that he'd ever had a Thanksgiving dinner. His landlady had invited him to share her family's celebration last year, but he hadn't felt much like it. It was such a family holiday, and he wasn't family to anyone here—maybe not to anyone anywhere. "Just the milk."

With a shake of his head, Pete left. The only other person in the diner took his place. "Mind a little company?"

Martin offered a silent invitation, and Frank Sanderson sat down opposite him. The police chief looked tired. "What are you doing out so late?"

"We had a domestic dispute call."

"You have officers to handle those for you."

"This one was family," Sanderson said grimly, and Martin didn't say any more. "What are you doing out?"

"Some nights I don't sleep."

The chief nodded as if he understood completely. With one member of his family beating another, he probably did. "I'm getting too old for this business, Martin. You know, I've been a cop longer than you've been alive. I've seen things you wouldn't believe." He gave Martin a piercing look. "Well, you probably would, but the average person wouldn't. I've arrested friends, sent family to jail and buried my fellow officers. I need a break." His voice softened, and his expression grew distant. "There's a cabin up in the hills about sixty miles from here, right on the edge of the most beautiful lake you ever saw. The wife and I built it ourselves back when the boys were young. Back then, I loved being a cop. I lived for it. When I wasn't working, I was thinking about working. Now…"

Now he was thinking about the cabin and the lake. "Sounds as if you've earned it."

"That's what the wife says." Sanderson grinned. "Actually, she says *she's* earned it for putting up with the job all these years."

For a moment they sat in silence, Martin thinking idly about how tired he was and the sleep he needed but might not get. Just when he'd decided to give it a try, the chief spoke again.

"I had a visit from Hal Stuart the other day."

Martin tensed, waiting for the inevitable warning.

"He said you and the computer person were at his sister's house, asking questions about their mother's murder."

"Juliet."

"Hmm? Oh, yeah. Anyway, he wasn't too happy and wanted me to order you to stay away. I told him it was no crime to ask questions about a murder. If it was, I'd have to lock up everybody in town. But as long as you don't do anything illegal, like use Julie's—"

"Juliet's."

"Position to gain access to protected records, then I don't much care." Sanderson subjected him to another of those piercing looks. "You haven't done anything illegal, have you?"

"No, sir."

"You don't *plan* to do anything illegal, do you?"

He thought of the credit report he'd asked Juliet to get, then forget, thought of her own brushed-off suggestion that they let themselves into Olivia's house for a look around. "No, sir."

"Good." The chief stood up and stretched. "Can I interest you in a ride home? It's on my way."

"No, thanks. I'd rather walk." Martin watched him leave, then slumped lower on the stool. *The computer person.* Sanderson was the second person in the department that Martin had heard call Juliet that. Even when the chief had made a stab at her name, he'd gotten it wrong. How must that make her feel? Insignificant. Damn near invisible.

Hell, she was the most significant person he'd ever met.

"Need a refill, Martin?"

"No, thanks, Pete. I'm heading home." He left a couple of bucks on the counter on his way by.

"Good luck sleeping. Hope I don't see you tomorrow night."

Except for the diner and the police department in the opposite direction, the downtown area was deserted. The streets were empty, the stoplights flashing. The shops were locked up tight, and there was no sign of life until he reached the Monroe Building. The three-story building housed a print shop and dental offices on the first floor, an accounting firm and insurance agency on the second. Maxwell Brown, who owned the building and a good deal of the town, claimed the third floor for his own.

There were lights on up there, and Brown's Lincoln was parked in the narrow lot on the side. Martin supposed late hours weren't uncommon for businessmen—and the more prosperous the business, probably the later the hours—but if he had half of Brown's money, influence and success, he would be satisfied, and he would spend his nights at home with a family. With Juliet.

He turned the corner onto the side street that would take him home, via a short detour. The sound of car doors caught his attention as he approached the alley. Instinctively, he stopped, eased around the corner and pressed tight against the building in the shadows as he watched.

There was a car parked behind the Monroe Building, an older one, full size, a popular model in an indeterminate dark color. Two men stood on one side, their conversation loud enough for him to hear, distant enough that he couldn't understand. One was smoking, the other jangling a set of keys

Burglars planning a break-in? Martin didn't think so. There was nothing covert about their behavior. They acted as if they had every right in the world to be where they were at three in the morning. They probably had business with Brown, or were waiting for someone who did. It was no big deal. No reason for him to stand here in the darkness like some sort of spy.

But when he moved, it was only to creep farther into the alley, to take cover behind a garbage can, crouching in the shadows, staring hard at the men and the car. It seemed like forever, but the dim glow of his watch showed only ten minutes had passed when the back door of the building opened and two more men came out. One was Maxwell Brown, dressed as impeccably as if it were the middle of the afternoon instead of after midnight. The other, his face visible only for the few seconds the door was open, was a stranger.

The men talked for a moment, then Maxwell returned inside. The two men who had first caught Martin's attention climbed into the front seat of the car, and the third man, a briefcase in hand, slid into the back. They drove away, lights off until the driver made the turn onto the street a block away.

Martin remained where he was. Two businessmen conducting business in the middle of the night. It was unusual, but not unheard of. It shouldn't interest him in the least. But it did. It gave him a funny feeling centered right at the base of his neck, a niggling little what's-wrong-with-this-picture feeling. Something was odd.

His calf muscles were cramping and he was about to stand up when the light above the back door came on, illuminating the width of the alley and twenty feet in each direction. Odd that Brown hadn't turned it on for his business associates. It was almost as if they hadn't wanted to be seen.

Brown came out, locked the door, set the alarm and turned toward his car. Martin crouched closer to the wall and the trash can, cutting his view down to a narrow slice. He was dressed in dark clothes, but without the black knitted cap he normally wore when he did this sort of thing, his hair—

Brown passed out of sight, and Martin sank to the ground. A black knitted cap. He could see it, could damn near feel it warm and close against his head. Who the hell wore dark clothes and black knitted caps when they went out at night? Who the hell worried about staying hidden, invisible?

Thieves, burglars, drug dealers, rapists, murderers. Criminals. And him.

Long after he heard Brown's Lincoln drive away, he sat there, shaken. Finally he forced himself onto his feet, out of the alley and back onto the sidewalk, which he followed to Juliet's house. Everything was quiet, with the usual light burning in the front hall. She was probably sleeping soundly with Hunter curled up somewhere nearby. Lucky dog.

He turned toward home. He didn't think sleep was going to come easily, but sooner or later sheer exhaustion would gain him a few hours' rest. Until then he would lie in bed and pretend that he wasn't tense and desperate for sleep, that he wasn't dreading the lack of control that came with it, that allowed the dreams to slip in. He would pretend that he wasn't the sort of man he feared he was, the sort of man Juliet would never settle for. He would pretend, wish and hope. He would pray.

For all the good it would do a man like him.

Before the library opened Tuesday morning, Juliet wandered through the stacks looking for Tracey. She found the reference librarian curled up in a cozy chair with a cup of convenience-store cappuccino in one hand and the latest issue of a popular magazine in the other. "You know, home delivery *is* an option with that publisher," she remarked as she sat down in the nearest chair.

"Not when the library's paying the bill. How're you doing?"

"Fine."

"I heard you're seeing a lot of Martin Smith. Are things getting serious between you?"

She thought about the kiss, the touches, the looks and the things he'd said and uncomfortably shrugged. "Where did you hear this?"

"Well, let's see... I saw him in your office a week ago. Everyone in town knows about the little incident with Jimmy Ray at the Saloon. My aunt—your neighbor—has seen him coming and going from your place practically every day. Her best friend—his landlady—saw you at his place one day. My brother-in-law Tom says you were in the hardware store together on Saturday, and—"

"Enough already. You have quite a little network of informants, don't you?"

"What can I say? My life is nothing, so I live vicariously through gossip and innuendo."

Juliet wasn't fooled. Tracey needed so many informants because she was much too busy herself to snoop. She'd dated every eligible man in town except Martin, and she'd tried with him, she admitted, but he just wasn't interested. Further proof, along with his attraction to *her*, that the man was certifiable. "You used to date Hal Stuart, didn't you? Tell me about him."

"Oh, honey, you don't want to trade Martin for Hal. Martin's gorgeous, mysterious, dangerous. Hal is..." She shrugged. "Hal."

Martin wasn't hers to trade—though he wanted her to think he could be—but even if she wanted to move down to someone more her type, Hal wouldn't make the list. No man who was capable of telling anyone over the age of two to toddle off ever could. "I met him the other day, and I was just curious about him."

"Yeah, we dated for a while. He's not a bad guy. He's handsome. He takes his dates to the best places in town. He has money and likes to spend it."

"Family money?"

"Investments. He takes risks, and sometimes they pay off big time. No, his family never had a lot of money. His father died when he was just a kid, and his mother worked and scraped to support them and put herself through school. She was a lawyer, you know, but she never went after the big-bucks business. She wanted to help people who needed it, and then she went into politics. But you don't want to know about his family. You want the personal stuff, right? Let's see... He's the best kisser I've ever met."

No way. That title already belonged to Martin. Any kiss better than the one he'd given her in her bedroom last night couldn't be survived.

"He was engaged to Randi Howell last year, but the marriage didn't happen. He was in his tux, all the wedding guests were waiting, and she disappeared—wound up with a rancher someplace. It was all for the best, because it was on their wedding day that Olivia was attacked, which certainly would have made for some lousy anniversaries. The funny thing about it, though—about Randi running off—is that Hal wasn't really upset. I mean, she was about twenty minutes from being his wife, and he never acted the least bit heartbroken."

Maybe he hid his troubles well, or maybe he hadn't been heartbroken. Maybe he'd had reasons other than love for proposing marriage. "How did he get along with his family?"

"Eve didn't live here, you know. She left before Molly was born and came back when Olivia died. I guess they got along fine. He admired his mother. She was the reason he became a lawyer and got involved in politics himself.''

"Was there anything about him you didn't like? A quick temper? An attitude? Any quirks?''

Tracey gave it a moment's thought, then shook her head. ''He's a nice guy. Maybe a little overbearing with people he considers subordinates, but no attitude, no temper.'' Her smile was quick and teasing. ''If you're through with Martin, how about tossing him my way? And put in a few good words on my behalf. Tell him I'm every woman he ever dreamed of, all wrapped up in one. I'll make him forget his name—oops, too late for that. Tell him I'm the best time he'll ever have.''

"No, thanks. I don't need the competition.''

"I don't believe you have any—except maybe his past. You know, there's something exciting about a dangerous man who doesn't know who he is. But from his viewpoint, it must be scary as hell.''

Scary and restrictive. He wouldn't ever be free to fully commit himself to anything—or anyone—as long as he couldn't remember. And what if he did remember and couldn't deal with it?

No, he could deal with it. Knowing the worst was better than not knowing anything. Besides, maybe there was no "worst.'' Maybe the worst thing in his past was that he had a wife and children who loved him dearly and wanted him back—which would be the worst only for her. It would be heaven for him.

Murmuring about the time, she left Tracey and returned to her office, but the morning seemed to crawl. She couldn't keep her mind on work. The mundane task of writing and adapting software to the library's specific needs couldn't begin to compete with the more intriguing questions of Martin, Hal Stuart and Olivia's murder. After the third time she came out of a daze to find herself staring at garbage on the computer screen, she left her desk and headed for the reference desk.

One of the more interesting items she'd been shown in her initial tour of the library was a series of yearbooks put together by one of the women's clubs in town. They were nothing fancy—scrapbooks, basically, with newspaper articles, photos and personal remembrances. They represented a fairly comprehensive history of the city for the last thirty years, according to the head librarian. She had advised Juliet to look them over when she had time.

Mrs. Hilburn surely hadn't meant on library time, but since her mind wasn't good for much else this morning, that was what Juliet intended to do. She would make it up to the library by working late today and coming in early Thursday.

She selected five of the yearbooks from twenty years ago, returned to her office and closed the door. The turning point in Olivia's life had been her husband's death and her son's disappearance. Those two events had given birth to the woman whose death both interested and frightened Martin, and Juliet wanted to know more about them.

The books were divided into sections: local news, births and deaths, social news and an honor roll that included everything from the winner of the citywide spelling bee to the high school basketball champs to Maxwell Brown's young businessman of the year award. In the first book she paged through, she found the news of Roy Colton Stuart Sr.'s death in one section and Roy Colton Stuart Jr.'s disappearance in another.

The death announcement was accompanied by a photograph of a handsome man with blond hair, a strong nose and a narrow jaw. He didn't look like a man who would beat his wife and son. Of course, if wife-beaters *looked* like wife-beaters, they would never have wives to beat. There was no mention of the beatings in the obituary, of course, or of the drinking that he had no doubt used as an excuse. Just a simple sanitized version of the way he had died: in an accidental fall at home. It went on to list his surviving family—Olivia and the three children, his parents and two brothers in Denver and a grandmother in Colorado Springs. It also gave the time and place of his funeral—Grace Tabernacle, the church where Martin was working.

Could one of the Stuarts in Denver be responsible for Olivia's murder? It wasn't uncommon for an abusive man's parents to free him of responsibility for his actions, to place the blame instead on his victim. If Olivia had been a better wife, if she hadn't made him angry, if she hadn't failed him so miserably, he wouldn't have drunk, he wouldn't have hit her, and he wouldn't have died. Over the years, they had grieved for their son even as they watched Olivia go to college, become a lawyer and make a better life for herself and her children. They had seen her prosper, becoming the most influential person in the city of Grand Springs, all while their son and brother lay dead in the ground. Such grief could easily become hatred. Sorrow could fester into vengeance until finally they had to do something or die.

But according to the phone bills, Olivia had been in regular contact with the Stuart family right up until her death. Maybe one of them had fooled her into believing they were still friends.

Or maybe Juliet was grasping at straws.

With a sigh, she turned to the news section. Local Boy Missing, the headline read, with a smaller subhead: Police Seek Help. There was a photograph accompanying this article, too, a school picture of a stern-faced sixteen-year-old boy. He'd had his father's blond hair, straight nose and thin jaw. Had he also had his father's temper? Had Roy Stuart Jr. grown into a bully like Roy Sr.? Had his abusive tendencies put him in an early grave, like his father?

According to the story, Roy Jr. had run away following a fight with his father. It sounded so simple and stereotypical—a rebellious teen, a strict father, a disagreement over curfew, use of the car or grades. It didn't mention that the fight had been physical, that it had involved fists, pain and the violation of the most sacred trust—a child's trust in his parents.

Who had dictated the slant of the story? Roy Sr., who'd probably considered the beatings for his son's own good? Or Olivia, who'd spent sixteen years of her marriage protecting her husband instead of the son who was her first responsibility?

Juliet studied the photograph, finding a faint resemblance to Hal Stuart, an even fainter one to Eve Redtree. The picture gave her a chill. She could go out there to the high school yearbooks and find thousands of pictures of how sixteen-year-olds should look. Even among thousands, this one would stand out. Roy Jr. had been old beyond his years. Why hadn't anyone noticed? A teacher, a neighbor, a pastor—some adult should have stepped forward and said *No more.* His father wouldn't do it, and his mother couldn't, so someone else should have.

Instead, the teenage boy had been left to do it himself, by running away to live—and possibly die—on the streets.

Martin had been right, she thought with a sad sigh. Olivia had owed her eldest son so much more than that.

Seven

Martin stood two dozen feet in front of the window that looked into Juliet's office and tried to talk himself into leaving without speaking to her. After a half-dozen hours of dream-ruined sleep, he'd awakened making deals with himself. He could get out of bed if he didn't leave the apartment. He could leave the apartment if he stayed away from the library. He could go to the library if he didn't go to her office. He could see her if he didn't speak to her.

Plenty of agreements, and every one of them broken. Hell, he couldn't even keep a promise to himself. How the hell could he be expected to treat Juliet fairly?

Treating her fairly, in light of what he now knew, translated to one thing: staying away from her. She deserved better. With what little he knew of himself, he deserved nothing.

But here he was, a few strides away, watching her like some kind of lovesick—or just plain sick—fool. She hadn't noticed him. Ever since he'd arrived, her attention had been focused on something on her desk. She seemed a thousand miles away, and he wished she was, literally as well as figuratively. Then she would be out of his reach. He would never know she existed, and she would be safe from him.

Abruptly, she looked up, her gaze locking with his. He tried to look away, but instead, for one long, greedy moment, he continued to look at her, to study her, to want her. She was so sweet, so innocent. He was neither and suspected he had never been.

Finally he forced himself to break the eye contact, to

turn his back to her. He still felt her gaze, though, even when he crouched on the pretext of finding something on the shelves, even when solid wood and a forest of paper blocked him from her sight. He stared blindly, wishing she'd never come to this town, wishing he'd never come, wishing *he'd* gone over the side of the mountain with his damned car if this was what he had to live with. Pain, fear, doubt. Ugly truths and impossible wants. He wished—

She crouched beside him, her pale summer dress brushing the floor, the faint scent of her fragrance competing with the smells of papers and inks. "Can I help you find something?" she asked, her voice impossibly soft, her tone unmistakably hurt.

"No. I can find—" He pulled a book from the shelf, but he couldn't read the title because his peripheral gaze was on her, a soft blur of colors, scents, sensations.

"Interested in college? Since part of my salary is paid by the local college, I feel obligated to recommend them first. However, that one's good, too. I believe you're a little old to become a cadet or to think about a career in the military, but since you can't prove your age..."

Finally he forced his gaze to the book. It was a catalog for the U.S. Naval Academy. His face burning, he let her pull it from his hands, then sank back to lean against the bookcase behind him.

"What's wrong, Martin?"

"Nothing."

"Has something happened? Did you find out anything?"

"I don't want to know anything. I don't want to know who killed Olivia—" because damned if it might not have been him "—and I don't want to know anything else about myself."

She sat down, too, gathering her skirt close. "You remembered something, didn't you?"

He shook his head.

"What is it? What do you remember?"

"Nothing. Not a damn thing. The doctor says I may

never remember anything. The shrink, however, says these things usually resolve themselves. One minute I know nothing, and the next I know it all. One minute I'm the freak, and the next I'm—'' He clamped his jaw shut to keep from finishing the sentence, but he couldn't stop the words in his mind. *A murderer.*

''One minute you're a man with amnesia, and the next you're a man with a full set of memories. The amnesia doesn't define you, Martin. It's a condition you have. It's not who you are.''

No, the memories determined who he was, and the few he had now weren't pretty. His only comfort was that anything else he remembered could only get better. After all, what could possibly be worse than killing a man?

Only one thing that he could imagine right now: telling Juliet that he'd killed a man. Last night he'd thought he could do it, and she would understand. She would make excuses that they both could believe in. She would say that was another life. He'd been a different man. That past was ended. It had nothing to do with the man he was today.

But that was in the night, in the shadows where he'd lived too much of his life. In the hard light of day, the truth and his wishful thinking were about as far apart as they could get. The truth was, a woman like Juliet should stay hell and gone from a man like him. She shouldn't have an affair with him. She sure as hell couldn't be allowed to fall in love with him. They didn't stand a chance, not in the long run. Better to accept that now, while he could, while he might survive it, while she *would* survive it.

''Martin, talk to me, please. Tell me what's wrong.''

He looked at her, so pretty, so worried, and smiled bitterly. ''Everything's wrong, darlin'. You're wrong. I'm wrong. This whole damn relationship is wrong.''

A woman walked past on the opposite side of the low bookcase, giving them a curious look, distracting him for one blessed moment from the hurt that turned Juliet's eyes liquid blue. The moment passed, though, and he had nothing to look at but her. Nothing to think about, nothing to feel, nothing to regret but her.

"Would you come in my office, please?"

"No."

She had started to get up but sank back again at his blunt answer. "So you're giving up."

Giving up hope. Giving in to the past.

It was possible, the shrink had told him ten months ago, that there was a hysterical aspect to his amnesia. The head injury he'd suffered in the accident hadn't been severe. Medically they wouldn't have expected such a blow to cause anything more significant than a headache, certainly not full-blown generalized amnesia. Dr. Jeffers had suggested that his subconscious had seen the blow as an opportunity to be free of a life he no longer wanted to live and so had blocked off all those memories, giving him a chance to start over.

Some chance, when he remembered just enough to keep him trapped in that past he'd no longer wanted.

"I don't have anything to give up," he said flatly.

She opened her mouth as if to speak—to offer herself?—then thought better of it. After a moment of awkward, hurtful silence, she murmured, "I don't understand."

"There's nothing to understand, darlin'—"

"Don't call me that. My name is Juliet."

He acknowledged that with a nod. Endearments at a time like this were more than a little cruel. "I don't want to know anything. What's hard to understand about that?"

"Why don't you trust me enough to tell me what's happened?"

"I trust you. It's *me* I don't trust. You shouldn't, either."

"I do trust you."

"You do, huh? Well, hell, what do you know? You're a timid little librarian who lives her life with her computers, who doesn't do well face-to-face and whose only friends use fake names and live somewhere out in cyberspace." Who was looking at him now as if he'd struck her. Whose eyes were so full of unshed tears that he was drowning in them. Muttering a curse, he scrambled to his feet. "Do yourself a favor, darl—Juliet. Stick to your computers and stay the hell away from me."

He left the library, feeling sicker than he'd ever been. Leaving the sidewalk for the shelter of a weeping willow, he leaned against the trunk and ground his palms against his stinging eyes. He was one hell of a bastard who didn't deserve to even know her...which was the point of this whole ugly mess. He needed to know that Juliet was safe, and the one thing in the world she needed to be safe from was *him*.

There was a soft rustle of sound, followed by the certain knowledge that he was no longer alone. Gritting his teeth on a curse, he dropped his hands from his eyes and slowly opened them. Juliet was standing primly a few feet in front of him. She still wore a wounded-angel look, but she wasn't crying. Her lip wasn't trembling, and she didn't look as if she might dissolve into a sorrowful pool of tears.

"Most people I meet never get to know me well enough to figure out what hurts most. You did it in only a week." She didn't wait for him to speak. It was just as well. There was nothing he could allow himself to say—no deliberate insults, no apologies, no pleas for forgiveness. "I suppose this was for my own good. Better to hurt me now than later?"

He still said nothing. He simply stared at her.

"Did I give you the impression that I was expecting anything from you? Did you think I believed the things you said last night?"

I kissed you because I've been wanting to ever since the first time I saw you. Because you're a beautiful woman and you're sweet and you have a voice to make a man ache. I did it because I wanted to. Because I wanted you.

Her smile was tremulous. "Frankly, I thought you were crazy. I thought you'd been alone too long. I thought you felt more comfortable with someone not too demanding and easy to please, which, of course, describes me perfectly. I didn't think it meant anything spec—''

"You are so damned naive.''

She blinked and closed her mouth.

"I meant every word I said last night—and, darlin', if you thought that kiss was nothing special, then you're even more innocent than I thought.''

For a long moment, she stared at him, obviously confused. Finally, carefully, she said, "Maybe I am, because I don't have a clue what's going on here. But I still want to help you. I can keep things strictly business between us—''

"But I can't.''

She stared a moment longer, then shook her head. "I don't understand,'' she said in a small voice. "Just tell me what's wrong.''

"What's wrong is that I want you more than you can even begin to imagine. What's wrong is that you're sweet, naive and innocent, and I'm not. What's wrong is me in your life.''

She made an obvious effort to steady her voice. It trembled, anyway. "What did you remember, Martin?''

"Nothing important.''

"But important enough for all this. What is it?''

He let himself touch her then, just the simple brush of his palm across her hair. "Trust me. You don't want to know.'' *He* sure as hell didn't.

"I do trust you, and I do want to know.''

She sounded so sure, but he knew she wasn't. Once he told her, once she knew the truth, it would change the way she looked at him. It would definitely change the way she felt about him.

"Please, Martin.''

He looked away, folded his arms across his chest, then met her gaze evenly and blurted his confession. "I killed a man. Maybe I regretted it later, I don't know, but at the time, I was glad. I killed him, Juliet, and I was *glad*.''

Juliet wanted to look away to hide the shock that she

knew must be on her face, but he expected that of her. Instead, she looked straight into his eyes, never wavering or flinching. Details. Before she reacted to this news, she needed details. "How did you figure this out?"

"I've suspected it for a long time. After last night, I'm sure."

"And what happened last night? Another dream?"

His only response was a shrug. With his arms folded, he looked both chagrined and incredibly stubborn.

"It was a *dream*, Martin. Dreams are generally not real."

"This one was."

She rested one hand on his forearm, her fingers curving over taut muscle. "I had a very vivid dream once that took place in colonial Massachusetts. In it, I was an American spy in the Revolutionary War. It didn't mean that two hundred years ago I was a spy in the war. All it meant was that the dozens of Revolutionary War novels I'd been reading had had a really strong impact on me."

"Yeah, well, I haven't been reading any murder mysteries lately. This wasn't just a dream, Juliet. I killed a man. I *know* it."

She wanted to argue, but she respected him too much. If he truly believed this dream was a replay of an actual event, it might well be true. "But you don't know who this man was, or when or where it happened, or under what circumstances."

He shook his head.

"Then it could have been self-defense."

"And it could have been cold-blooded murder."

She studied him for a long moment. She didn't doubt that he was capable of killing. She believed everyone was, with the right threat. But cold-blooded murder? Not Martin, with his charming grins, his sizzling kisses and his empathy for mistreated kids and abandoned puppies.

But he had been Martin only since last June. The man he'd been before that could have been capable of anything.

It wasn't a comforting thought.

"We know you weren't arrested for it, or you would have been fingerprinted. Maybe the man's death was ruled self-defense and no charges were brought against you."

"Or maybe they never caught me and his murder is still unsolved."

He really believed this. He was convinced that he was a killer. How did she feel about that?

Juliet believed anyone who had died at Martin's hand had deserved his fate. She believed he would never hurt anyone unless that person was threatening harm to someone else. She believed that if he had killed some unknown man, he had paid ever since with guilt and remorse. She believed that he was a better man than he believed himself to be.

Didn't she? Or was she kidding herself because he was handsome, because his grin was charming and his kisses were sizzling, because he empathized with others less fortunate than him? Because she was falling for him?

No. If she were rationalizing, somewhere deep inside she would still be the slightest bit afraid of him, and she wasn't. She'd known from the first night he'd shown up at her door that he'd been no stranger to violence, but she wasn't afraid. He would never hurt her, unless he broke her heart or tried, as he just had in the library, to protect her from himself.

"You can't make judgments about yourself based on bits of a dream, Martin. Until you know who the man was, how he died and why he died, you can't blame yourself for his death. You could have been protecting yourself or others from a madman. You could have saved the life of an innocent woman or a helpless child. You could have been a hero."

"A hero," he repeated, his voice edged with scorn. "Don't think that, Juliet. I'm not hero material."

She smiled gently. He could be *her* hero. "The fact that you worry so much about the kind of man you used to be suggests to me that you couldn't have been the kind of man you fear. That knock on the head didn't give you morals and ethics, Martin. You already had them.''

"So what am I hiding from? If there isn't something awful in my past, why can't I remember?''

"I'm no expert on amnesia,'' she said, though she had waded through countless Net sites on the subject, "but I know the workings of the mind aren't that simple. You'll recover your memory eventually, and I'll bet you dinner at Randolphs that there's not going to be anything awful in it.''

Mention of the most expensive restaurant in town brought him a faint smile. It wasn't the sort of place either of them could afford on even a semiregular basis, but the return of his memory would be an event to celebrate.

It could also be goodbye.

At last he uncrossed his arms and slid one around her waist. "I hope you win.''

So did she—not just the bet, but a chance, a wish, a future. Everything.

His expression grew more serious. "I'm sorry.''

Finally she was able to look away, lowering her gaze to his chest. "It's okay.''

"No.'' His fingers gently forced her chin up. "I thought—I still think you would be better off away from me. You don't know what you're getting into.''

"No one ever really knows that, do they? Everything's a gamble.''

"But you can improve the odds in your favor by getting involved with the right kind of man.''

"And what's the right kind?''

"Someone normal, average, who knows who he is, what he's done, where he's going. Someone whose life isn't full of questions and fresh out of answers. Someone you can trust.''

She moved a few feet away and rested one hand on a branch just above her head. A slight breeze blew past her, rustling the leaves, brushing her skirt against her legs, bringing with it the lovely scent of flowers. "You just described the last guy I dated. He was an account rep with the company I worked for. He was an up-and-coming executive, bright, ambitious, with a desire to get ahead and make a name for himself. In the business world, he was perfectly normal and average."

A strand of hair fell across her face, and she brushed it back, catching it behind her ear. "We went out a half-dozen times. He spent a lot of money on me, said all the right words, made all the right moves. We seemed well suited, and the sex was incredible. I imagined myself well on the way to falling in love with him." She hadn't been, of course. She hadn't dated since the illness that had led to her mother's death, and she'd been lonely, hungry for companionship, affection and sex, and he had been so very charming. She'd been more in love with the whole relationship than with him.

"One evening, when he came over, he said he had something to ask me. I actually thought it might be a marriage proposal. I was a little giddy and excited and frightened and trying to decide what my answer would be when finally I heard what he was really asking. He wanted me to hack into the computer of his rival in the company. They were competing for a new account, and he needed the inside track to be sure he got it. That was why he'd gone out with me, why he'd gone to bed with me." She smiled and realized that it wasn't forced or embarrassed at all, but rather relieved. Neither the story nor the man responsible for it still held the power to hurt her. "By your standards, he's exactly the right sort of man for me. By mine, he doesn't come close. I'd much rather take my chances on someone with questions and no answers."

Martin came to stand in front of her, his hand resting on the branch next to hers. "I knew the first time I saw you that the men in Texas were blind or fools or both."

"Thank you."

Then, his expression fading into bleakness, he returned

to his earlier subject. "I don't want to hurt you, Juliet. I don't want to disappoint you. I sure as hell don't want to frighten you."

"Hurt and disappointment are a risk in any relationship."

"But they're a bigger risk in ours."

"So maybe the payoff is bigger, too." And maybe the heartache would be bigger. Maybe the emptiness would be emptier, the loneliness lonelier.

Moments rustled past on the breeze as they stared at each other. Finally he blinked, gave a little shake of his head and almost smiled. "Do something for me, would you? Expect something from me. Believe everything I said last night and today about wanting you."

She had to swallow before she could answer. "All right. And you do something for me. The next time you have one of those dreams, come to me. No matter how late or early. We'll talk."

After a moment, he solemnly nodded. It was the only answer he offered.

"I have to get back inside. I haven't gotten much work done this morning."

"Let me take you to lunch."

She hesitated, wanting very much to say yes. "I'd better work through lunch, or I'll feel guilty. You're coming over this evening?"

He nodded.

She started to leave but stopped with her hand on his. "Everything will be all right, Martin. Whatever you remember, whatever we find out, it'll be okay."

"I hope you're right, darlin'."

She was a dozen yards away when he called. "Hey, how's Hunter?"

"He's stubborn and smelly and manipulative as hell." Then she grinned. "He's all right." So was Martin. And so was she.

* * *

Martin stopped inside the door of the deli and gave the room a quick survey. It was lunchtime, and most of the tables were occupied, with only a few empties here and there. Eating alone was one thing he'd never minded, not from the start, even when he'd been treated like an oddity on display by everyone around. He figured he'd spent most of his life doing things alone. It just came too naturally to him.

He intended to spend as much of the near future as possible with Juliet, even though he shouldn't. Even though she claimed she understood the risks. Even though he did believe she was better off without him. If she had let him walk away from the library without an argument this morning, maybe he would have been able to manage, but when she'd come after him… Well, a man could be strong for only so long. Maybe he could stay away from her if she cooperated, but if she was willing to take a chance on him, wasn't taking his own chances the least he could do?

He was heading toward a table near the television mounted on one wall when a table across the room caught his attention. Hal Stuart sat there, the remains of a sandwich in front of him, and across from him was none other than Maxwell Brown. On impulse, Martin turned in their direction, taking the nearest empty table.

The idea of Hal and Maxwell as friends was a difficult one for Martin to get his mind around. The two men knew each other socially, of course. They were both prominent in town. They were just different. Maxwell's interests seemed focused entirely on his business—even in the middle of the night—while Hal's biggest interest was himself.

Maybe their lunch was business and not social. Hal was a lawyer. Maxwell could be one of his clients. Or perhaps Maxwell had some business with the city council and hoped to win Hal to his side. Whatever the purpose, Hal didn't seem in a particularly good mood, and nothing Maxwell said changed that. In fact, there were a few times when, judging from his body language, Hal's responses to

Maxwell were definitely hostile and, once, bordering on threatening.

Interesting. Something was definitely going on with Hal. Whether it was in any way connected to his mother's murder was another question entirely, but something was wrong. After lunch and before work at the church, he would stop by the courthouse, Martin decided, and find out what he could about Hal. Maybe there was nothing to learn…but maybe there was.

Before Martin finished his sandwich, Maxwell Brown left, greeting other diners on his way out. He was well known in town, not only from his diversified business interests but also from his generosity. There was a clinic over at the hospital with his name on it. His various companies supported more than a dozen of Grand Springs's Little League teams. He was a major contributor to the Grand Springs Historical Society and one of the top-level supporters of Olivia Stuart's own favored charities. No fundraising effort was complete without Maxwell Brown.

Back at the table, Hal was scowling at everything and nothing. When his gaze settled on Martin, his face darkened and his expression turned contemptuous. He tossed a stingy tip on the table, then came to Martin's, sliding in across from him. "I had a talk with Chief Sanderson about you and that woman."

"You did."

"If you two don't stay out of police business, he's going to lock you—"

"That's not what the chief told you, now, is it? It's no crime to ask questions about a murder, you know. If it was, why, the chief would have to lock up everybody in town." Martin watched Hal's face turn red and finished quietly, "I had a talk with Chief Sanderson, too."

"This case is none of your business. You're interfering with the real investigation and making it more difficult to find the man who ordered my mother's murder."

"We're not interfering with anything." Except possibly

Hal's peace of mind. Why was that? "You know, if my mother had been murdered, I think I would appreciate all the help that was offered in solving the case, no matter where it came from."

Stuart got to his feet and gave Martin one of those arrogant, straight-down-his-nose looks that Juliet had gotten the other day. "You expect me to be grateful for the 'help' of a part-time handyman who doesn't even know his own name and a mousy little computer clerk who's afraid of her own shadow. Get a grip on reality, Smith. Go back to your little painting-and-hammering job, and leave the police work to the police."

He should have been put firmly in his place, Martin acknowledged as he watched the other man walk away, but Hal's insults didn't bother him—at least, not the ones directed at him. He was too curious about Hal's overall response to take offense. Why was he so dead set against anyone but the police—who'd made zero progress in the last six months—looking into Olivia's death?

It was a question he puzzled over through the afternoon and finally asked aloud of Juliet as they sat on her back steps after dinner. It was a warm evening, the dinner dishes were done, Hunter was enjoying the freedom of the backyard, and Martin was enjoying Juliet, almost too much to bring up business. When he did, she seemed almost as reluctant to answer.

After a long silence, she glanced at him. "Maybe he's afraid that we'll mess up everything—that something we do could jeopardize the police investigation."

"What investigation? For all practical purposes, the case is closed. Until something happens, it's sitting in the files with all their other unsolved cases. They have no leads, no clues, no theories. Entire weeks go by that they don't put in even a minute's work on that case."

"Maybe he has more faith in them than we do. Maybe he's kidding himself that they're making progress."

"Maybe he doesn't want a new perspective on the case."

She looked at him, waiting for more.

"The first rule in a murder investigation is to look at who profits. Find out if there's a life insurance policy, how big it is and who the beneficiaries are. Look at the will and see who's inheriting. Find out who stands to gain from the victim's death and investigate those people first."

"And you learned this…?"

He shrugged. It was easier than saying, I don't know. "Hal was never a suspect, even though he profited from Olivia's death. No one ever looked at him. Everyone in the department knows him. Half the officers grew up with him. He's an attorney, the ex-mayor's son, a council member. Hell, he's the city council's liaison to the police department. He helps them get their money, goes to bat for them whenever they need anything. It's damn hard to suspect someone you like and respect in a murder."

"But you and I are strangers. There's no friendship to get in the way. So maybe he's afraid that his relationship with his mother and any actions he might have taken regarding her can't stand up to closer scrutiny."

Martin nodded, then watched the dog for a time. In twenty-four hours, Hunter had marked the entire yard, dug two holes and broken enough ground-hugging branches off a bush at the back of the house to allow himself to wriggle into its shade. At least he had better manners indoors, or Martin would probably be looking for a new home for him.

When Juliet spoke, her voice was soft, as cool and welcome as a breeze on a hot summer day. "Do you really think Hal is involved in Olivia's murder?"

He wanted to answer in the negative, but gut instinct held him back. "I don't know. I think he deserves a closer look. His behavior is odd. Everyone in town likes and respects him, which suggests that he's a decent guy, so why is he so hostile to us? What sets us apart from everyone else?"

"Our interest in Olivia."

"His sister excused his behavior as grief over her death.

No matter how much he loved her, ten months later, he should have some measure of control."

"Unless it's guilt and not grief. But why would a decent guy play any part at all in his own mother's murder?"

That question had Martin stumped, too. They knew Hal had been in trouble that had required twelve thousand dollars from Olivia to fix, knew that he had expensive tastes which his income probably didn't cover. But was simple greed reason enough to kill his own *mother?*

"I went by the courthouse before work. There's never been an arrest warrant issued for Hal, and he's never been sued. He's never married, so there's no divorce. Other than his condo on Greeley, which is mortgaged, and a one-third share in his mother's house, which isn't, he doesn't own any property in the county. He's late paying his property taxes every year, but so is half the county."

She didn't ask how he knew that that information was public record. Most of the public didn't.

"We really need his credit report."

She looked at him, her eyes wide, her expression concerned.

"I don't want you involved in this. I can get it myself." He couldn't put her job at risk. Helping him was one thing. Losing her job and/or getting a criminal record in the process was totally unacceptable.

"How?"

He could make a clandestine, middle-of-the-night visit to the local credit bureau offices. Breaking in and circumventing the inevitable alarm system would be the easy part. Getting the necessary information out of the computer without Juliet's help would be damn near impossible. Fortunately, he had a better idea. "There's a woman who works there...."

She gave him a sharp, narrowed look. She knew his plan immediately—probably had already considered it herself.

"It shouldn't take more than lunch, maybe dinner." The look on Juliet's face made him think that maybe breaking

in was a better idea, after all. It wasn't jealousy, posses-
siveness or anything like that. He could appreciate and deal
with those emotions. No, this was uncertainty, insecurity
and fear. Sliding his arm around her, he pulled her snug
against him. "It would be a sacrifice, having to sit through
an entire meal with any woman besides you," he said, his
tone gently teasing, "but, hey, I'm willing to do it just this
once."

Slowly, deliberately, she looked away. "Tell her the
things you tell me, give her that grin, and it shouldn't take
more than a simple *please*."

"What things? Should I tell her how much I want you?
How much I like being with you, talking to you, watching
you? Should I tell her about the first time I came to your
house, when you were walking down the hall buttoning
your dress? How your hair was loose and your feet were
bare, and I could see just a little strip of skin all the way
to your waist, how it looked so soft and pale and I would
have given a year off my life to fasten those buttons for
you, to touch you there, to brush my fingers across your
skin the way you were doing? Should I tell her that I
thought it was the most erotic image I had ever seen in my
life?"

As he'd spoken, his voice had gotten thicker, huskier,
and she had turned to look at him again. Her expression
was soft, her eyes hazy, her lips parted just a little, just
enough to tempt him. He leaned toward her, coaxed her to
lean toward him and touched his mouth to hers. The heat
was instantaneous, consuming. In a flash, the night went
from pleasantly warm to unbearably steamy, and the
ever-present ache in his groin exploded through his entire
body.

He knew nothing about his past, but he *knew* he had
never wanted like this, knew he could never forget a need
like this, a kiss like this, a woman like this. The only way
to satisfy this hunger was to get close, to crawl right inside
her and stay forever. The only way to ease this arousal was

in loving her, long and hard, tonight and always. The only way to survive the need was to hold tight to Juliet, to never let her go, to love her forever.

She stroked his tongue with her own as her thin, slender fingers curled with surprising strength around handfuls of his shirt. The soft little whimper that passed from her mouth to his intensified everything—the heat, the swelling, the desire, the pain, the torment. It gave him a sense of incredible power and humbled him tremendously.

His skin tingling with raw need, he freed himself of her mouth one small kiss at a time, then drew a desperate breath. He was shaking, trembling from the pure sweet pleasure of her mouth. "Oh, darlin', you're killing me."

"Come inside." She said it simply, quietly, her words sending one message, her voice, her eyes, her body promising another. It was the second he wanted—to strip off their clothes and bury himself deep inside her, to thrust and arouse and build and pleasure until his body could endure no more, to come inside her in the most intimate sharing two people could ever achieve.

Her hands were folded together in her lap. He wrapped his fingers around them, able to secure both of her small, delicate hands in one of his. "I don't have any condoms."

There was a hint of relief in her eyes that his objection was one of common sense and safety rather than lack of desire. "I do. I stopped at the store...."

He had carried in the twenty-five-pound bag of dog food this evening, while she brought the plastic bag with Hunter's new collar and leash. She'd given no hint that it had contained anything else, certainly not anything as personal, as hopeful or as potentially embarrassing as condoms. He was surprised that she'd found the courage to make such a purchase—and found it incredibly erotic that she had.

Getting to her feet, she stood in the moonlight, slender and lovely, and offered the invitation again. "Come inside."

Taking her hand, he went.

Eight

Leaving Hunter to chase imaginary prey, they entered the house. Juliet retrieved the bag she'd tucked in a drawer while Martin locked the door. She led the way to the bedroom, and he followed, his gaze so intent that she could feel it. It made her self-conscious of every step, every sway of her hips, but at the same time, it made her feel graceful. Sensual. Womanly.

"I'm kind of new at this, you know," Martin said, his grin less than confident, his lack of assurance endearing.

"I think it's like riding a bike. You never forget."

He slid the bag from her hand, removed the box inside and left it on the night table, then claimed both of her hands. "There are a few things I'd like you to forget, starting with the bastard in Texas and the incredible sex."

"What bastard in Texas?"

He backed up until he was sitting on the bed and drew her between his legs. In the dim light from the single lamp burning on the night stand, he raised his hands to the first button at the point of her dress's V-neck. He slid it open, then moved to the next one, his palms brushing her breasts. He opened it, too, and the next and the next, all the way to her waist, where he stopped.

Just as she'd done last week, he drew his fingertips along the opening to her waist, easing fabric back, exposing skin, stroking. Just as she'd known last week, his heat, rougher skin and stronger hands felt incredibly different from her own tentative touches. Sexier, full of promise and pleasure.

Each time he stroked her, his hands explored a little further, sliding underneath the cotton, brushing the sides of her breasts, teasing her nipples, then covering her, pressing his palms against her flesh, kneading, teasing, massaging. Her legs grew weak, and his touch became both vital and unbearable. Her skin quivered everywhere he touched, the heat so intense that she was damp with it, the sensations so potent that she trembled. If he stopped touching her, she might die. If he didn't stop, she surely would, an erotic death of pleasure so pure it would destroy her.

He unfastened a few more buttons, slid the dress off her shoulders. It caught on her bent arms, exposing her breasts to his gaze, his deliberate caresses and the sweet torment of his kisses. He kissed her breasts, suckled her nipples, bit and soothed and drew hard on them, sending heat through her body, sending wicked need to pool between her thighs.

"Oh, Martin."

He pressed his cheek to the warm, shivery skin between her breasts. "You like that?" She heard his smile, felt his tongue making lazy circles. He must know the answer she couldn't give voice to, must know that her lungs were tight, her every breath needed for things more important than talk. "You like this?"

He slid his hand underneath her skirt, gliding it quickly along her thigh to the heat and moisture that awaited him. Stroking her through the thin cover of her panties, he chuckled softly. "You're ready for me, aren't you, darlin'?"

From some wicked place inside, she found the strength to raise her head, to gaze into his intense blue eyes as she feather-stroked her fingers over faded denim and swollen flesh. "No more than you are, sweetheart," she said with her own husky laugh.

For an instant her boldness surprised him, but when she would have withdrawn her hand, he caught it, spread her fingers over the length of him, pressed her palm hard against him. "Juliet..." His groan made her name barely recognizable. "Please..."

She pulled free of his hand, then stroked him again and again as she claimed his mouth. Tangling his hands in her hair, he took control of the kiss. It was harsh, demanding, greedy. There was no gentleness, no tenderness, just pure passion, pure determination.

Their touches clumsy, their movements frenzied, they stripped off their clothes and fell across the bed. He knelt between her thighs, fumbling with a condom while she tried without success to pull him closer, so close they could never find their way apart again. Then he was there, pressing in, one deep, stretching inch at a time. She thrust against him, wanting more, needing more, none of this slow and easy, but hard and fast and full and *now*. Oh, please, now.

Her cries were soft, felt rather than heard, but Martin understood. *Oh, please, now.* Yes, he needed her now. Sliding his hands underneath her, he pushed hard, filling her in one powerful thrust. Her hips cradled his, and her body fitted his as tightly, as heatedly and perfectly as he could have wished. His head told him to remain still, to give her a moment to adjust, but his body insisted he didn't have a moment. He stroked her, kissed her, moved with her and against her, faster, harder, deeper, and the release he was struggling for built inside him, stronger, stronger, threatening to explode, to destroy him, to—

It washed over him, over and over, racking his body with violent shudders, robbing him of all thoughts, all fears, all needs but this one. Dimly he was aware of her own release, of the tightening of her body around and beneath his, of her trembling and helpless cries. He wanted to comfort her but had no comfort to offer, wanted to soothe her but couldn't find his voice. All he could do was hold her, kiss her, rock with the tremors that shook her.

Moment after moment passed. Her fingers eased their grip on his arms, and the tension eased its grip on his body enough so he could breathe, enough so he could control the twitchy responses of his muscles, enough so he could see her in the lamplight. She was beautiful, her pale face flushed, the delicate pink extending down her throat to the still-swollen tips of her breasts. Her lips were parted, her breathing uneven, but her eyes were clear and free—thank God—of embarrassment, shame or regret.

Her smile faint and packing a punch, she raised her hands to his face. He pressed a kiss to one palm before she evaded his mouth and slid her fingertips across his cheeks, his jaw, his forehead, into his hair. They were simple touches, the sort lovers indulged in, the sort she'd never had the courage to try with him. Her hand on his arm was about as intimate as her gestures had gotten before tonight, and he'd been grateful for even that.

After tonight he would always want more.

"See? You didn't forget." Her voice was throaty, her smile satisfied.

"No," he agreed. He'd remembered the mechanics, but not the emotions. Now he was more convinced than ever that there was no woman waiting somewhere for his return. He could never forget this. It was part of his heart, part of his soul, always and forever part of him.

She slid her hands down to his shoulders, across his chest, brushing his nipples and making him shiver. "Again."

Her command made him grin. It also made his body jerk and start to swell inside her. "*Again.* What kind of request is that?"

"It's a demand. An entreaty. A plea." Her fingers were tickling across his belly now, working between their bodies to touch him where they were joined.

"What happened to sweet, shy, innocent Juliet, who doesn't do well face-to-face, who blushes when a man looks at her the way he looks at a woman?"

"It's hard to be shy and innocent when you're naked and in bed with a man," she said primly.

"Especially when your fingers are wrapped around his—"

She cut him off with a kiss and yet another intimate caress, her hand sliding lower to cradle him. By the time she let him breathe, he could think, want, need only one thing.

Again.

Juliet lay on her stomach, supporting her weight on her elbows, her hip pressed snugly against Martin's, and studied him in the shadowy light. He was on his back, with one arm at his side, the other loosely around her. His head rested on her pillow, his skin was slick with sweat, and his breathing was almost back to normal.

Hers might never be normal again.

She had insisted just this morning that she had experienced incredible sex before, but she'd been wrong. Sex—making love, the romantic in her whispered—with Martin was incredible. Amazing. Exquisite.

He raised his free hand to stroke her cheek. "Why aren't you married and raising babies?" His tone was lazy, sleepy, a little bewildered. It was sweet of him to think that surely some man in the last fourteen years should have wanted her, but the truth was, none had.

"I never planned to be thirty-four and alone. It just happened."

"I'm glad it did." He found the energy to raise his hand where it rested against her and stroked her breast. Odd, how what had made her ache a short while ago was now comfortable and soothing. "I'd like to think you were waiting for me."

All her life, she agreed. And she would spend the rest of it being grateful for however long she had him.

She forced a smile to lighten her mood. "Maybe *you* were waiting for me. Maybe that's why you were coming to Grand Springs and that's why you had the accident and developed amnesia—to keep you here until I got here. Maybe the fates and the heavens conspired to bring us together."

"Then it was worth the price. Who needs memories, after all?"

He did. He needed to know that he wasn't some awful, horrible person not fit to walk the streets free. He needed to know that he deserved to be wanted, that it was all right to be loved.

She rested her arm on his stomach, patted her hand gently on his chest. "Tell me about last night's dream."

Immediately his muscles tightened and his features shifted into a scowl. "No."

"Please, Martin."

"There's nothing to tell."

"It was enough to convince you that you killed a man. Please."

He turned his face away from her, then, after a long silence, spoke. "It was just images. Impressions. Feelings. Angry voices. The smells of fear, blood, something burning, someone— Someone dying. And a woman whispering, 'He's dead. Oh, my God, you've killed him!' She was talking to *me,* Juliet."

As far as she was concerned, it was a bad dream and nothing else. But he saw it as so much more. Truth. Verdict. Damnation.

"You can't accept it as real until you have proof. You'll get that proof when you remember."

"And if it is real? What then?"

If it was real, it would be self-defense or some other form of justified killing. She was convinced of it—but he wasn't. "Then we'll deal with it."

"How? Pretend it didn't happen? Accept it and forget about it? How do you accept, then forget, that the man you're sharing a bed with is a killer? How do you pretend—"

She bumped her entire body against his, jarring him into silence. "We'll deal with it *then.* Right now I'm not going to worry about something that might not have even happened. Right now I'm going to deal with *you.*" She was going to turn onto her side and take a long, leisurely look. She knew how he tasted, how he felt, how he moved. Now she wanted to know how he looked. She wanted to see his broad chest, flat belly, lean hips and his long, strong-muscled legs. She wanted to see the part of him she knew most intimately now, wanted to behave like a giggly teen-age girl seeing a naked man for the first time and see, examine, appreciate *everything*.

He was beautiful…which made the scars even uglier. She'd felt them earlier, one thick and raised, the other a smooth line, pale against his tanned chest. Someone had shot him, had tried to kill him, not once but twice. Why? What had he done to deserve such hatred?

"If you want to rub something, darlin', I can make a suggestion."

Subconsciously her fingers had rubbed back and forth across the surgical scar. He pulled them away and slid her hand down his body. Her cheeks turning pink, she pulled away. "Let me see the others."

"No."

"I know you don't like them. I know they've been the cause of a lot of concern for you about what kind of man you were when you got them. Let me see them, just this once, and I won't ask again." When he was still resistant, she offered her coyest smile. "Let me see them, then I'll rub whatever you want."

After a moment, he rolled onto his stomach, his face hidden in her pillow, and lay very still. The gunshot wound and surgical scar on his lower back were virtually identical to the ones on his chest. There were a few smaller scars, including one higher, a few inches below his shoulder. It was no bigger than a quarter, raised and ridged, particularly ugly. In his dream he had smelled something burning. His own flesh? Had this burn been an accident, or had someone deliberately inflicted it on him, then died for his brutality?

She touched his skin lightly beneath the scar. "How old is this?"

"Old."

"How old?"

"Doc Howell couldn't say, just that the scar is mature."

If the dead man in his dreams had been responsible for the burn, then he'd deserved to die a vicious and painful death, and Martin had had every right to be glad about it. He didn't owe the bastard a moment's regret.

He continued to lie utterly motionless. Leaning over, she pressed a loud, smacking kiss to his spine, then murmured near his ear, "Roll over here and tell me what you want me to do. Tell me where to touch you, where to kiss you and how it makes you feel."

He turned over and settled her close against him. "This guy in Dallas...the incredible sex—"

"It wasn't."

"Were you in love with him?"

I imagined myself well on the way to falling in love with him, she'd told him this morning. Had he interpreted it as a face-saving remark to cover a broken heart? "No." She offered no explanations. The answer didn't require any.

"Under normal circumstances, I think this would be where you ask me if I've ever been in love." His tone was dry. "All I can tell you is I don't think so."

She tightened her arm across his waist. "If you have, I don't think I'd want to know."

"Why not?"

"Because if you were, you probably still were, right up to the time of the accident. Because she would probably be waiting somewhere for you to come back."

"If anyone out there wanted me back, don't you think they would have filed a missing persons report by now? But no one has. No one cared enough."

If that were true—and it seemed to be—then he must have been even more alone than she was. Knowledge like that must be hard to live with. "We could try one other thing," she suggested, her fingers straying back to the scars high on his chest. Immediately he captured her hand and held it, clasped in his, on his stomach. "It's a requirement of law that gunshot wounds be reported to the local police. Granted, big cities might have thousands of gunshot victims a year, but smaller cities and towns might have only a few. According to your doctor, one set of scars is probably a couple years old, and the other is double that. Maybe we can send out a bulletin to all law enforcement agencies in the country, asking that they check their records for the last…oh, five or six years for a shooting victim who matches your description."

"Kind of a long shot, isn't it? There must be thousands of possibilities."

"There were over 250,000 aggravated assaults with fire-arms in 1995." She shrugged at his questioning look. "I read the FBI Uniform Crime Report. But how many of those people are likely to be blue-eyed, blond males who are six-three, with two sets of gunshot wounds suffered several years apart?"

He grunted in grudging agreement.

"I don't know if I can do it, but I'll find out tomorrow. If I can, I imagine it might take a while. For a department that's computerized, it wouldn't be much trouble, but for someone like us, it could take some time. Still, at least it's a chance."

He grunted again, then began moving her hand back and forth over his stomach. Closing her eyes, she flattened her palm and enjoyed the lazy caresses as they dipped lower. Once she was touching him intimately, he released her hand and brought his own hand to her body, tickling her belly, making her skin quiver, rubbing her breast. When he shifted to lean over her, she sighed. When he covered her mouth with his, the sigh became a groan, low and needy.

"You're a beautiful woman," he murmured as he filled her again, stretched her again.

He'd called her beautiful before, and she'd heard it with a large dose of skepticism. She was much too familiar with her own face to consider it anything but plain. But right now, right this moment, with the way he was looking at her, touching her, making love to her, she had no problem believing. She *felt* beautiful. Overcome, head-over-heels, definitely-in-love beautiful.

The credit bureau was downtown, a half block off the main thoroughfare. Martin stood across the street for ten minutes, watching through the plate-glass windows as the two women inside chatted and worked. In another few minutes one of the women would be going to lunch while one remained to keep the office open. He hoped Sherri was the one who stayed, but it didn't really matter either way, as long as he could talk to her alone.

He didn't know Sherri Stevens well, but she'd always been friendly, and she'd made it clear over the winter that she was interested in a relationship. He hadn't been at the time—hadn't been in a long time, since even before last June, he was certain—and she had accepted that graciously. He hated to come back now, when any interest he might ever have in a woman was all tied up in Juliet, but they needed Hal's credit report.

Thoughts of Juliet sent his temperature up a few steamy degrees. After they'd made love the last time, he'd left her in bed only long enough to let Hunter in, then they had all gone to sleep. The dog had snored, but it hadn't disturbed Martin. Hell, with Juliet's slender body curled close to his all night, nothing could have disturbed him, not even dreams. If he'd had any at all, they'd been about Juliet, because the only time he'd awakened, he'd been hot and hard. He hadn't awakened her, but had eventually drifted off to sleep again.

Tonight, though… Tonight would be a different story.

Across the street, the older woman left the credit bureau. She was followed a moment later by a man in shirtsleeves and tie, carrying a suit coat over one arm. That meant Sherri was alone in the office.

He waited for a car to pass, then crossed the street. The

electronic bell connected to the door dinged as he walked in, bringing her attention from the computer straight to him. Her smile was welcoming, her voice surprised but warm. "Martin. Long time, no see. How're you doing?"

"I'm fine. How about you?"

"I get by. What brings you to my part of town?"

He knew the act—what to say, how to say it, with just the right degree of male interest. He'd sweet-talked things more important than credit records out of people less friendly than Sherri—though he didn't know what things or which people. But when he opened his mouth, the smooth delivery, the easy invitation, the sexual interest, just wouldn't come. Instead, he stumbled over his response. "I came downtown to get some lunch before—before I head to work. I thought maybe—maybe you'd want to go with me. To lunch. If you don't have other plans."

She gave him a long, steady look. "I do believe that's the most unenthusiastic invitation I've ever received."

"I didn't mean—"

She brushed him off. "It's okay. I don't go to lunch until one. What time do you go to work?"

"One-thirty."

"Too bad." She spoke with only a hint of disappointment. "Though it's been a long time since we've talked, I've seen you around town—lately with that new dispatcher."

He was blank for a moment, then blinked. "You mean Juliet. She's the records supervisor."

"Whatever. Rumor is you two are pretty tight."

The latest rumor was probably that he'd spent the night at Juliet's house. He wished she didn't have to be subjected to gossip, but the talkative folks in town still considered him enough of an oddity to warrant their attention. If he were truly concerned about gossip, he should have left her house well before dawn, and he certainly shouldn't have kissed her in the driveway until her knees were weak, until his chest was tight and he was ready to explode.

"We're close," he admitted. It wasn't the right answer when he was supposed to be charming Sherri into risking her job for him, but he couldn't lie. He couldn't diminish the relationship he shared with Juliet for any reason.

"So why aren't you over at the police department asking her to lunch?" She left the desk and came to stand directly in front of him. "Exactly what is it you want here, Martin?" When he hesitated, she smiled. "Go ahead and say it. The worst that can happen is I'll turn you down. Why are you here?"

"Because I need a credit report. I have no legal authority to request it, but it could certainly help clear up some questions for me, and I was hoping to talk you into giving it to me." He didn't think he'd been totally honest often in the past, but he liked the way it felt.

Her smile faded, and her light tone disappeared. "I could lose my job for that."

"I know."

"Is it important?"

"I wouldn't ask if it wasn't."

She simply looked at him for a time. "You're friends with Stone Richardson. Why don't you ask him to get it for you?"

"Because he'd tell me no."

"Which is exactly what I should do." But she didn't, not right away. Instead, she continued to study him. "How many reports are you looking for?"

"Two." The answer surprised him. He hadn't given any thought whatsoever to snooping into anyone else's business, but there *was* a second report he wanted. It might be of some use.

"Whose?"

"Hal Stuart's—"

"Hal Stuart! Oh, geez, why don't you just ask for the mayor's, too? And the police chief's and Father Kinneally's? How about Maxwell Brown's and—"

"Well, now that you mention it..."

"Hal Stuart and Maxwell Brown." She grimaced. "You know, if I get caught, I could expect a little mercy from most people, but not those two. Firing wouldn't be enough to satisfy them. They would want blood. What could they possibly have to do with finding out who you are?"

He felt a twinge of guilt at misleading her but didn't correct her. "I don't know. It's just a hunch."

"For a man who didn't want to go out with me even once, you're asking a lot."

More guilt. "It wasn't you. I didn't want to go out with anyone. There was just so much going on—"

"It's okay. I'm over it." She fell silent, and he didn't speak, didn't disturb her in any way. It couldn't be an easy decision for her. Taking a risk for someone important to you was one thing. Doing it for someone who barely qualified as an acquaintance was, as she'd said, asking a lot.

After a while, she clasped her hands together. "I've liked you from the beginning, Martin. You've made the best of a bad situation, and you haven't asked for help or handouts from anyone. I can't even imagine what it's been like for you, having no clue who you are. If you can promise me that no one will know about these—at least, no one besides Juliet..."

"You have my word."

She returned to the desk, typed a series of commands into the computer, then, only moments later, presented him with the two reports. He folded them to fit into his hip pocket. "You don't know how much I appreciate this. If there's ever anything I can do..."

She smiled sweetly, a little sadly. "Oh, the answers I could have come up with to an offer like that four months ago. Good luck."

"Thanks, Sherri. Thanks a lot." He left the office and headed for the police department a few blocks over. Through the window in her office, he saw Juliet facing the computer. Her hair was pulled back at her nape and tied with a ribbon, and she was wearing his favorite of her dresses, the watercolor he had watched her button that first night at her house. He had helped her put it on this morning, had fulfilled one of his fantasies by buttoning the long row of small buttons himself, gliding his fingers over her skin, straying far from the task to caress and tease. Considering how easily he was aroused, she was lucky she'd gotten out of the house before noon.

He exchanged greetings with Stone, Jack and a few of the uniformed officers before going to her office. By the time he got there, the chair was empty, the computer unattended. She was sitting on the floor in front of the file cabinets, a thick file open in her lap, her head bent over the papers. He closed the door quietly, bent and pressed a kiss to her exposed neck.

The smile she gave him was sweet and a bit timid. She'd lain naked with him all last night without the least reticence, but today, fully clothed and in the businesslike confines of her office, she was shy. "Hi. Have a seat."

He ignored the chair and sat on the floor near her. "Want to have lunch?" When she didn't answer immediately, he offered another option. "Want to go home and make mad love? Or would you rather go over Hal Stuart's credit report?"

"You have it?" One moment her face was alive with interest. The next she looked as if she had serious reservations. "You're not having lunch with *her?* Why? Because you're seeing her tonight?"

"Why, darlin', it sounds almost as if you're jealous. Good." She still waited for an answer, so he gave it. "No lunch, no dinner. She gave me the reports free and clear."

"You must have been very good."

"I think I was. I think maybe I was a con artist. I was definitely a liar. Telling Sherri the truth felt awfully good, as if I hadn't done it much in the past." He considered that a moment, then gave her a nudge. "So…what would you like to do? Lunch, sex or work?"

She gave him a look that made his skin prickle and left

no doubt whatsoever as to what was in her mind. The look was so intimate, though, that he knew he wasn't going to get the most desirable answer. "How about if we go over the reports over lunch? Then we won't have to do it to-night."

Maybe that *was* the most desirable answer. She put the file away, exited the computer program and took her purse from a drawer before leading the way outside to her car.

They picked up burgers and fries from a drive-through, then went to Vanderbilt Park. With an old quilt from the back of her car, they found a sunny place that looked on distant mountains and settled in. While Martin unpacked the food, she smoothed the papers he'd pulled from his pocket. "Why did you get a report on Maxwell Brown? Isn't he just a local businessman?"

He handed her a cheeseburger before unwrapping his own. "Monday night, after the dream, I was afraid to go back to sleep, so I went for a walk. I do that a lot. Brown was in his office downtown having a meeting with some guy. There were two other men waiting for them out in the alley. I'd been watching them for about ten minutes when Brown and the other guy came out. The three men got in their car and drove away, and Brown left in his own car."

"What time was this?"

"Around 3:00 a.m. It gave me a funny feeling in the back of my neck. It just didn't feel right." He paused to take a few bites, washing them down with soda. "The next day I saw Brown and Hal having lunch together. Hal was not in a good mood."

"So you think that not all of Maxwell Brown's business is legitimate and that Hal might possibly be involved with him."

"I don't know. I just thought that getting his records was too good a chance to pass up."

When they finished eating, she moved closer to him, and they studied the papers together. Hal's risk score wasn't very good. His credit cards—and there were plenty—carried high balances, and he was frequently late with his payments on everything from his car to his condo to his utilities. The sixty-six thousand dollars Olivia's life insurance had paid would have made a good dent in his debt, but he still would have been up to his ears in it. Hell, maybe that was where he'd spent it and he still owed this much.

Maxwell Brown was a different story. He had A1 credit ratings all the way down the list, reasonable balances, sensible debt and regular, on-time payments. There was no mortgage for a house or cars, which meant he must own those outright.

"So does that satisfy your curiosity about Brown?"

"It should." Financially the man was as upstanding as they came. But that funny feeling was there again. If Martin knew only one thing for a fact, it was that he could trust that feeling.

"But it doesn't. All right. Tomorrow why don't you go by the courthouse and find out everything you can about him? I'll check at the library." She folded the papers, offered them to him, then slipped them inside her purse when he refused. "Grand Springs is such a pretty place," she remarked with a look around. "It's no surprise that Olivia loved it."

"Coming here was a big deal for you." Leaving her home, her family and friends, the only place she'd ever known, for someplace strange and new took courage that she probably hadn't realized she possessed. "I hope you never regret it."

"I never will. No matter what."

He didn't like the ominous undertones his mind supplied to her last words. Even after last night, she wasn't convinced that there was no one in his past who could take him away from her. Truthfully, she was right to have doubts. There *was* the very strong possibility that someone in his past could separate them, though not another woman. The man he had been before the accident, the man who had killed, the man who knew too well how to live in the shadows—*that* man could come between them. He was his own biggest worry.

She withdrew a paper from her bag, then settled again even closer. "After talking with Stone this morning, I sent this out."

He recognized the printout as being an NCIC entry—but how did he know that? It listed his name as John Doe, gave a physical description, including details on the scars, and asked each agency to check its records on shooting victims for the last six years.

"He says it could take a long time to get an answer, but unless you were shot outside the country, the chances of hearing something are pretty good."

The suggestion that he might not have been in the country when the shootings occurred didn't feel as foreign as it should. Had he traveled overseas often? Had he lived there? Maybe. It could explain why no missing persons report had ever been filed. It could also explain his fluency in Spanish.

After a time, they shook out the quilt and returned to the car. Juliet dropped him off at the church, drove the short distance to the library and went inside. Instead of going to her office, though, she headed for the reference section. With two rubber-banded files in hand, she found an out-of-the-way table and sat down.

The clip file on Maxwell Brown was thick. There was coverage of business triumphs and charitable contributions. There was a yellowed wedding announcement, detailing a lavish wedding and featuring a picture of a handsome young man with a beautiful young bride. A few years later, there was a one-line mention of a divorce in the legal news column. He received honors and tributes by the handfuls and was active on Grand Springs's social scene, though rarely with the same woman on his arm twice. His generosity apparently was exceeded only by his business acumen. His home, the site of charity balls and civic events, was nothing less than a mansion. He gave freely of his money and his time, the townspeople admired and respected him, children adored him, and he was kind to small animals.

He was almost too good to be true.

If Martin's suspicions were correct, he *was* too good to be true.

Hal Stuart's file was much smaller, his career much less stellar. Most of the clippings regarding him dealt with city council business. There was an announcement of his engagement to Randi Howell, the bride who'd fled her own wedding and fallen in love with someone else. An older story covered his graduation from law school and setting up practice in Grand Springs, and there were mentions of his election and subsequent reelections to the council. There was nothing new or interesting.

With a sigh, she returned the files to their cabinet, left the library and made the short trip to the police station. There was nothing more she could do for Martin. Now she needed to concentrate on her own work. Even if it was nearly impossible. Even if the hours did drag until the afternoon was finally over. With more relief than she would have believed possible, she shut down the computer, said goodbye to Mariellen and headed for the church.

She hadn't offered to pick Martin up after work, and he might have already left, but it was only a few blocks out of her way. When she parked at the curb out front, she saw that she wasn't too late. Several people were inside talking, and one was Martin.

The sidewalk led straight to the porch, where the double glass doors were propped open. She stepped into the hallway and hesitated until one of the men saw her and smiled. Martin turned and smiled, too, and held out his hand to her. He introduced her to the group—the Reverend Murphy and three of his parishioners, two older women and a man.

After a polite hello, one of the women continued talking. ''Now, you see here in this picture, the carpet is definitely burgundy—and pretty new, too. This was taken thirty-three years ago at our oldest daughter's wedding.'' She beamed at Juliet. "She's still married to the same man, and they have four children and three grandchildren. Now, this picture is of Emma's grandson's wedding, and it's this same green carpet, and pretty new, too. This was taken—" She looked at the back, squinted to read the writing, then looked at the woman beside her. "When, Emma?"

"That was December. December 17, a Christmas wedding. His mother had always wanted a June wedding—"

"Of what year, dear?"

"Let me think. Their oldest boy just turned eighteen this month, so that means they've been married..." Emma's fragile skin flushed a delicate pink. "Eighteen and a half years."

No one blinked at the discomfort her grandson's marriage-of-necessity still caused all these years later, but, out of sight, Martin gave Juliet's fingers a squeeze.

The minister turned to Martin. "So you were here at some point at least eighteen and a half years ago but probably not more than thirty-three years ago. That's more than a fourteen-year span. Not much help, is it?"

Martin was shaking his head when the other man spoke for the first time. "I don't remember you. I've been here every time those doors opened for a service. I've known every family who worshiped here. I've been to every wedding, every christening and every funeral, but I don't remember you."

"He was a boy, Henry," Emma said. "Maybe he's changed."

Henry stubbornly shook his head. "You look faintly familiar—it's something about your eyes—but no. You weren't a regular here, not even a semiregular."

His very certainty gave Juliet cause to hope, and she said so to Martin once they'd said their goodbyes and reached the car. He gave her a flat, disappointed look. "Then you're an incurable optimist, darlin', because he didn't leave room for hope."

"What is the one physical feature that doesn't change

with age?'' When he didn't offer an answer, she did. ''You can gain weight or lose it. You can straighten a crooked nose or put a crook in a straight one. You can cover a high forehead, reshape cheekbones, reconstruct jaws and straighten teeth. You can make your nose bigger or smaller, and you can change the way your ears lie in relation to your head. You can cut, curl, color or shave your hair. But the only thing you can do to your eyes is a tuck on the lids or change the color with contacts. Henry said there's something familiar about your eyes.'' She smiled. ''They *are* your best feature.''

''They are, huh? And here I thought you were more interested in my—'' He finished the sentence in a whisper, his mouth pressed to her ear, making her shiver and squirm before he kissed her mouth. It was the same sort of kiss he'd given her before work this morning, the sort that made her forget everything, including her name.

Sitting back in his seat, he fastened the seat belt. ''How about stopping by my apartment? You can keep me company while I clean up.''

For a moment she looked blankly at him, her mind still occupied with sensations and not processing information. Finally, giving herself a mental shake, she started the car and pulled into the street.

His apartment was quiet, dimly lit and still full of the day's warmth even though outside the temperature had begun its usual evening slide. Juliet wandered around the single large room, half her attention directed to the bathroom, where Martin was in the shower. Naked. Washing, touching himself. Such a simple, everyday task. Such erotic images. They left her throat dry and sent an edgy, dissatisfied feeling through her.

If she were bold, she would take off her clothes and be waiting in his bed when he came out. If she were brash and bold, she wouldn't wait for him to come out but would shed her clothes and join him in the shower. She would take the soap from him, work up a lather in her hands and rub them over his body. She would tease and torment them both until they couldn't stand any more, and then she would take him, first in her mouth, in a sinfully wicked kiss, then in her body, right there in the tub, with the water beating on them and around them, until—

Catching her breath on a groan, she stopped in front of one window and stared out sightlessly, all too aware of her body's needs, of the tightness in her chest, of the tension deep in her belly. She had indulged in a few fantasies before—what woman hadn't?—but the fantasy of Martin was more appealing, more enticing, than the reality of any other man she'd known. He wasn't even in the room, but her breasts were swollen, her nipples achy, her muscles trembly. The man embodied pure, raw sexual fantasy, and he was a danger—

His arm wrapped around her from behind, and his fingers slid between buttons to stroke her midriff. He hadn't made a sound crossing the room, but she could feel him now, could smell him—warm, damp, aroused, masculine. He came closer, until his legs brushed hers, until his erection was pressed against her bottom. Moving his hand lower, he worked a few buttons loose, then slid his hand inside her dress, his fingers leaving a damp, quivering trail across her belly, beneath the elastic band of her panties, probing between her thighs.

She gasped when he touched her, when he found her hot, damp and craving his attention. When he slid his fingers inside her, whatever sound she might have made was lost in the flood of sensation. He stroked deep inside her, then outside, concentrating his touches where her response was most powerful, his talented fingers drawing her closer and closer, coaxing her to feel more, to want more, demand more.

She clenched her fingers, then flattened them against the cool glass pane. She was so hot, so desperate, able to breathe now only in soft gasps that threatened tears, and still he tormented her, robbing her of everything but need, aching, killing need. It became unbearable, but she bore it, became painful, but she loved it, until finally, her body quivering, her back arched, with one great rush, with one writhing, whimpering shudder, she collapsed against him. She trusted him to hold her, to keep her on her feet, and he did. He wrapped his arms around her waist, held her tightly against him and spoke for the first time. "Hey, darlin'."

Nine

Maxwell Brown's house sat on the highest hill in Grand Springs, a monument to money, ego and the determination to succeed. With its Mediterranean styling, lush grounds and elaborate security fence, it would have looked more at home in the Caribbean or on one of the tiny exclusive islands between Miami and Miami Beach, but even high in the Rockies, it was beautiful. Both the house and the grounds were brightly lit in the night. No one would ever slip in there unnoticed. No doubt, there were perimeter alarms, motion-sensitive detectors and burglar alarms all over the place.

"What a great place to live."

Martin glanced at Juliet, who was staring up at the house from their place on the dark street. Frankly, he couldn't imagine her in a place like this, maybe because he identified her so strongly with her neat little green house. Oddly enough, though, he *could* see himself living in a place like this. Maybe…

Damn, how he hated that word.

She smiled at his fierce look. "Feeling cranky? You should have taken me up on my offer."

Tension born of frustration was immediately replaced by tension of a sexual nature. Back in his apartment, once she'd found the strength to lift her head from his shoulder, once she'd been able to speak coherently, she had made him several offers—to take off her clothes, to take him to bed, to do things to him that he might never have had done to him before. She'd offered earthy, lusty promises, made all the more indecent by her utterly innocent face, and he had been tempted, heaven help him, more than ever before. But the condoms were at her house. She hadn't minded, but he had. No matter how urgent the desire, he couldn't risk her future, maybe even her life, not even for the most incredible lovemaking that existed.

So he had torn himself away from her, dragged on clothes that she'd kept trying to remove and made himself a promise. *Later.* He could have her later. The prospect was enough to give him some measure of control.

"Exactly what kind of business is Maxwell Brown in?"

He looked back at the house. "He used to be a stockbroker. Now he's into a little of everything. He owns both residential and commercial rental property. He has a construction company, a trucking company and a couple of car dealerships. He owns an interest in the mall, one of the banks and in the commuter airline out at the airport. He's also part-owner of the Squaw Creek Lodge."

"So he's a respectable businessman whose interests are diversified. But you still have this feeling."

"I know it sounds silly—"

"Not at all. I work three days a week with people who get paid for heeding their 'feelings'—only they call them hunches. Instincts."

He gestured toward the endless wrought-iron fence that circled the property. "I know there's money in business, but look at that house. There's no mortgage on it. The fence alone cost more than most houses in town. Grand Springs is a small city. Just how much money can one man make here legitimately?"

"Do you have any theories?"

He looked at the house, then closed his eyes and saw similar houses in south Florida. He thought of the trucking company, the airplanes, the auto dealerships where nondescript cars could be easily brought in or disposed of, and the bank. "A wild guess? I'd say drugs. If I didn't know he was a respectable businessman."

Juliet's voice was soft in the darkness. "I think of drug lords as South Americans who have no heart or soul, who live surrounded by armed men and kill anyone who gets in their way."

"They come in all nationalities, darlin', including middle-class American. And not all of them are heartless. Some of them love their families very much. They're generous with the people around them. They're protective, almost fatherly. The drug business is just that—business."

"Dangerous business."

"Extremely so. The cops either want to stop you or bleed you dry, and the competition wants you dead—" Abruptly he stopped. Why was he speaking with such authority? Because he'd lived that life before? Was that why someone had tried to kill him? Why he spoke Spanish fluently for an apple-pie American? Why the pictures of Miami had seemed so familiar? Why he knew that there were little islands in Biscayne Bay where houses like Maxwell Brown's were abundant? Was that why Juliet heard trucking company, airline, car dealers and bank, and thought business, while he heard them and thought drugs?

Was that why he dreamed of killing men?

"What is it?"

Ignoring her question, he stared away from her. Maybe Maxwell Brown was nothing more than a legitimate businessman. Maybe the only person involved in the drug trade around here was *him*. And maybe that was why no one had tried to find him after his disappearance: they simply assumed that he was dead, that whoever had wanted to kill him had succeeded.

Juliet wrapped her fingers around his hand, squeezing tightly enough to make him wince. "Not you, Martin. Maybe someone you knew, but not you."

She sounded so sure, but she could be kidding herself. She wanted to believe the best of him, but he had to face the fact that there might not have been any "best" in him. He might have been the worst sort of person imaginable.

In the silence that followed her assertion, headlights appeared at the top of the hill as Brown's Lincoln came into sight. "Duck," he commanded, sliding Juliet half under the steering wheel, bending low over her. The lights bounced across Juliet's car as the Lincoln turned toward town. Martin waited a moment, then another before lifting his head in time to see the taillights disappear around a curve.

Juliet started the engine and swung the car into a tight U-turn.

"What are you doing?"

"I want to see where he's going."

He smiled faintly. Prim, shy Juliet, tailing the most influential man in the county. Who ever would have believed it? Then he thought of last night in her bed and this evening in his apartment. Prim and shy, yes, but also sensual, sexy, uninhibited, wild, tempting and seductive. "I think I've been a bad influence on you."

She flashed him a smile. "If you've been bad, I don't think I could survive good."

They came out of a curve into a straightaway just as, several blocks ahead, Brown made a right turn onto the main road. "Slow down," Martin instructed. "Wait until he's almost out of sight."

"But what if we lose him?"

"We won't." He watched the Lincoln for a moment, then nodded. "Now. You know, one-car surveillance is damned hard to pull off. Ideally, you should have at least two cars and radios or cell phones to stay in touch. Then if your guy gets suspicious, you can turn off and let your partner take over."

She was giving him a curious look. "Spoken like a cop."

"Or the subject of too much surveillance."

Brown's car was several blocks ahead as they entered the main part of town. When his brake lights and turn signal flashed, Martin instructed Juliet to pull over and shut off her lights. She obeyed, stopping behind a delivery van that blocked them from sight, and he slipped from the car and moved to the side of the van to watch.

Brown pulled into the parking lot beside the Monroe Building, took a quick look around, then headed for the alley entrance to the building. He was carrying a briefcase and looked as if he were just starting his business day, not ending it.

Martin returned to the car. "He went to his office."

"Oh, wow, that's exciting."

"Who ever told you that surveillance was supposed to be exciting?"

"So now what?"

"Want some dinner?"

"What if he leaves while we're gone?"

"Then we go home."

"Aren't you curious about what he's doing in there?"

"Yes, but we're not going to find out from here." He looked at her for a moment, then relented. "All right. Let's find a better place to park."

She backed up, went around the block and parked near the corner on a side street. Their position gave them a good view of the parking lot, part of the alley and the front entrance to the building without being too noticeable. As soon as she shut off the engine, Martin unfastened his seat belt. "I'm going down the block to the Saloon to get some burgers. Don't go anywhere. If he leaves, let him go and wait for me. Don't get out of the car for any reason. Don't do anything."

"I'm not a child, Martin, and I'm not going to do something foolish."

"I know. Just don't get carried away. If anything happened to you..." He stopped, unwilling to finish the statement, unwilling to admit the truth aloud—if anything happened to her, it would destroy him.

"I'll stay here. I'll lock the doors, and I'll be good."

He got out quickly so the dome light wasn't on one second longer than necessary. Sticking close to the building, he backtracked half a block to the alley, then made his way to the Saloon, placing their order at the bar, waiting impatiently. Maybe he shouldn't have left her. Maybe he should have forgotten about dinner or insisted that they go home. Maybe—

"Hey, Martin, Stone and the chief and a couple of the guys are over there in the corner. Come join us."

He glanced at Jack Stryker, then at the long table of cops before shaking his head. "Thanks, but not tonight."

"Haven't seen you around the department lately, though I hear you met Juliet there for lunch today."

Martin let that slide. "Anything new on the Stuart case?"

"Dean Springer has gone to ground, and he might never come back up. We reinterviewed everyone in town who knew him, and we still can't connect him to anyone with reason to want Olivia dead. Of course, part of the problem is we can't *find* anyone with reason to want her dead. And it's easy for someone like Springer to hide. He's one of those forgettable sorts. Hell, he lived here for twenty years, and only a few people knew him."

Martin was one of those forgettable sorts, too. He'd been missing for more than ten months, and no one had missed him yet.

"Sure you won't join us?"

"Thanks, but Juliet's waiting." He pulled some money from his pocket as the waitress brought his order. He was across the bar and on his way out when he met a crowd coming in. One of them bumped into him, then released the woman with him and stuck out his arm to block Martin's way.

"Hey, why don't you watch where you're going?" the man demanded, his tone belligerent, his manner blustery, posturing for his girlfriend.

Martin switched the paper bag to his left hand, then tilted the cowboy's hat back so they could see eye to eye.

"Jimmy Ray," he said softly. "Haven't we danced this dance before?"

The cowboy's eyes widened, and he swallowed hard. "Man, I'm sorry. I didn't mean— I didn't know—"

"That's right. You didn't know. That's why you need to be nice to everybody, because you *never know*." He leaned closer to emphasize the last words. "The next time you bump into somebody, you handle it right. You say, 'Excuse me. I didn't mean to do that.' Try it now."

"Ex-excuse me. I didn't mean to—to…" Jimmy Ray's Adam's apple bulged as he swallowed again.

"Close enough. Nice seeing you again." He stepped around the cowboy and left the bar. A glance down the street showed the lights were still on in Brown's office. A closer glance showed just the front end of Juliet's car on the next street over. It wasn't attention grabbing, since there were other cars parked nearby. Of course, Maxwell Brown hadn't seen any of those other cars parked outside his house a short while ago.

He returned down the side street and through the alley, tapping on the window so she could unlock the door. He handed her a burger, Coke and napkins and unwrapped his own burger before speaking. "I ran into a friend of yours at the Saloon."

"Really? Who?"

"Jimmy Ray."

"Jimmy— Oh, the cowboy."

"You say that as if it's something special," he teased. He could afford to tease because, in fact, she'd said it as if the other man was totally inconsequential. "Of course, being Texas born and bred, I imagine cowboys do carry some significance for you."

"Not in the least, though if you put on a pair of boots and a Stetson, I imagine it might raise my temperature a degree or two."

"I could do more than that, darlin'. In my apartment this evening you were steaming."

She blushed in the dim light and picked for a moment at her hamburger before asking, "You don't think anyone could see...do you?"

The window was set high enough that his hand underneath her skirt had been hidden from view. But anyone with any imagination whatsoever would have known what he'd been doing to her, where he'd been touching her, what she'd been feeling. The look on her face, the taut line of her body and the arch of her back had all but shouted pure sexual delight.

"No," he said quietly. "I'm sure no one saw a thing."

For the next hour, they talked, sat in silence and listened to music. Martin was about to suggest that they call it a night and head home when finally something happened. The lights went off in Maxwell Brown's office, and a moment later he came out of the building and climbed into his car. If he turned toward home, they would let him go, Martin decided. If he didn't, they would follow.

When Brown turned the other way, Martin opened the door. "Let me drive, Juliet." They switched places, then he pulled to the corner. As soon as the Lincoln was out of sight, he turned.

Once the road left town, it wound through valleys and over passes. Eventually, it reached the interstate, and from there it was easy going to anyplace in the country. Brown didn't go that far, though. Only a couple of miles out of town, he turned into a broad driveway, slowed at the security gate, then went inside. Martin drove past, pulled to the side of the road and cut the engine and the lights. "Wait here—"

"No way. I'm going with you."

"You're not dressed for a nighttime walk through the woods." Her skirt was full and would snag on bushes, and her shoes, while sensible flats, weren't designed with hiking in mind.

"I'll be fine."

"That dress will reflect every bit of light in the sky."

She reached in back and came up with a black trench coat. Her smile was smug. "I like to be prepared. I don't trust Colorado weather."

He wanted to argue with her, but he didn't have time. If there was anything to see inside the fenced-in compound, he needed to get close enough. "You do what I say without question. Stay behind me. And if I tell you to run, you run like hell and don't look back. Understand?"

Her only response was to shrug into the coat, then climb out of the car. With the coat covering her to the ankles and its hood drawn tight around her face, she was less visible than he was, making him wish once more for a knitted black cap to cover his blond hair.

What little light the moon gave disappeared as they moved deeper into the woods. They followed the concertina-topped fence, keeping to the shelter of the trees, around to the back of the compound. There, a drainage ditch that ran the length of the fence provided them cover. Martin found a good vantage point and eased onto his stomach, his feet braced on chunks of granite in the bottom. With a rustle of nylon, Juliet joined him.

The back of the warehouse was brightly lit, and there was a good deal of activity going on. Three tractor-trailers marked Grand Springs Trucking were backed up to the loading dock, and another three sat off to one side, motors running, awaiting their turns. On the dock Brown stood out in his suit. Everyone around him wore jeans or work clothes.

"How's your neck?"

Juliet's whisper tickled his ear, but he didn't twitch. "Itchy as hell," he whispered back.

"It's not really unusual for deliveries to come in at night, is it?"

"I don't know. But do you think Brown comes out to personally oversee the unloading of every nighttime shipment?"

"Probably not." She wriggled around, then came up

with a small rock that had been somewhere underneath her. She was about to toss it aside when Martin grabbed both it and her hand. With a weak smile, she gave him the rock, which he laid silently in front of them.

As he watched the men work, he made up a mental wish list: electronic equipment for listening in on Brown's conversation, binoculars for closer examination of the crates being unloaded, and a gun, a nice little Sig-Sauer. He felt damn near naked without the comfortingly familiar press of the pistol in the small of his back.

He became still, his thoughts distracting him from the activity at the loading dock. He'd carried a gun. His subconscious must have been aware of that—after all, guns were the weapon of choice for killing, and he knew he'd killed—but it was still a disconcerting idea. A lot of people carried guns. Cops. Burglars. Thieves. Rapists. Murderers. Drug dealers.

Maybe his business in Grand Springs had had something to do with Maxwell Brown. Maybe he'd been looking for work. Maybe he'd been checking out the competition.

"Martin."

Maybe he had come here to make a deal…or a hit or—

"*Martin!*" Juliet whispered his name and tugged his jacket even as she slid further down into the ditch. A big, burly guy was coming their way, and he didn't look particularly friendly.

Snapping out of whatever bleak possibilities he'd been contemplating, Martin moved quickly, silently, to the bottom of the ditch, pulling her with him. For a long time they lay motionless, listening as the footsteps came closer. Just when it seemed as if the man must be walking right up to the fence, a truck door opened, then closed. A moment later the engine rumbled to life, the gears ground and the truck pulled away.

With her face pressed against Martin's thigh, Juliet let her breath out in a whoosh. She was scared to death—and exhilarated beyond belief. Never in her life had she done anything the least bit daring or dangerous. It was fun. It was exciting. It turned her on.

He wriggled free of her and worked his way back up the sloping side of the ditch. She followed, but this time there was no sign of Maxwell Brown. Men continued to unload the trucks, but Brown and the person who appeared to be his right-hand man had disappeared.

"Let's go," Martin mouthed, and gestured for her to lead. She picked her way carefully over the rocks until they reached the woods. Once the darkness swallowed them, she loosened the hood, unbuttoned the coat, then turned, stopping so abruptly that Martin ran into her. Before he could react, she kissed him long and hard, thrusting her tongue into his mouth while her hands roamed restlessly, greedily, over his body.

Once the shock passed, he grabbed her hands, then pushed her back. "Juliet!" he whispered.

"That was fun. It was neat."

"It was dangerous, not fun."

"Fun. Exciting. Arousing." She tried to free her hands but couldn't, so she satisfied herself with rubbing sensuously against him. "I want to make love to you. Now. Right now."

"Here? In the forest? On the ground? Right next to Brown's place? I don't think so."

"I need you." She got one hand loose and slid it down the front of his body, over hard belly and soft denim to the beginnings of an impressive erection. "Now, Martin, please."

Choking back a laugh, he trapped her hand again. "Not here. At home, darlin'."

"Oh, please... Where's your sense of adventure?"

"You're the only adventure I can handle, Juliet. At home. Come on." Still holding her hands, he pulled her behind him through the woods, and she followed docilely.

It was no surprise that he'd been shocked. Heavens, she had shocked herself. She had never behaved so brazenly in her life, but then, she'd never done anything so risky in her life. No wonder people liked to live dangerously. It was a potent feeling—a rush of power, of fear, of being incredibly *alive*.

They reached her car and drove home in silence. She stripped off the trench coat and returned it to the back seat. When they pulled into the driveway, she held out her hand for the keys, walked up the sidewalk and let herself into the house, all without saying a word.

The screen door banged behind her. She didn't stop, didn't turn on any lights, but walked down the hall and into her bedroom. She was standing beside the bed, a condom in hand, when Martin walked in. He came straight to her, sliding his hands under her skirt, kissing her as if his survival depended on it. She fumbled with his zipper as he carefully, deliberately ripped her lace panties. She wrapped her fingers around him, and he groaned. She freed him from his jeans, rolled the condom into place, and he cupped his hands to her bottom, lifting her, bringing her down hard so that she gloved him.

It was fast, greedy, raw need. He offered no tenderness, but she wanted none. Rough, hard, deep, purely physical, he drove into her and she rode him, giving, demanding. Her release hit her first, her body clenching around his, giving his the last push before he exploded, too.

Moments passed—hours—then he slowly lifted her away, letting her slide down his body until her feet reached the floor. He brushed her hair back and gave her a faint, sexy smile. "You could kill a man before his time."

She smiled, too. Her breasts were soft and achy. The heat was still building, cooled for only an instant by their play. Her muscles were trembling, her nerves quivering, her heart thudding. "You're amazing."

"Amazing, huh. I don't have a past, I may not have much of a future, I can't remember my own name, but I can make you weak."

"Amazing." Her gaze locked with his, she began unbuttoning her dress. When she reached the buttons below her waist, she pulled the straps off her shoulders and let the dress fall to the floor.

Still looking at her, he raised his hand to her breast and flicked his fingertips across her nipple. "You're greedy."

"I never was before." She had enjoyed sex and had always had a healthy regard for it, but she hadn't indulged often, and she hadn't really missed it when it was absent from her life. Of course, she'd never been in love before.

Now, that was a scary thought. Granted, love never came with guarantees, but she had even fewer than usual. All she could say for certain was that Martin would never deliberately hurt her. But so much was beyond his control. Someday he would remember, and when he did…

She wouldn't think about it. Not when he was standing in front of her, fully clothed, fully aroused and effortlessly arousing her while she was naked. Not when he was looking at her as if he could never get enough of her, as if he would never stop wanting her, as if… As if he might love her, too.

She helped him undress, then drew him down on the bed, pushing him onto his back, shifting to sit astride him. It was an intimate position, their bodies snugly joined, and yet she was able to look at him, to appreciate everything about him. He was so incredibly handsome, his body nothing less than beautiful despite the scars. Handsome, sexy, charming, powerful, intense—he was exactly the sort of man who never paid attention to her, who never looked twice at her.

But he was doing a whole lot more than looking, she marveled as he moved deeper inside her. It was incredible. If, by some chance, fate gave them that future he wasn't sure he had, if they grew old and gray together, she would always be amazed.

Their lovemaking was as slow and lazy as the first had been quick and frantic. They played with each other, spent long minutes doing nothing but stroking, touching, kissing.

The fever built so slowly, so gradually, that the release that followed was little more than a warm, shivery, pleasure-filled moment. Once, then again, then he pulled her into his arms, cradling her against his slick skin.

"So," he murmured after a sleepy, soothing kiss. "You're not a virgin anymore."

"Excuse me?"

His chuckle tickled her ear. "We're in bed naked. We just had sex once and made love twice. I don't think you have to be quite so polite."

The fact that he recognized the difference between the acts pleased her inordinately, but she remained focused on the conversation. "I haven't been a virgin since—well, a long time." Since she'd met a fellow computer geek her sophomore year in college and let him coax her away from the machine long enough for a vaguely disappointing introduction to the physical side of life. Over the next four years, the sex had gotten better, of course, but it had never been a major part of their relationship. It had become a non-existent part once Jerry met Veronica, with her big hair, drop-dead-gorgeous body, big baby blues and IQ equal to her bust size.

"You successfully completed your first surveillance tonight."

"How successful could it be? We didn't learn anything."

He patted her reassuringly. "We're alive, babe, and that counts as successful in anyone's book."

Long after his breathing slowed and evened out, she lay awake, her mind too active to sleep. Finally she got up, dressed in a faded old T-shirt and let Hunter in from the yard. He sniffed her hand, accepted a cookie, then trotted off to the bedroom. She headed for the dining room.

Her computer had never been so neglected. Before meeting Martin, if she was home and awake, she was staring into a monitor. Since meeting him, she'd spent precious few hours on-line. She was behind in her mail, she hadn't caught up on any of the on-line discussions that she subscribed to, and she hadn't read the *Washington Post* or the *New York Times* in days. No, instead of living vicariously through the computer, since meeting Martin, she'd been *really* living. It was so much more fun.

She read and answered her E-mail, browsed through a few news stories, checked the weather maps, then called up the Net directory and selected a search engine. She typed in Maxwell Brown and methodically worked her way through the entries that popped up, usually able to tell from the opening lines whether it might be their Maxwell Brown. As she tried Hal Stuart's name, Hunter wandered in, circled the room twice, then curled up directly behind her chair. In less than two minutes, he was snoring.

A search for drugs yielded nearly thirty thousand hits, drug smuggling almost three hundred. Narrowing the subject to drug smuggling in Colorado had only five hits, but none of them were of interest. Swallowing a yawn, she paged back to the screen that displayed the first ten hits on drug smuggling, then drew her feet into the chair and rested her chin on her knees.

Personally, she never would have suspected Maxwell Brown of any wrongdoing, but then, she wasn't a suspicious person by nature. She could look at his incredible house and all his holdings and see nothing more than a very smart—and lucky—businessman. But Martin saw more, and she trusted his instincts.

So how did they prove that Brown was up to no good? And how did they prove that Hal Stuart was or was not involved? And what would it mean regarding Olivia Stuart's murder? Would it prove that Martin had nothing to do with it?

So many questions, so few answers. If they were cops, if this were an official investigation, it would be much easier. They would have access to bank and tax records. They could find out exactly how much money Maxwell Brown made legally and whether it was enough to support his lifestyle. If it was obvious that his outgo substantially exceeded his legitimate income, that would be enough to justify a closer look into all of his business enterprises.

But they weren't cops, and if they got a closer look, they might not like what they saw, especially Martin.

Her eyes were tired and gritty, making it difficult to focus on the screen. She wasn't accomplishing anything here, and she was sleepy, and Martin was down the hall in her bed, where she should be.

After shutting down the computer, she started to roll back, but her chair wouldn't budge. "Let me up, Hunter." She poked the dog with one foot, which stopped his snoring and prompted him to give her a narrow-eyed look. It didn't make him move. "Come on, Hunter, it's bedtime. Want to go to bed?"

The mutt yawned, opening his mouth wide enough to accommodate a person's head, then lumbered to his feet and out of the room. Juliet was smiling as she followed him. A month ago she'd been alone, restless and lonely in Dallas. Now she was living in Colorado with a smelly, none-too-trusting dog and in love with a handsome, mysterious man with a questionable past.

How life had changed.

Martin and Juliet were talking over the remains of their lunch at the deli Friday afternoon when Eve Redtree joined them. She slid into the empty chair between them and greeted them both with a smile. After a moment's small talk, she came quickly to the point of her visit. "Have you learned anything from my mother's papers?"

Juliet gave Martin a look, but left it to him to answer, and he did so carelessly. "No, I'm afraid not." Only that Olivia had been bailing Hal out of money trouble and that even at a very young age, Roy Jr. had been terrified of his father, but there was no way he was going to discuss those things with their sister. "There were just those calls to Jason Scott in Miami Beach. I don't suppose you've remembered him."

Eve shook her head. "I asked Hal about him. I told him I was looking through the condolence cards we got after Mom's death and came across one with his name. Hal didn't recognize it, either. What is it about the calls that interests you so much?"

"Your mother called him every week—"

"Every Saturday evening," Juliet clarified.

"For the three months before her death. She made the calls between seven and eight, and they lasted at least an hour."

"Saturday evening…" Eve looked puzzled, as if trying to remember something. Martin waited silently, giving her time. "When I lived away, Mom and I talked for a couple of hours every week. Usually she called me on Sunday afternoon, but once last spring I called her on a Saturday night because Molly and I had plans for Sunday. Mom was kind of distracted, and after twenty minutes or so, she insisted that she needed to get off the phone. I thought it was odd—I mean, she hadn't even said hello to Molly. I let her go, then called back a while later so Molly could tell her good-night, but her line was busy, and it stayed busy the rest of the evening."

So Olivia's weekend conversations with Jason Scott had been important to her, important enough to brush off her daughter and granddaughter. Why?

"Have you been able to locate this Scott person?"

Martin shook his head. "We tried calling the number, but it's been disconnected. Juliet tried every Jason Scott in the Miami area, but none of them ever lived at his address."

"Maybe…" Eve's smile was faint. "Maybe he was a long-distance boyfriend. Maybe they met while he was passing through the state or on one of her business trips. Or maybe…" The smile faded, and she offered the same theory Juliet had come up with last week. "Maybe he's my brother. Maybe he changed his name."

Martin gently discouraged her. "If she'd finally located

the brother who disappeared twenty years ago, don't you think she would have told you and Hal?''

''Probably. That was her fondest wish—that Roy Jr. would come back, alive and well. Everyone thought he was probably dead, but she never accepted that. She always believed, always hoped... She always regretted that she hadn't protected him. She was convinced that someday he would come walking back into her life.'' Her smile this time was bittersweet. ''It was kind of like living with a ghost. Mom very seldom talked about him, but we always knew he was an important part of our family, even years after he disappeared. When we moved into the house on Poplar, she had a room set aside for him. She called it a guest room but we knew it was really Roy's room. She bought cards for him on his birthday. We'd be driving along the highway, and she'd say, 'Cole likes to go camping right up that road,' or she'd see a leather jacket and say, 'Cole has a jacket just like that.' Always in the present tense, as if she knew in her heart that he was still alive. Maybe she did.''

''Your mother called your brother Cole?'' Juliet asked.

At Eve's nod, Martin gave a shake of his head. That explained Olivia's dying word easily enough. It had had nothing to do with strip mining, after all. Just a mother's dying wish for her son.

''I doubt that Jason Scott has any connection to your brother,'' Martin said quietly. ''If he did, don't you think he would have contacted someone when the calls from Olivia suddenly stopped?''

''Probably. It would be nice to know who he was, though, and why she talked to him every week but never mentioned him to us.'' Eve gave a sigh, then made a move as if to stand. ''I wanted to tell you that I need Mom's stuff back before tomorrow afternoon. Hal needs some papers regarding the house for the insurance company, and he's coming over tomorrow to pick them up.''

"No problem," Juliet answered. "We'll pack everything up and bring it by your house this evening."

"I appreciate it. I wish I could have—"

"What the hell's going on here?"

Speak of the devil, Martin thought as Hal Stuart advanced on them. The man looked seriously annoyed with his sister and way beyond that with him and Juliet.

"What are you doing, Eve?"

She gave her brother a cool glance that should have put him in his place. "Talking to friends. What are you doing?"

"I came in to get some lunch and find you—" Breaking off, he turned his gaze on first Martin, then Juliet. "I thought I warned you two to mind your own business. I won't tolerate your interference in my family business. If Chief Sanderson can't make you back off and leave us alone, then maybe Judge Walters can. Eve, come with me."

She refused to be hurried away. Instead, she shrugged free of his hand, stood up and gave them a warm smile. "Juliet, Martin, it was nice seeing you." As they walked away, the warmth left her voice. "You may be my older brother, Hal, but you do not run my life. Don't you ever interfere…"

Her voice trailed away, and a moment later, the door swung shut behind them. Martin looked at Juliet. "She may be only half his size, but I'd put my money on her any day."

"I hope we haven't caused any trouble for her."

"She'll deal with him." Thinking of Hal's last comment to them, he said, "I hope we haven't caused trouble for you. If he goes to the chief again—"

"What can they do?"

"Gee, I don't know. Fire you?"

"Then maybe you and I can go into business together. Smith and Crandall, Private Investigators."

Or Smith and Smith. Or Whoever-the-hell-he-was and Whoever-the-hell-she-would-be-if-she-married-him. He didn't allow himself to dwell on such a possibility, though. Instead, he shook his head. "No P.I. work. Not for you. It's too dangerous."

"But it's not dangerous for you?"

"I'm better equipped to deal with it. I'm a man. I'm able to take care of myself."

"'I'm a man.' Now there's a chauvinistic answer if ever I've heard one. News flash, Mr. Smith—this is the nineties. Women are quite capable, too."

"I'm not talking about women. I'm talking about *you*. Every other woman in the world can go out and risk her life every day if it's what she wants, but you… I want you safe." It wasn't what he wanted to say, didn't come close to touching on how he really felt, but it was the most he could offer. He could tell her that he wanted her, that he wanted her to always be safe, maybe even that he needed her, but he couldn't tell her that he loved her. Not yet. Not until he knew everything he'd forgotten. Not until he knew he was a man deserving of her love.

Maybe never.

Juliet stood up, slung her purse over her shoulder, then fluttered her eyelashes. "My goodness gracious, it's time for me to go back to work, but I surely do hate to walk those mean old streets all by my helpless, feminine self. I would feel so much safer with a big, strong man like you by my side to protect me from whatever evil might await."

He grinned. "You're a smart ass, Juliet."

"Thank you." She led the way out, then walked beside him on a leisurely stroll back to the police department. "After we return Olivia's papers to Eve, want to find out what Maxwell Brown is up to this evening?"

"I'd rather stay home and spend a little quiet time with you and Hunter."

"Aw, come on. If he does something exciting, I'll ravish you when we get home."

"If we stay home, I'll do something exciting. *I'll* ravish *you*."

She walked a block in silence, then settled her blue gaze on him. "You think I'm getting carried away, but I'm not. It's just that you're the most fun I've ever had. In Dallas, my idea of daring was downloading a file that might possibly have a virus in it. It was leaving the house without my umbrella when the forecast called for rain or making eye contact with a stranger. Last night was exciting. It was a totally new experience, and it was fun."

"It would have stopped being fun real quick if they had caught us out there at the trucking company."

"I know. They would have called the sheriff—"

"Only if everything going on out there is on the up-and-up. If it's not, if they're involved in something illegal and they suspected that we'd seen something, they would have killed us." Saying it aloud made him realize how incredibly stupid he had been to take her along when he'd left the car last night. He should have ordered her to wait, and if she had refused—*when* she had refused—he should have forgotten about Brown and driven her back to her house.

For a moment she looked subdued and chastened, and he thought he'd made his point. Then she grinned. "But they didn't catch us, and they didn't kill us, and that's a success in anybody's book. So let's do it again. Let's tempt fate."

"*No.* The only thing you're going to tempt is me. If I have to spend all my free time making love to you to keep you out of trouble, well, I guess I can make the sacrifice."

She stopped, only a few yards from the doors of the police station, and faced him. "That's so generous of you."

Before he could agree, the glass door swung open and Hal Stuart came out, scowling as if he had a grudge against the world. His expression turned scornful and smug when he saw them. "The chief's looking for you, Ms. Crandall," he said as he walked past.

"Hey, Mr. Stuart?" As he turned, she raised one hand, obviously intending to give him further cause for anger, but

Martin grabbed her hand and forced it to her side. Instead, she offered her sweetest smile. "So nice to see you again."

Shaking his head in disgust, Hal walked away.

"Oh, Juliet, what am I going to do with you?"

She shifted the smile to him, and its innocence stirred the ever-present ache inside him. "You can have your way with me. Tonight. After we return Olivia's papers to Eve. After we see what Maxwell's doing."

He gave her a long up-and-down look and brought to life the same sort of ache in her. He saw it in the sudden softening of her eyes, the relaxing of her mouth, the purely sensual look that claimed her. "I reserve the right to try to change your mind about that last."

With a brush of her gentle fingers across his cheek, she walked to the door, then looked back. "I reserve the right to let you."

Ten

Being called on the chief's carpet wasn't so bad, as Juliet related it that evening to Martin. He'd told her about Hal's complaint, and she had explained very calmly that she'd simply been having a conversation with Eve—a conversation initiated by the other woman, no less. She'd played innocent for all she was worth, and the chief had sent her away with a request to please not further antagonize the councilman.

"I keep forgetting that Hal's a public official," she remarked as she placed the lid on one of Olivia's repacked boxes and taped it in place. "The next time he takes that attitude with me, I'm going to remind him that I'm part of the public he's sworn to serve. By the next time he comes up for reelection, I'll be registered to vote, and I'll vote against him."

"You probably don't live in his district."

"Then I'll campaign against him."

"He's been a good friend to the department. He was instrumental in getting the money that allowed them to buy the computers that required them to hire a computer expert. You owe your job to him."

"A fact he no doubt gravely regrets. He's an idiot." She taped the last box, then looked at the stacks. "All those papers, and nothing helpful. Do you suppose Eve would let us take a look around Olivia's house?"

"We're not asking, and we're not breaking in, either."

"But there could be something there—something Eve and Hal and the police missed, something hidden."

"Something everybody else in the world missed that you and I could waltz in in the middle of the night and find on our first look through?"

She ignored his skeptical question. "If Jason Scott were a gentleman friend, wouldn't she have told someone? Maybe not her children—though I can't imagine either of them begrudging her a relationship with a man twenty years after their father's death—but her friends? I mean, women confide in people. Who did Olivia confide in?"

"Maybe there was nothing to confide. Jason Scott may not mean anything. The person she was calling could have been someone who lived in his house—an old friend or a long-lost relative."

His explanation was entirely too reasonable and made her frown as she picked up the top box. They loaded everything in the car, then drove past Hal's condo on the way so she could reassure herself that they weren't likely to meet him while at his sister's. One run-in with him was enough for one day. After picking up fried chicken in a box, they returned home for a quiet dinner with Hunter, who drooled but didn't beg. She rewarded him with the meat stripped from a piece or two.

After disposing of the bones where the dog couldn't reach them, Martin suggested, "How about a bath?"

Juliet blinked. Her fantasy yesterday about joining him in the shower had ended so delightfully that the mere implication of naked and wet was enough to make her hot. Before she could agree, though, he grinned and gestured to the dog. "For him. See if we can make him smell a little better. What do you say, Hunter? A bath, and then a walk so you can drip-dry outside."

They coaxed the dog into the bathroom and the tub. As the water began rising around him, he tried once to escape, then resigned himself to the indignity. After wetting him down, Juliet squirted a dollop of her own shampoo over his fur, then began lathering it. It was an herbal blend that smelled of jasmine blooms in the summer, and she loved it.

"No self-respecting male dog should smell like that," Martin complained. "When he goes out, every poodle in the neighborhood's going to come sniffing around."

"You wouldn't have a prissy little poodle, would you, Hunter?"

"He'll probably take after his mother—"

"Owner."

"And show a decided preference for strays."

She gave him a chiding look before opening the drain and turning on the handheld shower massager. With a long-suffering look on his scarred face, Hunter let her rinse away the suds, then, the minute she turned her back to reach for a towel, he bolted. Dripping water, he wrenched free of Martin's hold on his collar, forced his way between them and hit the hall at a run.

"Well." Martin's voice was low, carefully level and undeniably amused. "I guess he'd had enough of that."

Her dress was wet in great splotches from neck to hem, and his clothing was also damp. Water soaked the rug and puddled on the floor in the hall. No doubt as soon as the mutt had been sure he was free, he'd given a good, hard shake and splashed water on everything in sight. He'd made a mess, and she couldn't find it in herself to care.

Martin stood up and offered her a hand. His gaze was dark and intimate, his voice husky, when he spoke. "We could forget that walk. He's probably already shaken himself mostly dry, and you…" He turned her to face the mirror. The bodice of her dress had taken the brunt of the contact with Hunter, and the thin cotton was soaked, molding to her breasts like tissue. Not even the flowery print material could hide the swelling of her nipples.

He buried his face in her hair and was sliding his hands up her bare arms when, with a low bark, Hunter commanded their attention. He stood in the doorway, his curling tail dripping over his back, his leash dangling from his mouth. Maintaining a hold on the nylon, he barked again, then took a few steps toward the door.

"Someone used to walk him," Juliet murmured as she leaned back against Martin's chest. "That's kind of a chore. Why would someone go to that much trouble, then mistreat and abandon him?"

"Maybe the person who walked him lost him, and whoever found him mistreated him."

There was another bark, followed by a peek around the door frame. His look was so serious, his big brown eyes solemn and accusing. Even though she hadn't promised the walk, Juliet felt guilty. "All right, Hunter. I'll change clothes."

Five minutes later they were walking down the sidewalk, the dog's leash secured around her wrist, her hand clasped in Martin's. If the dog noticed that he was wet in the cool night air, he didn't care. He was too busy sniffing, exploring the limits of the leash and testing his strength against hers.

"Do you miss Dallas?"

Juliet glanced at Martin. "I thought I would. I thought moving away would be terribly hard, that it would take months, maybe even years, to get over being homesick. And I was homesick in the beginning. I got into town early on a Saturday morning and spent the entire day unpacking, shopping and keeping busy. But at bedtime I'd never felt so lost and alone in my life, not even when my mother died. I knew I had made a terrible mistake, and I wanted nothing more than to jump into my car, rush back home to Dallas and beg for my old job and my old house back."

"But?"

She shrugged. "I liked the town. My new jobs were challenging and interesting. This part of Colorado is certainly more impressive geographically than Dallas. And then I met you." He had made such a difference in her life. His leaving would make such a difference, too. If he left. If he had someplace to go back to once he remembered.

They reached a corner and went where Hunter led. Juliet glanced up at the street sign. "This is Poplar Street."

Martin's response was little more than a grunt.

"Olivia lived on Poplar."

Another grunt.

"Do you know where?"

He walked in silence for nearly a block before stopping to face a house. "Right here."

It was a nice middle-class house in a nice middle-class neighborhood, two stories with a yard that needed mowing and a garage at the back of the property. It didn't look any emptier than some of the other houses on the block, but it felt it. It felt…sad.

"I wonder why Eve and Hal haven't put it up for sale."

"There might be a problem with the will. Olivia left the house to all three children. Since no one knows where Roy Jr. is or if he's even alive, they would have to go through some legal maneuvers to be able to sell it."

The house was a nice accomplishment for a woman who'd spent her married life as a victim and hadn't gotten an education until her husband was dead and her oldest kid practically grown. Olivia had matured into a strong, capable woman who had provided a comfortable, loving and safe home for her younger children. Too bad it'd been too late for Roy Jr.

Curiously, Juliet looked around. The houses on either side both had lights on, but the ones across the street were dark. It would be so easy to walk up the driveway, around to the back of the house. While the front door would require a key or a skilled lockpick, the back door might be a simpler prospect—

"You're not going in."

She looked up. The nearest street lamp cast a yellow glow over Martin's features, highlighting the warning in his expression. "Did I say I was?"

"No, but you have that look. You're not breaking into

a dead woman's house. You know nothing about picking locks, and you don't even have a flashlight.''

With a grin, she pulled her free hand from her jacket pocket. She'd grabbed the compact flashlight while changing into jeans and a dark T-shirt in her bedroom. ''Just in case we wandered off onto any poorly lit streets. Do *you* know how to pick a lock?''

He was shaking his head, but more at her audacity, she suspected, than in response to her question. The question he intended to ignore. There were things about his past that he didn't like to admit to because he didn't like the obvious implication. Being skilled at breaking and entering was one of them.

''Just a quick look around.''

''No.''

''Look at those windows. The drapes are closed on every one, and they're so heavy that there's no way this little flashlight would show through.''

''Juliet—''

''Martin.'' She grinned again. ''We might find out who Jason Scott is.''

''The police have been through her house.''

''They went through all her papers, too, and they missed Jason Scott. Maybe they missed something in there.''

''Do you know what the penalty is for breaking and entering—and into the beloved Mayor Olivia Stuart's house, no less? You wouldn't have to worry about losing your job or finding another one because Hal Stuart would have us both strung up on the courthouse lawn.''

''Let's just walk around back. Let's see how easy it would be.''

''No.'' He tightened his fingers around hers. ''We're getting out of here, and you're not coming back alone. Do you understand?''

Hunter, traitor that he was, happily took off when Martin began walking again. Juliet had no choice but to move or be dragged along. They walked to the end of the block in silence, turned onto another street, then Martin stopped in the shade of a tall oak. "I'm waiting for an answer. You're not going to break into Olivia Stuart's house, right?" At her silent, mutinous look, he cupped both palms to her face and brushed his mouth across hers, then rephrased the question to one she couldn't help but answer. "You're not going to prove that I'm a bad influence who has no business in your life, are you?"

"No."

"You won't come back to Olivia's without me."

"No."

He kissed her before reclaiming her hand and moving onto the sidewalk again. She was disappointed. Maybe it was just wishful thinking, but she was sure that they could find something of help in Olivia's house. But she couldn't blame him for being so insistent. In the past he'd forgotten, he had most likely been the breaking-and-entering kind, and he was convinced that he'd been the murdering kind. He was afraid that he might once again resort to such practices, to succumb once again to such a life-style.

So whatever clues might be hidden in Olivia's house would have to remain hidden. And maybe he was right. Maybe there weren't any clues. Maybe she would be risking her job, her reputation and her freedom for nothing.

As they walked, the houses grew shabbier. The streetlights came farther apart, the sidewalks gave way to paths in the grass, and the curbs disappeared from the street. At one time the houses had been decent—twenty, maybe thirty years ago—but they'd gone into a steady decline since. The yards were junky, the houses in need of regular maintenance. They had reached the part of town called the Downs. If she were alone with Hunter, she would have turned around at the last intersection. Even with Martin at her side, she would prefer to go back, but he showed no such interest. In fact, something about this sadly rundown part of town captured his attention.

They moved into the street, walking near the edge in the

shadows of overgrown trees and distant street lamps. She clung a little tighter to his hand, but he didn't notice. He didn't seem to remember that she was even there.

His steps slowed until finally he stopped in front of a dilapidated house. It was abandoned now, with boards over the windows and the front door missing from its hinges. It was two stories, and the front had last been painted yellow, with the sides weathered gray.

Martin gestured to the overgrown lot next door. "There was a house there that burned down. This house used to be blue. And that stop sign was put in—" he gestured toward the corner ahead "—after an accident killed three people."

She didn't know whether to ask questions that might help him remember more or to remain silent so she wouldn't disturb his concentration. She chose silence.

"There was a fence around this yard—little white pickets—and roses in that yard. The police came here—" his open arms encompassed the entire neighborhood "—a lot."

Juliet looked for an address and found none, not on this house or the next. She made a mental note to stop by the courthouse and find out who owned these properties, then track down the police department's old records. If the death in his dreams had really happened, maybe it had happened here on this street.

Suddenly he shivered and looked at her. His eyes were particularly vulnerable. "Let's go home, Martin," she suggested softly.

He nodded, and they started back. But all the way down the street, he kept looking over his shoulder as if to make sure that they weren't being followed. They were, of course. By memories. By ghosts.

After breakfast Saturday morning, Juliet dropped Martin off at the church. The pastor had asked him to come in for a few hours so at least one of the classrooms would be ready for Sunday services. Initially she'd welcomed the morning alone. She could clean house, do laundry, run to the grocery store—all the boring things she never got done while he was around—but it didn't take long at all for her to start missing him. After all, there wasn't that much cleaning or laundry or shopping to do. She didn't want to pass the rest of the morning on the computer, wasn't in the mood to answer E-mail or particularly curious about what was going on in the rest of the world. She only wanted to be with Martin.

In anticipation of a dusty job, she traded her dress for jeans and a T-shirt, then drove downtown and parked in her reserved space at the police department. Though she hadn't expected to see Stone Richardson, she was pleased to see his car in his usual space.

She found him at his desk, doing the old hunt-and-peck. When she sat down, he sprawled back in his chair. "What can I do for you?"

"I have a couple of questions. Is there any conceivable way a cop's fingerprints wouldn't be in the FBI's database?"

"Nope."

The swiftness and certainty of his answer deflated her hopes. She'd known it was a long shot, but there was so much about Martin that suggested some law enforcement experience. Of course, it could be twisted around to also suggest some criminal experience, but she'd hoped… "None at all? What if a federal agent were working undercover, trying to identify dirty cops? Would those cops be able to run his fingerprints and find out that he was an undercover agent?"

"No."

"Then it's possible—"

He held up one hand to stop her. "Say a DEA agent is working in deep cover. The DEA gives him a fake identity and all the documentation to support that identity—a driver's license, birth certificate, automobile registration, et cetera. The place where he lives, the utilities, his credit cards and everything else will come back to that name. If, for the purpose of the investigation, he needs to have an arrest record, they'll create that for him, too. If he gets arrested and his fingerprints are sent to the FBI, the bureau will know who this person really is. They'll also know that his prints have been flagged or blocked, so the first thing they'll do is notify the DEA. The DEA might contact the police department and find out what they want to know and why, or—in a situation such as you described—they would have the bureau verify the guy's fake identity and then contact him directly to let him know that he's making his subjects suspicious." He gave her a curious look. "Is this about Martin?"

She shrugged.

"If he were a cop or a fed, even working undercover, they would have responded to the initial missing persons bulletin we sent out. I mean, it said in plain English that we were trying to identify a John Doe suffering from amnesia. Somebody would have been on the phone to us in an instant. So…now that I've shot down that theory, what's your other question?"

"The old police records. Where are they stored?" That was the reason for her jeans and shirt. Old records tended to be dusty and musty and stored in old boxes. She'd wanted to be comfortable for her search through them.

"The department has a warehouse over on Third Street. Everything's all boxed up and dated. What in particular are you interested in?"

"Any unsolved murders that happened longer than eighteen years ago but no longer than thirty-three."

"Open homicides are in the files right here. I'll get them." He left his desk and returned a moment later with only a few slim folders. She'd expected a heftier stack, and the expression on her face must have indicated as much, because he grinned. "We're good around here. We have about a ninety-five-percent solve rate."

"Except for Olivia's," she said softly, and his grin disappeared.

"We're still trying."

She opened the files one at a time and scanned the reports inside. There was a man killed by his next-door neighbor in a feud over the property line; the neighbor had fled town immediately following the murder and never been located. The second was a woman found shot to death outside the company where she worked; her estranged husband was the only suspect, but he, too, had disappeared. There were three murders whose victims were also women, and that was all.

Martin was certain that the person he'd killed was a man. There was no question of that. If it had happened in Grand Springs, it had been ruled a suicide, an accident or self-defense. But maybe it hadn't happened in Grand Springs.

Maybe it hadn't happened anywhere, except in the dreams of a troubled man.

"Anything else I can do you?"

She smiled vaguely and shook her head. "Thanks for the help." She was about ten feet from his desk when she abruptly turned back. "Stone, what do you think of Maxwell Brown?"

"What's your interest in him?"

"I met him the other day," she lied. "I don't find him as likable as other people seem to. I was just curious about what you think."

"I don't like him much, either. He makes a lot of money, and he likes to flash it around."

"He's very generous with the local charities."

"And he's very public about it. It's part of his showing off—his way of saying, 'Hey, look, I have so much money that I can afford to give hundreds of thousands of dollars to you losers.'"

"Other than being condescending and flashy, you don't think there's anything a little off about him?"

He looked puzzled. "He's never been in any trouble.

From what I can tell, he never does anything but work and spend his fortune.''

With another vague smile and a thanks, she left the department. It was only eleven o'clock and Martin wasn't scheduled to finish at the church until one, but she intended to show up, anyway. Maybe she could help out. If not, maybe she could just sit and watch him. That was always a pleasurable pastime.

Martin switched off the headlights, pulled onto the shoulder of the road, then eased onto the right-of-way before shutting off the engine. For a moment, he sat there, scowling so hard that his jaw ached. What the hell was he doing here yet again? How had he let Juliet talk him into another damn fool evening of tailing Maxwell Brown?

At least this time he'd come better prepared. He'd used heavy-duty duct tape to ensure that the interior light wouldn't come on when the doors were opened. Juliet's powerful little flashlight was in his pocket, and a hunting knife in a leather sheath was tucked in the small of his back. It wasn't as comforting as the gun he usually wore there, but it was better than nothing. And he was good with a knife. He knew how to use one to protect himself, knew how to defend himself against one.

Better prepared or not, he would still rather be safe at home. No, that wasn't entirely true. He was curious as hell about Maxwell Brown's activities, and he wanted to see what was going on out here at the trucking company warehouse tonight. He wished *Juliet* was safe at home. Keeping himself safe and out of sight was problem enough. He didn't want to worry about her, too.

She was dressed in black—jeans, shirt, windbreaker with a hood to cover her hair. He wore dark clothes, too, and a similar windbreaker, but where he looked sinister, the all-black get-up somehow merely emphasized her innocence. Not even the most suspicious person in the world could take one look at her and think that she was up to something. She looked so damn angelic.

"Are you ready?" she whispered, though they hadn't left the car yet. He didn't comment on it, but climbed out and slid the keys deep into his pocket.

The trip through the woods to the drainage ditch was no easier this time than the time before. They slipped and stumbled through the darkness. As he worked his way down the sloping sides of the ditch, Juliet lost her footing and slid into him. He reached back to steady her, then felt her hand at his waist.

"What is this?" she whispered, her mouth over his ear making him shiver.

"Just a little protection."

She groped the shape of the knife and recognized it. "Martin?"

He turned to face her. Moonlight showed the concern on her face. "You don't go into a potentially dangerous situation unarmed. I normally carry a gun, but I don't happen to have one."

"You remembered that."

"Last time we were here." He held her gaze for a moment, then turned away.

The bottom of the ditch wasn't much easier going. The ground wasn't level, and the chunks of rock scattered across it shifted under their weight. All he needed was to fall and break an ankle out here behind Brown's warehouse. Then they would be in a fine mess.

At about the same place they'd stopped before, he motioned for Juliet to wait, then inched up the slope. A tractor-trailer was parked parallel to the fence, but he had a perfect view between the wheels to the loading dock where all the activity was centered. Brown was there, as well as his second-in-command from the other night. In fact, from what he could tell, all the men who were here tonight had also been here Wednesday night. That made sense, of course. No doubt, part of Grand Springs Trucking's business was strictly legitimate, and so were some of their employees. The illicit part of their business would be restricted to the same crew of trusted workers.

As the men unloaded wooden crates from one truck and took them inside, Brown paced back and forth, looking every few minutes at his watch.

"You think he's in a hurry or expecting someone?"

Martin glanced at Juliet. She had moved into place beside him without making a sound. She was getting good at this covert stuff. *Too* good. He didn't want her to develop a taste for excitement and danger. He wanted her to prefer a quiet evening home alone over sneaking around in the dark and risking her life.

He shrugged in response to her whisper, then turned his attention back to the warehouse. If he could get inside the fence, get up close enough to hear what was being said… It wasn't impossible. He could cut the fence on the far side just wide enough to slip through, make his way through the shadows to the building and find cover among the pallets and crates stacked around the loading dock. But no matter how strenuously he insisted to Juliet that she had to wait behind, he had no doubt that he wouldn't make it fifty feet before he found her tagging along like an overeager puppy.

No, he would have to be satisfied with watching. And wondering.

Headlights came from around the corner of the building, sweeping across the ground where they lay. He ducked his head so that nothing showed but a dark hump, like all the other dark humps of rocks, and made sure Juliet did the same. As soon as darkness settled again, he eased his head up and watched as the car parked next to the trailer being unloaded and the driver climbed out.

It was Hal Stuart.

He joined Maxwell Brown on the platform, his hands in his pockets, his expression grim, and watched the men work. Where it appeared business as usual for Brown, Hal seemed uneasy, as if he'd rather be anywhere in the world than here. He paced back and forth, gave only brief answers whenever anyone spoke to him and used impatient gestures when he spoke.

When the last crate was unloaded, a driver climbed into the cab and pulled the truck away. A second trailer, painted dark blue and bearing the name of a different shipping company, backed into the same space, and Hal and Brown went inside.

Why a different company? There was nowhere Big Blue Shipping out of Cheyenne, Wyoming, could go that Grand Springs Trucking couldn't. Maybe there was some odd stipulation in a contract specifying that separate companies handle each leg of the shipment. Or maybe it was simple subterfuge. If a law enforcement agency suspected that Grand Springs Trucking was involved in smuggling, they would pay closer attention to those trucks. They might search a Grand Springs truck or put a dog through it, but not look twice at a Big Blue truck.

Last time, once Brown had gone inside, they had left. Tonight Martin waited. Five minutes stretched into ten. Ten became twenty. He became aware of a rock pressing against his knee and moved to a more comfortable position. Beside him, Juliet did the same, sending a small shower of dirt down the hill to bounce off the rocks below.

The men were loading the second trailer with packing boxes of the sort used to move household goods. They brought them out on dollies, two and three at a time in varying sizes. Martin counted more than thirty before he gave up. Several loads later, they began bringing out furniture. A legitimate shipment?

The need to rub the back of his neck was the only answer Martin required.

Once the truck was loaded, the driver left. For a few moments, the rumble of the engine filled the night, then faded away somewhere toward the interstate. Hal and Brown came out once again and walked to the steps, where

Brown extended his hand. Hal clearly didn't want to take it, but did, switching the briefcase he carried to his left hand, giving Brown a swift handshake. He hurried down the steps, put the briefcase in the trunk, then drove away. Five minutes later Maxwell Brown drove away, and ten minutes after that, the workers shut off all but the perimeter lights and left.

Martin tapped Juliet on the shoulder, then moved down into the ditch. They worked their way back to the car, then drove home in silence. At the house, she went straight into the dining room and sat down in front of the computer. He watched as she clicked her way into a directory of business directories. There were nearly fifty listings, and she started with the first, running a search for Big Blue Shipping.

She worked methodically through directory after directory, but there was no listing for such a company, not in Wyoming, not anywhere. After the last futile try, she faced him and shrugged. "It seems funny saying this after seeing that big blue truck, but apparently Big Blue Shipping doesn't exist."

Why wasn't he surprised?

"You think it's drugs."

He nodded.

"And Hal's involved. Do you think he uses?"

"Probably not. Most dealers don't."

She looked surprised. He felt it. Granted, he didn't like Hal Stuart, but that didn't make it any easier to reconcile the popular image of a drug dealer with the clean-cut, well-dressed, respected lawyer. But major drug dealers were often clean-cut, well-dressed businessmen. They didn't use their product; they didn't sell to others to support their own habits; they considered the selling of drugs a business, nothing more.

"He probably got into it for the money," Juliet said softly. "It must have seemed an easy way to bring in a little extra cash, tax free and—with the right precautions—practically risk free."

"Until his mother found out."

"Do you think he killed her?"

Instinct said no. Hal Stuart might be many things, but a murderer wasn't one of them. He couldn't arrange his own mother's death just to protect his sideline, no matter how profitable. "I think Maxwell Brown killed her. Hal probably didn't know anything about it. He might still be in the dark."

She shook her head. "He must suspect something. He's not a stupid man. He doesn't want us looking into her death, and we both think that what everyone else excuses as grief is more likely guilt. Even if he doesn't know for a fact that Brown had Olivia killed, he must suspect it."

"I don't understand him. If I thought that my partner had killed a member of my family, I'd find out the truth, then kill the bastard. But Hal is still doing business with Brown. Maybe..." But he didn't have any maybes to offer. No excuses. And why would he want to make excuses for Hal Stuart, anyway? He didn't even like the guy.

"So what do we do now? Go to the police?"

"And tell them what? That Brown's shipping boxes out of his trucking company warehouses? You think that's going to make Stone sit up and take notice?" He shook his head. "We do what we've been doing. We snoop. We watch. We wait. And when we get proof, *then* we go to the police."

When Juliet arrived at her office Monday morning, Mariellen's desk was, not surprisingly, empty. She left her purse in her office, then went into the common area for a cup of coffee. Stone stood beside his desk, pulling on a jacket that hid his holster while Jack Stryker waited impatiently. She wondered where they were off to in such a hurry, but didn't ask.

Back in her office, she settled in front of the computer and wondered how late Mariellen would be today. She wondered what Martin was doing, how he would pass the next few hours until their lunch date at twelve. She wondered about the two bulletins she had sent out, the missing persons report and the request for information on gunshot victims, and when or if she would ever get back a response.

She wondered about everything in the world except work. This was so unlike her. She'd never been one to let her personal life interfere with her work...but then, she'd never really *had* a personal life. For thirty-four years she'd been so dull and dreary, the human equivalent of a bump on a log. This was the first time she'd ever felt truly alive and vital. It might not do much for her work, but she liked the feeling.

With a sigh, she forced her attention to the computer. Once the new system was completely up and running, she would be spending a good portion of her time offering instruction to the officers who would use it. She had a knack for stripping highly technical applications down to their simple, A-B-C bones. At her last job, one of her co-workers had commented that she'd be great teaching children. The only children she had any interest in teaching were her own, and at the time, she'd thought she would never have any. But maybe she would—tough little blond-haired, blue-eyed boys and sweet little girls. Maybe— .

She made a face at the computer screen, then concentrated hard. For all her careless talk last week about losing her job, she couldn't afford to find herself unemployed.

She was in serious working mode a half hour later when Mariellen came into the office. "Hi," she greeted, dropping into the chair. "You busy?"

Juliet unclenched her jaw. "You're late."

"Hmm? Oh, yeah. Just a little. Hey, did you hear the news? The Denver police arrested Dean Springer this morning. On a routine traffic stop. Can you believe it? The guy's driving through town just before the sun's up enough to turn his lights off, and he gets stopped for a broken taillight. He's got a fake driver's license, and there're no wants or warrants, but the cop knows he's seen the guy before, and boom, just as Springer's about to drive off, the cop remembers the wanted poster and pops him. The guy's evaded arrest on murder charges for *months,* and a little thing like a broken taillight brings him down. Can you believe it?''

A shiver of something—anticipation? excitement? fear?—rustled down Juliet's spine. What she knew—apparently, what anyone knew—about Dean Springer wouldn't fill the blank space on a postage stamp. Would he prove more closemouthed than his accomplice, Joanna Jackson, or would he readily name his boss? She supposed it depended on one thing: was he more afraid of prison or Maxwell Brown?

She had little doubt that, if Springer named names, Brown's would come first. She wasn't sure if she was trusting her own instincts or Martin's, but she was sure that Maxwell Brown had played a part in Olivia's death. Maybe he ordered it or maybe he merely arranged it for Hal, but he was responsible.

''Stone and Jack have gone to Denver to pick him up and bring him back here. This is the first break they've had in months, so they must be pretty excited. It's really bothered everyone, you know, that they're able to solve all their other cases but not the most important one. I mean, everyone wants to see Olivia's killers punished. Especially Hal and Eve. I wonder if they know—''

''If they don't, it's not your place to tell them.'' Judging by Mariellen's wounded look, Juliet's tone was sharper than she'd intended, but she didn't apologize. If Hal was as guilty as they believed, the last thing she wanted was for him to have advance warning that the police were about to close in on him. He was liable to flee, and they would never find him again.

Mariellen got to her feet. ''I would never take it on myself to break such news to anyone. I told you only because you're part of the department. You'd hear it, anyway. I'd better get to work.''

Now Juliet did feel as if she should apologize. But she

didn't leave her desk. Instead, she thought about Martin. He should know, but she couldn't just leave work and tell him. She couldn't call him, either, since he had no phone at his apartment. He might not be home, anyway. He might have had things to do before lunch.

Her gaze strayed to the clock. And strayed. And strayed. By the time the hands read eleven-forty-five, she was too antsy to wait any longer. She grabbed her purse, clocked out and headed outside. It was a warm day, and the restaurant was only four blocks away, so she bypassed her car and headed down the street.

She was crossing the street to the last block when two men came out of a building a few short yards ahead: Hal Stuart and Maxwell Brown. Hal was carrying a black nylon bag, the sort used for a laptop computer, and he looked agitated. Brown looked the same as always. His suit was impeccably tailored, his smile practiced, friendlier than the look in his eyes. Neither man noticed her right away, but her steps slowed, anyway. The sidewalk wasn't broad enough to leave her a comfort zone to pass them. She could cross the street, but it would seem odd if anyone noticed, and the last thing she wanted was to make either man think something was odd. Drawing a deep breath, she cast her gaze to the ground and forged ahead as if deep in thought and unaware that she shared the sidewalk with anyone.

It wasn't a smart move. She drew close enough to hear Hal murmur, "Not going anywhere with you!" then his hand closed around her arm and shoved her hard toward Brown. As she stumbled backward, he broke into a run, darting into the street and bringing traffic to a screeching halt, all the while shouting, "Help! Help! He's got a gun!"

Pedestrians stopped on the sidewalk, drivers climbed out of their cars, and, from down the block, two police officers came running.

Juliet staggered to a stop against the brick wall, banging her head hard enough to make her eyes sting. Before she could think, before she could make sense of what was happening, the two officers were crouched behind a car in the street, their guns drawn.

"Put the gun down, Mr. Brown."

Gun? *Gun?* Juliet swung around to look at the man beside her. He held a nasty-looking pistol in one hand and was muttering to himself. "Stupid bastard. I should have killed him when I took care of—" Abruptly he looked at her, and an unholy light came into his eyes. Too late she tried to move, tried to push away from the wall and flee, but her body was heavy, her brain too muddled to send the proper commands.

The same officer spoke again. "Mr. Brown, whatever the problem is, we can talk it out. Just put—"

He jerked her away from the wall, holding her as a shield with his arm tight across her shoulders. A murmur of shock went up from the bystanders when he pressed the cold, dark barrel of the gun beneath her chin. "You put too much faith in talk," he said, his voice loud in Juliet's ear. "I'll talk, all right. With someone who can guarantee me safe passage out of here. Get the chief over here. Oh, and tell him I've got a hostage."

Eleven

Martin was waiting outside the restaurant when a commotion arose down the street. From the sidewalk on the opposite side of the street, a man ran into the road, traffic skidded to a stop, and horns blared. The guy was yelling something, but Martin was too far away to hear the words. He saw great dramatic gestures, though, and, even from this distance, recognized fear.

Pushing away from the wall, he rubbed the back of his neck as he took a few steps in that direction. The rub didn't ease the sudden discomfort there. Neither did the distant wail of sirens. He glanced down the street in each direction. People were gathering, making their way toward the end of the block, talking excitedly among themselves. He should see Juliet among those people. It was nearly noon, time for her to meet him here. If she'd driven, her car should be among those stopped in the street. If she'd walked...

He began running, dodging people, pushing into the street where there were fewer obstacles. Just as he neared the cars where two cops had taken cover, a gunshot sounded, its noise muffled by all the surrounding sound but shattering just the same. Bystanders screamed, dropped to the ground or ran away. Martin ran even faster toward the commotion.

"Smith!" One of the cops grabbed him, yanked him down behind a car. "He's not going to hurt her. She'll be all right."

Twisting around to face the office building, he saw what

the fear had already known, what the ache in his neck had meant. Maxwell Brown was struggling with the door of the building. The gunshot had been a warning to the officers not to try anything while he forced his hostage inside.

His hostage. *Juliet.*

Finally Brown succeeded, dragging Juliet inside and out of sight. The last thing Martin saw before the door was kicked shut again was her face. Her eyes. Her terrified, pleading blue eyes.

He sank to the pavement, sick inside. He'd known better than to involve her in this mess. He'd worried about her safety, but he hadn't stopped. He hadn't backed off and done whatever was necessary to keep her out of danger. Now, thanks to him, she was in more danger than either of them had ever imagined. Now, thanks to him, she might die. Then he surely would.

How had Brown known? They had never come face-to-face with him. They had never done a thing to attract his attention. Sure, he'd seen her car parked out in front of his house one night, but people parked on the streets, even in his neighborhood, and he hadn't seen *them.* What in hell had made him suspicious of her?

Just then his gaze connected with someone in the crowd, and he knew he had his answer. There was such distress on Hal Stuart's face. Such guilt.

Martin surged to his feet and shoved through the crowd. At the same time, Hal began walking away, excusing himself politely at first, then shoving people out of his way. He was near the intersection when Martin caught him, grabbing handfuls of his suit coat, pushing him against the wall. "What the hell have you done?"

"I— I haven't— I didn't—" Hal drew a breath, then pulled his indignation around him like a cloak. "I don't know what you're talking about. The man is obviously crazy. Your little friend apparently angered him, and he—"

"Yeah, right."

Still holding Hal, Martin turned to see a boy of about

twelve leaning against the wall nearby. "You see what happened?"

"They came out of the building together—him and that other guy. The woman was just walking by, and he—" he jerked his head toward Hal "—grabbed her and shoved her at the other guy, then ran away." The boy's voice turned scornful. "He used her to get away."

For a moment Hal tried to bluster his way through. Then his shoulders sagged. "He had a gun. He would have killed me."

Martin could kill him. It would be so easy to wrap his hands around the bastard's neck and squeeze the life out of him one precious breath at a time. He could snap his neck, or he could just beat him to a bloody, lifeless pulp right here on the street. *So easy.*

But he didn't. He leaned forward, closer than he'd ever been to anyone but Juliet, close enough to make Hal flinch and try to press himself right into the stone at his back. "Big mistake, pal," he whispered. "Because if he kills her, if he hurts her in any way, I'll kill you, and it won't be as quick and easy as a bullet to the head. I'll make you suffer, you worthless son of a bitch. I'll make you beg to die. Do you understand?"

His expression one of pure terror, Hal managed a nod.

Martin backed off a step or two, released his hold on the coat, smoothed the wrinkles, then clamped his fingers around Hal's arm. "Get over here. The police will need your help."

Other officers had arrived and were blocking off the area, moving spectators back. One tried to block Martin's way, but took one look at his face and stepped aside.

"What the hell's going on here?" Chief Sanderson demanded.

"We have a hostage situation, sir," one of the first two cops on the scene volunteered.

"You told me that on the radio. What hostage? What situation? Where are they?"

"They're in Stuart's office building," Martin replied. "Seems Maxwell Brown got a little ticked off with Hal."

The chief looked from him to Hal, then back. "If he's ticked with Hal, why does he have someone else as hostage?"

"Being the big man that he is, Hal grabbed a woman walking by and used her so he could escape." Martin's voice dropped a tone or two and became thick with emotion. "It's Juliet."

The chief gave him a look of sympathy before turning to Hal. "Is anyone else in the building?"

"My secretary has gone to lunch."

The chief grunted acknowledgment, then began shouting orders. Officers started to evacuate the surrounding buildings. Others pushed the crowds back even farther, and still others began clearing the traffic stopped on the block preparatory to setting up barricades.

Martin stood where he was, staring at the building and listening to Hal explain the layout to the chief. The building was two stories and maybe fifty feet wide. Hal's offices occupied the first floor, and the second floor was empty, used only to store some cartons. Years ago a dance school had filled that space. There were a few cubicles in the corners—an office and dressing rooms—but the rest of the floor was open, one large expanse of hardwood floor with mirrors on the two long sides. The stairs came up at the back—half a flight, a large landing, then the remaining half flight.

Brown had taken Juliet to the second floor. Martin was convinced of it. There were two windows at the front of the building where he could keep an eye on what was going on out here, two windows covered with blinds that denied a rooftop sniper even a glimpse into the room. There was only one way in—the stairs—and the way Hal described them, it would be virtually impossible for anyone to sneak up them unnoticed. Even if he managed, cardboard cartons didn't provide much cover, and there were the mirrors, reflecting every move he made.

There was no phone on the second floor, but Brown, being the consummate businessman, had a cellular. Once they'd located the number, the chief called him. "Maxwell, son, I don't know what's going on here, but this is no way to deal with it. Let my computer programmer go, put the gun away, and we'll talk."

What *was* going on? Martin wondered as he stared at the second-floor windows. What had happened to make Maxwell Brown panic? Why had he gone looking for Hal Stuart with a gun, apparently intending to kill him? Maybe the Big Blue shipment had been diverted by untrustworthy employees. Maybe it had been discovered by the authorities. Maybe Hal had finally connected Brown to Olivia's murder and had threatened to go to the police. Maybe he'd tried to blackmail Brown. Maybe—

The touch of a hand on his arm startled him. He jerked around to see Stone standing beside him.

"She'll be okay," the detective said quietly.

Martin wanted to believe it, more than he'd ever wanted anything. While one part of his mind had been fixated on the situation, the other part had been frantically praying, offering God whatever deals were necessary to keep Juliet safe. He would leave her and Grand Springs, would give her up completely and live the rest of his life missing her if that was what it took. Or he would stay, would stay here forever, would marry her and spend the rest of his life loving and keeping her safe. He would do anything, would trade places with her, would trade his life for hers.

"She'll be okay," Stone repeated. "Maxwell Brown—"

"Is a killer."

Stone stared at him. "How did you—"

Now it was Martin's turn to stare. How did you know? the cop had been about to ask. Not, Why do you say that? Not, Are you crazy? Not, Brown is a respectable businessman, but, How did you know? Which meant that Stone knew, too. Which meant— "You found Dean Springer, didn't you?"

Stone's gaze narrowed. "Nobody outside the department is supposed to know that we picked him up this morning in Denver. Did Juliet tell you?"

Martin shook his head. No doubt she would have once she'd reached the restaurant, but thanks to Brown—and Hal—she'd never made it.

"Then how do you know?"

"We've been trying to prove a few theories of our own."

"Such as?"

Martin dragged his hand through his hair and watched the chief for a moment. Sanderson didn't seem to be making any progress with Brown. "We think Brown is using his trucking company and his car dealership and his airplanes to smuggle drugs. The mayor found out, and he had her killed."

"And you came to this conclusion based on...?"

"Instinct."

"You're right. Springer admitted everything." Stone's look was part chagrined, part disbelieving. "Instinct. A man without a past and a woman who eats, breathes and sleeps computers, and your instincts are better than the combined resources of the Grand Springs PD."

Staring at the building again, Martin shrugged. "I think...maybe I had some experience with drug smuggling."

Stone didn't immediately discount his words the way Juliet had. Of course, Stone was a cop, which was just another way of saying a cynic. He was paid to look twice at people, to not take them at face value, to look at actions and suspect motives. Juliet was an innocent, a woman who knew machines better than people, a woman in love. She wanted to believe the best of him.

"If Brown lets Juliet go, will the chief let him walk?" he asked abruptly.

"He ordered the murder of our mayor," Stone reminded

him, then reluctantly answered his question. "I don't think so."

Martin didn't like the answer, but it didn't surprise him. That wasn't the important question, anyway. What mattered—all that mattered—was whether Brown was desperate enough to kill Juliet. If he knew he had nothing to gain by holding her, he might let her go. But if he knew he had nothing to gain by freeing her, he might kill her. It would be his last defiant act, his last chance to flout the law.

Because, without Juliet, Martin would have nothing to gain by showing restraint, nothing to lose by venting his rage. He would have no choice at all.

He would kill Brown.

The air on the second floor was stifling and dancing with dust. Juliet sat in the middle of the floor, fifteen feet from the front of the building, in a straight-backed wooden chair, one of a dozen that had lined one wall. Her hands were tied behind her back with a length of faded pink ribbon, left behind by some long-ago ballerina, and her ankles were secured to one wooden chair leg with Maxwell Brown's silk tie.

She was hot. Hungry. Thirsty. And she had to go to the bathroom.

She tried to smile mockingly, to make fun of her urgent needs. She hadn't been here more than an hour, and it looked as if she would be here a lot longer, but suddenly everything she felt was intensified. The mild hunger she'd felt before leaving her office was now ravenous. Her throat was as dry as if she'd been days without water, and the bathroom... Well, the others might be exaggerated by the situation, but she really did have to go to the bathroom, more with each passing minute. As long as she concentrated on that, she didn't have to think so much about the situation she was in.

Brown stood at the front of the room between the two windows. Twice he'd talked to someone on his cellular phone—the police, she assumed—and both times he'd hung up in anger. Another half-dozen times he'd listened to it ring repeatedly before finally shutting off the power and laying it on a nearby chair. Since then he'd stared at the wall.

She would be absolutely terrified if Martin wasn't outside. As it was, she was pretty damn scared. After their first excursion to the trucking company warehouse, she'd thought she wanted more excitement, thrills and danger in her life, but she'd been wrong. All she wanted now was to lock herself inside her pretty little house with Martin and Hunter and never come out again. She never wanted to be excited again. God help her, if she lived through this, she would never go looking for danger again.

"Excuse me." When Brown gave no sign of hearing her, she cleared her throat and spoke louder. "Excuse me. I have to go to the bathroom."

"Forget it."

"*Forget it?* It's a natural function of the body. It occurs whether you want it to or not. I can't *forget* it."

"There's not a bathroom handy."

"Oh, please. This was a dance studio. Little kids came here for dance classes that lasted an hour at a time."

Finally he gave her a derisive look over one shoulder. "And your point is?"

"Kids go to the bathroom at the drop of a hat. They have to go all the time when they're supposed to be doing something else. One of those little rooms *has* to be a bathroom."

Acting as if she were more trouble than she was worth—*and if that's true, then, please, God, make him let me go!*—he checked first one corner, then the other. The third door he opened led into a bathroom.

He untied her hands, then stood guard while she undid the tie around her ankles. Nudging her with the gun, he followed her to the small room, backing off only when she closed the door.

The room was tiny and dusty. There was no window and only the flimsiest of locks on the door—probably so teachers could rescue small children who locked themselves in. If she'd ever been forced to take dance lessons, that was an option she would have considered.

After taking care of business, she washed her hands, then caught her reflection in the mirror. Her face was white, her cheeks bright crimson, and her eyes had doubled in size. She looked scared half out of her mind. She *was* scared. Maxwell Brown was a cold-blooded killer. He'd had no qualms about ordering the murder of a woman he'd known most of his life, a woman he'd chaired committees with, danced with at charity balls and publicly declared a friend. Apparently, he'd been ready to deal the same fate to Hal until she'd had the misfortune to walk past. He wouldn't hesitate to kill her, too, if he thought it necessary.

Tears welled in her eyes. She was too young to die. She had too much unfinished business. Who would take care of Hunter? Who would finish the work she'd started? Who would deal with her house? And who would love Martin?

The doorknob jiggled, and she rapidly wiped her hands across her eyes. She was turning toward the door when suddenly it swung open under the tremendous force of a kick, brushing just millimeters past her and bouncing off the wall.

"No more locking the door," Brown said. The twisted metal that had once been the lock ensured that.

With the gun pointed square in her back, she returned to the chair, where he tied her once again. "Why are you doing this?" she asked as he walked away.

"Over the last twenty years I've made a lot of money. I've lived quite a life." He smiled a chilling smile. "I've grown accustomed to luxury."

And, of course, prisons could hardly be described as luxurious. "This is pointless. They're not going to let you walk out of here."

"Don't tell me that, sweetheart. If a hostage can't guarantee safe passage, then what is she good for besides killing?"

She clamped her mouth shut for a time, then murmured, "I don't deserve this."

"No, you don't. I don't even know who the hell you are. Sanderson said something about computers?"

"I'm setting up the new systems at the library and the police department. My name is Juliet."

He snorted. "Too bad there's no Romeo around to save you."

But there was. He was outside, and he was looking for a way to rescue her. She knew he was.

The minutes crawled past. Her gaze kept straying to the big clock on the wall, but it had stopped working ages ago. According to it, it was eleven-eighteen forever. Her shoulders were starting to burn from the awkward position, and her fingers had lost some sensation. She was miserable, but misery she could deal with.

Terror, she couldn't.

After a time—a few minutes? a few hours?—Brown turned on the phone. It rang almost immediately. For the first time he gave the chief a list of demands: all officers pulled back at least a block, transportation to the airport, one of his own pilots and one of his own planes, fueled and ready to go. If there were no attempts at capture or rescue, if they got away safely, at the first opportunity, he would instruct the pilot to land and would release Juliet. If not, he would kill her.

She wondered if Chief Sanderson believed him. She wondered if she did. On the one hand, if he had a pretty clean getaway, why add another murder to the charges against him? That seemed foolish. On the other hand, she could see his face, his expression, his eyes. Why leave a witness who could testify against him? That was foolish, too.

Apparently, the chief tried to negotiate. Brown grew an-

gry and snapped, "You've heard what I want. Now get it!"
and disconnected the call.

Once his annoyance had slipped away, Juliet cleared her
throat and timidly asked, "Now what?"

"Now we wait."

Night had fallen. Only a few die-hard gawkers remained
on the sidewalk behind the barricades. Chief Sanderson had
turned control of the situation over to Stone and gone home.
Hal had gone home, too, hours ago, with a couple of officers assigned to keep an eye on him. With Brown holed up
inside the office building, he didn't need the protection, Hal
had insisted. They weren't there to protect him, the chief
had explained. He'd left it to Hal to figure out that they
were there to make sure he didn't go anywhere.

Twelve hours ago, if it'd been up to him, Martin would
have thrown Hal in jail. Hell, he'd have hurt him, maybe
even killed him. Of course, he wasn't bound by the con-
straints of the law, like the chief was. All Sanderson had
was the word of an admitted killer that Hal Stuart had been
part of Brown's drug operation. They needed corroborative
evidence before they arrested and charged one of the most
influential people in town, but they could keep an eye on
him until such evidence was found.

"Any suggestions?"

Martin didn't look at Stone but kept his gaze focused on
the blueprints of the building. Spread over the hood of a
police car, they confirmed everything Hal had said. Brown
couldn't have picked a better place to take a hostage if he'd
planned it. There were only two entrances—the front door
and an alley door. There was only one staircase. Unlike TV
movies, there were no convenient heating shafts running
overhead. "Any assault would have to be straightfor-
ward—through the windows or up the stairs. Rappeling
down from the roof and in through a window would give
us the element of surprise, but we'd be going in blind."
He glanced at Stone, but the detective didn't react to his

use of *we*. It was a done deal—in his mind, at least—that he would be part of any rescue attempt. There was no way in hell he was going to trust Juliet's life to anyone else. "We wouldn't know where Brown and Juliet are until we were actually in the room. That second or two to get oriented is enough time for him to kill her."

"But coming up the stairs, we'd be visible from here on up." Stone pointed to a spot about halfway up the second flight. "We would have to take him out immediately or we'd be sitting ducks." He glanced up at the dark windows. "The chief really wants to take him alive."

"That's not the chief's choice. If Brown's willing to be taken alive, he will be. If not…"

After a moment of silence, Stone asked, "Do you know how to rappel?"

"Yeah." He hadn't done it since before last June, but he knew. He figured it was something you never forgot. Like riding a bike. Like sex. Making love with Juliet, though… That'd been a whole different experience.

"You know how to use a gun?"

"I used to score around two hundred and ninety-five on range qualifications." He didn't waste time wondering how he knew that.

Stone gave him a long, level look, then shook his head. "You're an interesting man, Martin. You talk like a cop, but, according to the FBI, you're not. You seem to think you're a crook, but, according to the FBI, you're not that, either. I'd like to know what's locked away inside that head of yours."

So would he, he thought grimly.

"We can't do anything without the chief's go-ahead, but in case he gives it, tomorrow morning, go out to the range with me. I want to see just how good you are. We might be able to use you."

Martin nodded, then stared up at the second-floor windows. He was more afraid than he'd ever been in his life, but the fear was walled off. He could think, talk, plan. He just couldn't feel. He was cold, mechanical, fully in control. When all this was over, when Juliet was safe in his arms, that would be the time for feeling, for reacting, for falling apart. That would be the time to tell her he loved her, that no matter what secrets his past held, he would love her forever.

And if it ended badly? If he never held Juliet again, if she could never hear the promises he wanted to make? He squeezed his eyes shut, clenched his jaw a little tighter, clung to his control a little harder and detached himself a little further. No *ifs*. Just *whens*. It *would* end, and she *would* be safe. She had to be.

She was his life.

The cellular phone in Stone's pocket rang, and every man on the block swung toward him. He talked for only a moment, then hung up. "He wants food, and he doesn't want a cop bringing it in." His gaze connected with Martin's. "What do you think? Want to get a look at what we're up against?"

"You bet."

Stone sent a cop down the street to the diner, then opened the trunk of his unit and pulled out a bulletproof vest. "Put this on under your shirt."

Martin stripped off his T-shirt and pulled the bulky vest over his head. He'd done this before, he thought grimly. It felt too familiar to simply be a case of *déjà vu*. A criminal wearing a bulletproof vest. That was an interesting thought. But why not? By the very nature of their work, crooks were in a more dangerous field than cops. Cops generally only had to worry about the criminals. Criminals had to worry about cops, other criminals and victims who chose to fight back.

He pulled his shirt on again and smoothed it down. Already a snug fit, it stretched over the vest. Every bump, strap and seam were clearly visible.

"Here, try this." Stone pulled off his leather jacket and handed it over. The fit wasn't perfect—about a size too big—but that was okay. Under the circumstances, too big *was* perfect.

When the cop returned from the diner, he gave the bags to Martin. The smell of egg salad and chicken salad sandwiches made his mouth water. He hadn't eaten since breakfast—scrambled eggs and bacon at Juliet's kitchen table. He'd shared the bacon with Hunter, who had warmed up to him enough to rub against his leg and look pathetically hungry. Juliet had chided him that bacon wasn't good for the dog while munching her own, and he had teased her—

Deliberately he pushed the memories to the back of his mind. He needed all his attention on the task at hand. There could be no screwups, no slips because his emotions weren't under control.

Stone called Brown and told him the food was on its way. When he hung up, Martin crossed the street and walked through the door. The carpeted hallway led straight to the back, passing an open reception area that was still lighted, with the computer still turned on and a radio playing softly. Hal's secretary had gone out for a quick lunch, never expecting to be away this long.

There were lights on in Hal's office, too. A glance through the open door showed shelves of leather-bound law books, a massive desk, rich, dark paneling, thick carpet. Everything in the room was elegant, expensive, including the suitcase standing next to the desk, its sterling tag engraved with Hal's initials.

Martin continued down the hall, making no effort at muffling his passage. As he climbed the stairs, he made a point of rattling the paper bags, of placing his feet heavily on each tread. At the landing he stopped and, injecting a nervous note into his voice, called, "Hello? Mr. Brown?"

"Come on up."

The voice came from somewhere near the top of the stairs, but Martin couldn't see him. The only light on this floor was a single bulb in the stairwell that didn't illuminate much—a wood floor, shadowy mirrors, a stack of records storage boxes four high, two deep and four long.

And Juliet. She was in shadow near the opposite end of the room, slumped in a chair. Her hands were tied behind her, and her feet, judging from the awkwardness of her position, were also bound.

Fear tightened his chest and made breathing difficult. She was so still. Had Brown hurt her? Had he already killed her? Martin couldn't bear the thought, but it wouldn't be the first time some bastard had killed his hostage while continuing to negotiate for the hostage's release.

"Stop there."

Martin came to an abrupt halt at the top of the stairs. Brown was off to his left, hidden in the shadows, no doubt pointing his gun directly at him.

"Another late night, Mr. Smith? Insomnia, isn't it? Bet you never thought you'd be enlisted to deliver food to Grand Springs's newest most wanted, did you? You can put it down on the boxes right there and get out."

At the mention of his name, Juliet straightened in the chair and managed just the slightest of glances over her shoulder before turning back. A small sound of pain accompanied the movement and stirred his anger. His fingers clenched the bags. "I'm supposed to see that she's all right before I leave."

"You're fine, aren't you, Juliet?"

She didn't reply.

"I'm supposed to *see.* To look at her. To make sure. Stone said so." It was an easy lie—one that Brown shouldn't object to—and too good an opportunity to pass up.

"Make it quick. And don't try anything. I'm prepared to kill you both."

Martin wasn't sure whether that last was bluster or statement of fact. He wasn't about to find out. Setting a normal pace, he walked the length of the room, the rubber soles of his running shoes squeaking with every step. As he walked, he took notice of the high ceiling that showed bare steel beams supporting the roof, the long mirrors, the blinds at the windows, the depth of the shadows. He memorized the exact position of Juliet's chair in relation to both windows and to the chair where Brown had been sitting.

Finally he circled in front of her, put a good three feet between them and crouched. She looked as if she might burst into tears at any second. "You okay?"

She nodded, and one tear slid down her cheek.

"She's fine," Brown said impatiently. "She's tired, she's hungry, she's hot, she's cold, and she goes to the bathroom a lot. Other than that, she's a perfect little hostage. Just waiting for a Romeo, aren't you, Juliet?"

Mention of Romeo made her shift. "Hunter's hungry," she said plaintively.

"Oh, yes, she worries about her dog." Brown was scornful, as if the idea of worrying about anyone else when your life was in danger made no sense to him.

"I'll feed him." Martin lowered his voice. "Juliet—"

"Enough! You've seen her. Now, leave the food and get the hell out."

He set the bags on the floor, then slowly got to his feet. As he walked near her, he ducked his head and winked. She rewarded him with a weary, sweet smile.

On his way out, Brown gave him one last instruction. He left the building and walked to the middle of the street, standing motionless until he saw the blinds open slightly, then close.

"What's that about?" Stone asked.

"He wanted to make sure I'd left the building." Martin returned the jacket to Stone and removed the vest while relating everything he'd seen, including the suitcase in Hal's office.

"Maybe that's what set him off. Hal planned to leave town, and Brown panicked—figured it'd be safer to kill him than let him go."

"Why would Hal want to leave town? Why now?"

Stone was silent for a moment before slowly answering, "Because he knew Dean Springer had been arrested and that it was only a matter of time until we came looking for him."

"And how did he know about Springer? You said no one outside the department was supposed to know."

"Obviously someone told him."

"Someone *warned* him. It may have been innocent. It may have just been someone wanting him to know that one of his mother's murderers had been caught. Or Hal might have an informant in your department. Someone who knows he's dirty. Someone who protects him. Either way, you need to find out."

"Believe me, we will." Stone rubbed the back of his neck. "You look tired. Why don't you go home and get some rest? Nothing's going to happen tonight."

Martin's smile was thin and mocking. "Under the best of circumstances, I don't find it easy to sleep. I do need to feed Juliet's dog, though. I'll be back when I'm done."

Juliet had never been so miserable in her life.

Her head ached. Even when she thought it couldn't possibly get any worse, the burning in her shoulders and arms increased another degree. Her fingers might never regain feeling again. Her back hurt. Her eyes hurt. Even her throat hurt, from her refusal to cry.

She didn't know how many hours had passed—at least thirty. Activity outside this morning had roused her from an achy, restless sleep. They'd had breakfast and lunch, delivered by a man she didn't know, and there had been more phone calls, more demands and arguing and bad-tempered displays. For one endless moment this afternoon, she had feared that Brown was going to make good on his threat and kill her right then and there. He had backed off, but he remained edgy and restless.

"What time is it?" Her voice was small, thin. She was so tired that holding her head up was an ordeal, but trying to doze in this chair, in this position, was more of one. Maybe tonight— She cringed at the idea of another night like last night. If that was the only option, the most merciful thing he could do was kill her now.

"There's a clock on the wall."

"It's stopped." She had come to hate that clock in the last thirty-some hours. Not knowing the time—except when her infrequent trips to the bathroom freed her wrist so she could check her watch—was making her crazy, and that big clock stuck on eleven-eighteen didn't help any.

"It's nighttime. That's all you need to know."

"Can I get up and walk around?"

"No."

"Please… This is so uncomfortable."

"For God's sake, would you quit whining?" he snapped. "I have a few things on my mind more important than your comfort."

She sat silent for only a moment, then drew a deep breath and said, "You know they're not going to let you go. No matter what you do to me, they won't let you get away."

"You'd better hope you're wrong. I'll die before I'll go to prison—and I won't die alone. The only way you're walking out of here alive is with me."

She shook her head. "This is a mistake. You can't get away with it."

"You think some white knight's going to come riding in here to rescue you?" He was looking at her with pity, as if she were living in fantasyland. "You just told me yourself that they're not going to let me go, not even to save your life. They don't care whether you live or die. There's no white knight for you, Juliet. There's no Romeo."

"Maybe the police don't care, but someone does, and he's far more dangerous than you ever dreamed of being."

Brown came closer, right up into her face. "Sweetheart," he said softly, so softly. "There's *no one* more dangerous than me. Remember that."

* * *

Down on the street, out of sight around the corner, Martin slipped on a navy blue windbreaker over a bulletproof vest. The jacket, with Police stamped on the front and back in bright gold letters, was identical to the ones Stone and Jack Stryker wore. Where he and Stone were armed with automatic pistols, though, Jack was carrying an H&K MP-5 submachine gun. Weighing less than eight pounds and fitted with a laser sight, it was perfect for their needs.

"He's a civilian, Stone. We can't send a civilian into a hostage situation," Chief Sanderson said, a worried look adding ten years to his face. "This is very unorthodox."

"He's an unorthodox sort of civilian," Stone replied.

"He's not going to sit back and do nothing while we try to get Juliet out of there," Jack put in. "He knows what he's doing. We might as well take advantage of it."

The chief didn't look convinced but gave up the argument. "I'm getting too old for this," he muttered. "I should be at the lake catching fish."

Martin snapped up the jacket, then glanced around. "Who's got the best pitching arm?"

"We just happen to have two All-State pitchers in the department," Stone said with a grin. "Harris, Dailey…" he called.

The two officers who came forward couldn't be older than twenty-two. They were both wiry, and both looked more than capable of tossing the grenades through the front windows.

The flash-bangs were Martin's idea. The small canisters did exactly what their name said—exploded with a tremendously brilliant flash and a bang loud enough, under some circumstances, to rupture a person's eardrums. They momentarily blinded anyone nearby and left a ringing in unprotected ears that would last a half hour or more. They would distract and disable Brown long enough for him, Stone and Jack to free Juliet and take the bastard down.

Stone gave Harris and Dailey final instructions and confirmed the time needed for everyone to get into place, then they separated. Walking close to the building to minimize the risk of detection, Martin holstered his gun while inserting earplugs. That done, he drew the pistol out again, eased the door open and slipped inside. The lights were still on, the radio still playing. He led the way down the carpeted hall, then moved stealthily, cautiously up the stairs.

On the landing, he paused to pull on protective goggles as Stone and Jack did the same. He lowered himself to the floor, then eased up the next few stairs, just high enough to see across the room. Juliet sat in the same chair, her hands still tied behind her. After thirty-six hours, she must hurt like hell. Just one more thing for Brown to pay for.

Maxwell Brown was sitting down, too, in a comfortable padded chair pulled from the old dance school office. He had drawn a wooden chair close for a footstool and sat with his hands folded around his pistol. He didn't look like a man in a world of trouble, but as if he were merely contemplating the day just passed or the one yet to come.

Once Jack was in place, the laser ready to sight, Martin moved with absolute silence up the remaining steps and behind the stack of boxes. Stone followed.

Martin looked at his watch, then mentally counted. Five, four, three, two—

The shattering glass made Juliet jerk upright and brought Brown to his feet. The first flash-bang detonated, washing the entire room in intense light, vibrating the very structure of the building with its bang and sending a concussive wave through the air. Even with earplugs, Martin's ears ached. Even with his goggles and his face bent against his arm, the brilliant light distorted his vision.

As he crouched behind the stack of boxes, waiting for the second flash-bang, Martin suddenly doubled over. Sounds—loud, angry, pleading—assaulted him. A woman's cries that dissolved into a voice, his own voice, made barely recognizable by fury. *Leave us alone, you bastard, or I'll kill you.*

No, honey, it's all right. Please, your daddy didn't mean it. Please don't— A scream, long and panicked, then softer, horrified: *He's dead! Oh, my God, you've killed him!*

A nightmare come to life. It had plagued him for nearly a year, but this time there was a difference. This time he could see the faces—his own, much younger and distorted with shock, his mother's, tearstained as she frantically shook the unmoving figure below him, and that figure. His father. Lifeless.

This time he understood more than the intolerable fact that he'd killed a man. He knew that he'd killed his own father.

And he knew who that man was.

He knew who *he* was.

The second flash-bang exploded, the concussion so strong that Martin felt it as a real physical force pushing against him. He gave a shake of his head to clear it, to dispel the shock of remembering, and forced himself to cling to the knowledge that Juliet was only a short distance away and she needed him. He left the cover of the boxes and moved silently toward her as Stone, back behind him, called, "Drop the gun, Maxwell."

Brown stood hunched over, clutching both hands to his ears, unable to hear himself swear. "You sons of bitches! You lying, deceiving sons of bitches, I told you I'd kill her!" He pointed the gun blindly and fired, pointed and fired again, then drew aim on Juliet as surely as if he could see her.

"No!" Martin raced across the room, then made a flying tackle, knocking Juliet and the chair through the air as a burst of gunfire exploded through the room. They hit the floor and slid across the hardwood. Yanking the hunting knife from its sheath on his belt, he sliced through the bonds that secured her, kicked the chair away and shielded her body with his own. Even with his weight pressing her down, she was shaking. She clung to him, whimpering,

whispering something—prayers, he thought, and added his own.

The commotion ended as abruptly as it had begun. Slowly he lifted his head, turned to see Maxwell Brown lying motionless on the floor. At the other end of the room, Stone came out from behind the boxes and Jack was walking up the stairs, the H&K held loosely but ready to fire in an instant. Juliet was crying.

He sat up, scooted back to lean against the wall and lifted her into his lap. He pulled off the goggles, removed the earplugs, then kissed her forehead, her cheeks, her jaw. "It's all right, darlin'. We're all right."

"I was so afraid."

"So was I, babe. But it's okay. Everything's okay." He held her a moment longer, then pushed her back, brushed her hair from her face, dried her tears. "Juliet? There's something I need to tell you."

Sniffling, she looked at him, her eyes liquid blue and full of love, and patiently waited.

He tried to smile, but his mouth quivered. Hell, his whole body was quivering. Forcing a deep breath into his lungs, he looked into her eyes and found the peace he needed there. "My name is Colton Stuart, Roy Colton Stuart Jr., and I think I'm one of the good guys, and I love you more than anything in the world. Will you marry me?"

Twelve

Over the next two days, Juliet and Martin—Colton, she corrected herself—did little but sleep and talk. He'd had so much to tell—about the horrible fight that resulted in his father's death, running away at his mother's urging so the police wouldn't suspect him, years struggling to survive on the streets. He'd joined the army to stay alive, had used the GI Bill to put himself through college and then gone to work for the Drug Enforcement Administration in California, New York and Florida, in the Caribbean, Mexico and Colombia. He'd been shot the first time in Bogotá, the second in Jamaica, both in the line of duty.

He *was* one of the good guys.

But she'd known that all along.

It was Thursday afternoon, and they were standing in front of a grave marker at the cemetery. The stone was engraved with Olivia's full name and the dates of her birth and death. Inscribed underneath in fancy script was the legend, Beloved Mother. Mart—Colton crouched to run his fingers lightly over the letters, the look on his face one of exquisite sorrow. It broke her heart.

"When I killed my father, I wanted to stay here and take my chances with the law, but she wouldn't let me. I begged her, but she insisted that I couldn't risk it. I could claim self-defense, but I was a big kid—bigger than him—and I'd made no secret of the fact that I hated him. I wanted him dead. Everyone knew it, including the police." Closing his eyes, he shook his head. "They used to come to our house on a regular basis. They hauled him off, Mom refused to press charges, and he was back the next morning. Nothing ever changed. Until that night.''

He'd already told her about that night, how his parents had gotten into yet another violent fight. He had gotten between them, and his father had hit him, too, knocking him to the floor. With one knee in Colton's back, Roy held him down and, as punishment for his interference, used his cigarette to burn his own son's flesh. Colton freed himself, and, when Roy came at him again, Colton hit him. The force of the blow had carried him down the stairs, and the fall had left him dead of a broken neck.

Juliet felt no sympathy for the man who was buried in a distant part of the cemetery. She'd known from the moment Colton had told her about his dream, from the moment she'd connected the burn scar on his back to the smell of something burning in that dream, that Roy Stuart had deserved to die.

''I blamed her. I resented the hell out of her. She was my mother. She should have protected me. She should have made him stop, and if she couldn't, if he didn't, then she should have taken us far away from him.'' He stood, glanced around the cemetery as if he didn't know how he'd come to be there. ''Being on my own and on the streets was so damned hard. There were times when I thought jail couldn't possibly be worse than the life I was living. I wanted to go home, but I was so angry with her for making me leave in the first place, for putting me in a situation where I had to kill my own father, for not being a good mother. And I hated Roy Stuart even more. I dropped the Roy Jr. bit and became Colton Stuart.

''As I got older, I finally realized that life isn't always so easy, that people make mistakes, that my mother had made mistakes. I finally admitted how much I still loved her, and I called her. I talked to her last spring for the first time in more than twenty years. It was my birthday.'' He gave her a crooked smile. ''In the last five years, I'd spent so much time out of the country that I never really had a place of my own. I was in Miami then, staying with an old DEA buddy—Jason Scott. He's probably transferred out of there by now. That's why we couldn't locate him.''

''Olivia must have been so happy to hear from you.''

His expression saddened again. ''Yeah. The first night, we talked for two hours, and she cried the whole time. She apologized, asked me to forgive her. I said I did.''

''Why didn't she tell Hal and Eve?''

''In the beginning, she wanted to keep the news to herself for a while. She was the only one who always believed that I was still alive, and she wanted to...''

''Savor the moment.'' She said it with a knowing smile. *She* had savored every single moment with him.

He nodded. ''When she finally told me about the trouble Hal was in—the second call, I think, maybe the third—I asked her not to tell anyone. I arranged to take a leave of absence, to come here and try to help her with him. I wanted surprise on my side.'' He shook his head, his gaze distant, his thoughts a year distant. ''The shrink suspected all along that there was a hysterical aspect to my amnesia. He was right. I remember leaving the interstate and driving up the mountain toward Grand Springs, and the closer I got, the more desperately I wanted to be someplace else. I *hated* coming back here. I hated the fear and the old bitterness toward my mother. I would have gladly faced the toughest, most vicious and brutal dealers in the world rather than deal with my memories of Grand Springs. When I had the wreck, maybe subconsciously I *was* looking for a way out, for a way to forget.''

''Why didn't anyone recognize you? I realize Eve was just a baby, but Hal should have known. A lot of people should have known.''

He came to stand behind her, sliding his arms around her. ''I used to look more like Hal. When I got shot the first time, I was standing on a rooftop. I fell two stories to the sidewalk below. My face was messed up—lots of broken bones. Normally, in a situation like that, the doctors use a photograph to put you back together. If one's not available, they try to match the more seriously affected side to the other. They couldn't locate a photograph of me, and both sides of my face were pretty badly smashed, so they did the best they could. My nose came out crooked, they squared my jaw, and they altered a few other features. Considering the level of expertise at that hospital, I was just grateful that I didn't come out of it looking as grotesque as I'd felt.''

So twice in his life he'd awakened to find himself wearing a stranger's face. Whatever the face, she loved him more than she'd ever thought possible.

''Want to go home?'' he murmured, making her shiver.

''To sleep?''

''Maybe later.'' He nuzzled her hair from her ear, brushed his mouth across it.

''To talk?''

''That, too. Later.''

''Then what is it you want to do?''

He told her in explicit terms that left no questions and sent a heated flush through her body. ''Martin—Colton!'' She sounded scandalized. She felt turned on.

''Darlin', I'm not suggesting that I lay you down on the grass right here. Though it's not a bad location, considering.''

Giving him a chastening look that didn't leave him the least bit chastened, she claimed his hand and started for the car. Halfway there, she stopped, reached for his other hand and clasped them both tightly. ''I need to ask you something. Tuesday night you said…''

''That I love you.''

''And you asked…''

His smile was sweet and gentle. ''I asked you to marry me. You didn't answer.''

''It was a tense moment. Your adrenaline was pumping. We'd just been shot at. Our lives had been in danger.'' She hesitated before quietly continuing. ''I thought, if you really meant it, you would ask again when things calmed down. You didn't.''

"I wanted you to know what you were getting into. I wasn't a criminal, but...I don't look much like husband material, either. I come with my own baggage. That's one reason why I've been telling you everything. I want you to make an informed choice.''

"Martin—Colton, I've known everything about you that I've needed to know since the moment I realized I'd fallen in love with you. I'm sorry for all the things that went wrong in your past, but they don't make a difference. They can't change how I feel about you. They could never stop me from loving you.''

He studied her for a moment, then freed one hand to touch her face. "You really mean that, don't you?''

"With all my heart.''

"I love you, Juliet.''

"I love you, too, Martin—Colton—whoever you are.''

Grinning, he pulled her close against him. "You know, you could avoid the confusion by just calling me sweetheart. Or darlin'. Or husband. Or, in a year or so, Daddy.'' His mouth closed over hers in the sweetest, most tempting, most full-of-promise kiss she had ever experienced. Just as she was growing too weak to stand, he lifted his head and gazed down at her. "I have only two questions for you, Juliet. Will you marry me?''

"Yes.''

"And can I take you home and—'' Once again he whispered in her ear, offering wicked suggestions and sinful pleasures and love, more love than she'd ever known.

Laughing, she wrapped her arms around his neck and pressed a kiss to his jaw. "Yes. Yes. Oh, please, yes.''

Epilogue

Colton stopped in the open doorway of Juliet's office and tapped once to get her attention. "Are you busy?"

"That depends on who's asking whom. If it's the police chief speaking to the records supervisor, of course I'm busy. I'm always busy. I earn every penny you pay me and then some." Then she smiled, a sweet, provocative, God-how-he-loved-her smile. "If it's my husband speaking to his wife, of course not. I'm never too busy for you."

"How about the man who has that desk you requested for the new clerk you begged for?"

"I've got time. I'll help you move it in." She left the computer and walked to the door.

Colton didn't move but waited until she started to brush past to put his arms around her and nuzzle her neck. "You look awfully pretty today."

"Thank you. It's my favorite dress."

"It's my favorite, too." It had been, ever since one April evening when he'd watched through the screen door as she'd walked down the hall, buttoning soft fabric to conceal soft, pale skin. He'd entertained a few fantasies that night and later about removing the dress. Now he lived those fantasies on a regular basis, and they were good.

Life was good, better than he'd ever imagined possible. He'd resigned from the DEA and accepted the job of police chief when Frank Sanderson retired last month. He'd identified and brought charges against the dispatcher who'd been on Hal's payroll, the one who'd warned his brother and set in motion the events that had nearly cost Juliet her life. He'd tied up all the loose ends of his mother's murder and found peace with her passing. He'd given up his rather depressing apartment and moved into a pretty little green house, and he'd married the most beautiful woman in the world exactly four weeks ago today.

Life was *damned* good.

The only dark spot on his horizon was Hal. His relationship with the kid brother he used to protect might never be the same again. He didn't know if he could ever forgive Hal for setting into motion the events that had culminated in their mother's murder. After Hal's guilty plea on charges of narcotics trafficking in early May, though, Colton had eight to ten years to figure that one out.

"We have just enough time to get this office rearranged, then we have to get to the park," he said, reluctantly letting Juliet go. The city council had voted to rename Vanderbilt Park in honor of his mother and all that she'd done for Grand Springs, and he was scheduled to speak at the ceremony. He didn't care much for the idea of making public speeches—he'd lived so much of his adult life hiding in the shadows—but, with Juliet at his side, he could do it. He could do anything.

"It's going to be a tight fit," she said, thoughtfully surveying the room. "You know, the office space the chief shares with his secretary is quite a bit bigger than this. I think it would be only fair—"

"Fair doesn't count, darlin'. I'm the chief, and I get the best office. If we put Mariellen's desk over there—" he pointed to one side "—then there'll be room for Faye's desk over there. We can put them facing the wall, where the center of the room will be all open, or they can face each other, with a walkway between them to get to your office."

"Let's put them facing the wall. Mariellen doesn't need any more distractions than she's already got."

"You know, darlin', now that you've got Faye, we could probably do without Mariellen." The new clerk was older, responsible and mature. She had come to Grand Springs from the Denver PD, already a certified NCIC terminal operator, and she fully understood the concept of coming to work on time and putting in a full eight hours of work in exchange for eight hours' worth of pay.

With a smile, Juliet shook her head. "Mariellen's getting better. Besides…"

"You've learned to like her." He pulled first one, then a second, two-drawer file cabinet away from the wall to make room for the desk. As he pulled the second one out, a piece of paper caught behind it fluttered to the floor. He picked it up, then stared, disbelieving, at it. "Well…this solves our last little mystery."

"What is it?" Juliet came to stand beside him. She scanned the paper, then laid her hand on his arm. "Oh, Colton."

It was a fingerprint card, dated nearly a year ago, and the prints on it were his own. The purpose of the query, stated on the card, was to establish identification of a John Doe white male, approximately forty years of age—thirty-seven, he knew now—six-three, blond and blue, and suffering from amnesia following a motor vehicle accident. Stone had filled out two cards—one for the state crime bureau, one for the FBI—and had taken the prints himself, then passed the card on to the records clerk to forward.

On to Mariellen.

"But I thought—" Juliet went into her office and opened a file drawer. A moment later she returned, leafing through the documents inside. He looked over her shoulder at Stone's notes, the original unknown-persons bulletin, copies of the second bulletin and Juliet's request for matching information on gunshot victims. The last item was a teletype from the state crime bureau in response to the first bulletin, reporting that no record of the subject was found. There was no response from the FBI.

Everyone had assumed that his fingerprints weren't on file anywhere—that he wasn't a cop or a convicted criminal and therefore not easily identifiable—because Mariellen had claimed a not-on-file response from both agencies. In fact, she had never sent his prints to the FBI. If she had, he might not have remembered who he was, but he would have *known*. They would have identified him in a heartbeat. At least one important part of the mystery of his past would have been solved.

Instead, because of an empty-headed, careless and disorganized clerk, he'd spent more than ten months in the dark and troubled about who he was, about what he was.

"Oh, Colton, I'm sorry."

"Mistakes happen. Fingerprint cards get lost." And maybe it wasn't a mistake. Maybe it was fate that had caused his print card to literally slip through the cracks. If he'd been identified sooner, he probably would have left Grand Springs before spring. He would have missed Juliet, and his life would have been so much poorer for it.

"Want me to file that?"

He shook his head. "I'm keeping it for good luck. In getting lost, it's already brought me the best of luck of all—you." He laid the card aside, lifted the heavier end of the desk and said, "Grab that end so we can get out of here. It's a beautiful day, and I want to spend part of it alone with my beautiful wife."

Once the office was rearranged, Juliet dusted her hands. It was ten minutes until eleven—just time enough to get to the park for the rededication that, in addition to honoring Olivia, would also commemorate the one-year anniversary of the blackout. Grabbing her purse and the fingerprint card, she hurried Colton out to the car.

The park was packed. She clung to his hand as they made their way through the crowd, stopping to greet well-wishers and friends. Many of them had been at the wedding a month ago—Noah Howell, the doctor who treated Colton after the accident, and his wife Amanda; Stone and his wife Jessica; Jack and Josie Stryker. Tracey from the library had attended, too, and Sherri from the credit bureau and Pete, the night cook at the diner, and Reverend Murphy had performed the ceremony. He greeted them now from the new playground where children were crawling in, around and under anything that didn't move.

Some of the others were people she knew only to say hello to—the Frames, the Bennetts, the Montgomerys. They talked for a minute with Travis Stockwell, whose family had been a direct gift of the blackout, when he'd delivered a stranger's twins in the back seat of his cab and fallen in love with mother and babies, and with Tony and Bethany Petrocelli, who had been brought together by love for a baby born and abandoned during the emergency. Randi Howell, the runaway bride, was there with her husband Brady, and so was Juliet's doctor, Karen Sloane, with her family. Seeing Karen reminded Juliet of their appointment next week. She and Colton were eager to start a family, and though she'd rarely had a sick day in her life, she wanted the doctor's okay before the birth control went out the window.

They were all people whose lives had been changed in some way by last year's blackout. Some had suffered only minor inconveniences. Others had found someone to love. The entire town had lost someone they loved.

Finally Juliet and Colton reached the newly finished fountain, which bore a brass plaque dedicating it and the acres around them to Grand Springs's finest mayor. Colton slid his arm around her shoulders as they read the plaque praising Olivia's dedication and her achievements.

"I wish I'd known her," Juliet said wistfully.

"She would have loved you."

"You sound so sure of that."

"I am. Because *I* love you." He bent to kiss her, but drew back at a teasing comment.

"Knock it off, you guys. There are innocent children around here." Eve stretched onto her toes to kiss his cheek, then sweet Molly, looking like an ethnic china doll with her father's striking Native American features and her mother's—and uncle's—equally striking blue eyes, broke free of her father's grip and climbed into Colton's arms. "Hi, Uncle Colton. Do you know why we're here?"

"I do, sweetheart. Do you?"

"Uh-huh. Because it's a special day. Because Grandma went to heaven, and now she's an angel looking down on us."

"I bet she is, and she's thinking what a beautiful granddaughter she has."

"And what a pretty wife you have."

Grinning, Juliet leaned over to give the girl a smacking kiss. "Did I ever tell you that you're my favorite niece, Molly?"

"Of course I am, Aunt Juliet. I'm your *only* niece."

She returned to her father as the mayor called the gathering to order. He kept his comments brief, then turned the microphone to Colton. With a squeeze of his hand for reassurance, Juliet moved back, let Eve take her place at his side and listened to the calm, even sounds of her husband's voice.

"Our mother was a firm believer in second chances. Her second chance came when she was a widow with two young children to support, and she made the most of it. She went to college and became an attorney. She dedicated herself to making life better for those around her—not just her own family, but her neighbors, her friends and strangers, too. She accomplished so much, and those of us who loved her best are so proud." Stepping back, he relinquished the microphone to Eve.

"It is with pride that we announce the formation of the Olivia Stuart Foundation to provide assistance and aid to the people dearest to her heart—those in need. Those trying to make their lives better. Those who need a hand to get their lives back on track."

Her voice went on, but Juliet wasn't listening. She was looking at Colton, who was looking back with love in his intense blue eyes. "Thank you," he whispered, the words nearly soundless.

"For what?"

"Loving me. Believing in me. Being my second chance."

"Oh, darlin'," she murmured, unable to control the smile spreading across her face. "I'm your last chance. You're stuck with me forever."

As a moment of silence fell over the crowd, he leaned toward her. Just when she thought he might kiss her in front of everyone, the quiet was broken by a childish voice in the crowd. "Is it over yet?"

The plaintive question signaled the end of the ceremony as laughter rippled through and people began breaking up into neighborly groups to chat. Colton wrapped his arms around Juliet, and, just before his mouth claimed hers, murmured the sweetest words she'd ever heard.

"It'll never be over for us, darlin'. I'll love you forever."

*   *   *   *   *

Marilyn Pappano is a regular contributor to
our Silhouette Sensation® series.
Look for new novels from her in 2000!

COMING NEXT MONTH FROM

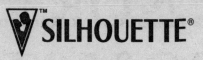
SILHOUETTE®

Intrigue
Danger, deception and desire

SHATTERED LULLABY Rebecca York
A FATHER'S LOVE Carla Cassidy
ONLY A WHISPER Gayle Wilson
TWILIGHT MEMORIES Maggie Shayne

Special Edition
Compelling romances packed with emotion

MAKE ROOM FOR BABY Cathy Gillen Thacker
THE RANCHER AND THE AMNESIAC BRIDE
Joan Elliott Pickart
A FAMILY KIND OF WEDDING Lisa Jackson
DR DEVASTATING Christine Rimmer
MARRYING AN OLDER MAN Arlene James
TERRIFIC TOM Martha Hix

Desire
Provocative, sensual love stories

CALLAGHAN'S BRIDE Diana Palmer
THE BEST HUSBAND IN TEXAS Lass Small
THE COWBOY'S SEDUCTIVE PROPOSAL Sara Orwig
THE OLDEST LIVING MARRIED VIRGIN Maureen Child
THE OUTLAW'S WIFE Cindy Gerard
THE FORBIDDEN BRIDE-TO-BE Kathryn Taylor

9909

NORA ROBERTS

Sweet Revenge

Adrianne led a remakable double life.
Daughter of a Hollywood beauty and an
Arab playboy, the paparazzi knew her
as a frivolous socialite darting from
exclusive party to glittering charity ball.
But no one knew her as The Shadow, a
jewel thief with a secret ambition to
carry out the ultimate
robbery—a plan to
even the score.

The Shadow was intent
on justice.

MIRA®   **Published 22nd October 1999**